T0357767

The
CORRUPTION
HOLLIS
of
BROWN

K. ANCRUM

HARPER

An Imprint of HarperCollinsPublishers

Library of Congress Control Number: 2024940345
ISBN 978-0-06-328583-5

Typography by Corina Lupp
25 26 27 28 29 LBC 5 4 3 2 1

First Edition

This is a love letter from a daughter of the city of the big shoulders.
The soil may be hard, but we can dig it with our hands.
Do not forget: we are all that we have.

HOLLIS

Hollis always grinned when this happened. He couldn't help it.

The aftermath wasn't his favorite, for obvious reasons. But this? The way James's knuckles felt as they slammed into his gut?

It made him clench his teeth.

Hollis was good at dodging—adrenaline always slowed down time, so he had the leisure of watching punches slice through the air. Hollis had taken enough hits in his life that he'd gotten good at making them miss. It wasn't like James was a slouch at this though; he was a haymaker for sure.

James's face twisted with rage, eyes darkening. The corners of Hollis's mouth ticked up.

Most of the time, when people fought Hollis, they were yelling at him too. But James was silent as he slammed his fist, sharp and violent, under Hollis's chin, cutting Hollis's smirk off. His head was still tilted, face warming in the midday sun, when James backhanded Hollis hard enough that his shoulder met pavement.

It felt real good to lie there for a minute.

James didn't even give him a second to breathe. He scraped Hollis off the ground, pinned him to the brick wall. Slotted close, thigh to chest, he shoved his broad hand across Hollis's throat. James pulled his arm back, biceps bunching with muscle to continue punching Hollis in the head, and Hollis realized at once that he couldn't take it.

He flinched, closed his eyes. Waited for his vision to explode in red and yellow, but the hit never came. When he got the courage to look, James was staring back at him hard.

Then James let him go. Watched Hollis's knees buckle without his support, saw the heels of his boots skid in the gravel, pathetic. But he didn't mock Hollis, or tease.

"Leave me alone," James said instead. Pulling his backpack onto his shoulders. "You don't always have to be such a dick."

BOY

Hollis Brown looked up.

Annie was staring at him, blocking out the sun.

He scrubbed the back of his hand across his face, smearing the blood beneath his nose.

Annie's frown got deeper.

"I didn't do anything."

She rolled her eyes. "You can't possibly expect me to believe that."

"Oh come on! There's nothing I could say that would hurt more than James Miller's right hook. He almost broke my fucking jaw."

Annie opened her backpack and pulled out her roll of Hello Kitty Band-Aids. She wiped his cuts roughly, spraying them with antiseptic, then she pressed a kiss to the scrape across Hollis's knuckles.

"Maybe if you bitched at him less, your jaw wouldn't be almost broken," she snapped, merciless. "Yulia isn't going to be happy."

Hollis let himself fall gently back until he was flat on the pavement again.

The thing about being friends with only girls was that they held him accountable for his actions. He got scolded and berated and pushed to be better. But he also got Band-Aids. Even kisses sometimes, if he played his cards right.

Annie sprayed antiseptic all over his face, then chucked the bottle at him hard enough to hurt.

ANNIE

Annie and Hollis lived next door to each other and walked to school together every day.

It was the only reason someone like Annie had become his friend in the first place.

Hollis was fine, but Annie was *cool*. She cut her hair herself and made her own clothes and jewelry. She had big brown eyes, wide sharp shoulders, and cheeks that flushed pink in any season.

She was the school photographer, so Annie knew everyone. She dated guys from student council, guys on sports teams, guys who did mathletes, guys who smoked weed and thought they were cool, no social group seemed off-limits.

She was the kind of girl who could sit down at any lunch table and no one would look at her sideways.

Annie Watanabe could do it all.

But instead, she was there. Right beside Hollis, always.

SCREAM

Yulia Egunyemi leaned against her Dodge Challenger and waited for Annie and Hollis to stumble across the parking lot. Hollis wasn't heavy, but Annie was small, and he had at least a foot on her. His long arm dangled over her shoulder, welts turning vivid and red.

"You're such a dumbass, Hollis," Yulia shouted when they got close enough to hear.

"It was James Miller," Annie yelled back. "Hollis won't tell me what he said to him, so I'm sure it was awful. As usual."

Yulia helped Annie shuffle Hollis inside so he could lie across the seats on his stomach. Then she slapped the back of his calf hard.

"Ow! Fuck!"

"Shut up." Yulia slammed the door.

She hopped in the front of the car, turned on the ignition, and squealed out of the parking lot.

"Where are we going?" Hollis griped.

"Urgent care. I heard that James got a scholarship for mixed martial arts. Who knows what he rattled around in there."

"I'm fine, just take me home."

"No!" Annie shouted.

"I'll pay the fucking copay, but you owe me," Yulia snapped. "I don't care if you don't have any money—figure it out."

Hollis stayed miserable and quiet until they pulled in to the urgent care parking lot. Yulia sucked her teeth in disgust as they helped him into one of the waiting room chairs.

Annie settled down beside him while Yulia handled the bill. She plucked at the thread from a hole in his jeans.

YULIA

Even though he had known Annie longer, *Yulia* was Hollis's best friend. She got him in every way there was to get someone. They just clicked.

Yulia was tall and very dark, like a supermodel. Eyes slender and lionlike, a jaw sharp and glamorous. She dressed like she was going to a casting and didn't let the stares stop her. She took to farm culture in furs and thigh-high tights. The only reason Yulia wasn't the most popular girl in school automatically was because she was the kind of New York chic that small-town people didn't like. Plus, her and her family were the only Nigerian immigrants for miles around.

A trust fund angel like her shouldn't even be in a podunk place like this.

Her pa was a real estate developer who moved their family to town to work on a nearby housing development. They were supposed to have stayed for just a year, but the project was taking longer. All projects near Rose Town did.

So here she was, three years in. Trapped with the rest of them.

GRAY

Hollis had nothing fractured and nothing broken, just bruises and burst vessels and shame. Annie and Yulia bundled him home, fast as holy chariot.

Yulia agreed to be paid back in bread and demanded Hollis bake it for her by the end of the week.

Annie helped Hollis into his house and put him to bed. She scraped her acrylic nails across his cheek, soft, while he held himself together.

Hollis watched them leave.

He waited until he heard the sound of Yulia's car peeling out of his driveway to cry.

ROT

Hollis didn't know any other way to be.

He had a temper. Not the kind that makes you lash out at your friends and family. But ... his mouth got away from him. You couldn't be like that when you were like him. It bucked the social order.

He wasn't a loser. But if someone popular asked to copy his homework, he shouldn't just snap "Go away" at them if he didn't want problems. If he missed a shot in gym and one of the jocks called him "butterfingers," he shouldn't whirl on them and ask about their parents' divorce. But he did.

James Miller was tall, blond, popular, and had about fifty pounds of muscle on Hollis.

Hollis told him he was going to die in this town.

No one's parents had much money for college, very few people figured out how to leave, but James was trying and trying hard. Punching Hollis into a brick wall a few times was the correct response to hearing his greatest fear tossed right in his face.

Annie was right, *he was an asshole.*

Not to her and Yulia, of course, but the fact remained.

Hollis turned on his side and coughed hard. He swallowed his own blood, wiped his tears on his sheets.

It was ironic though. That James was so scared of never leaving this place, when Hollis was sure he'd make it out.

Hollis would have to stay though.

His bones belonged to this soil.

HOME

They lived in a forgotten American dreamscape. A sliver cut from time.

There were other towns like it: coal towns, lumber towns. Places of Industry left to rot when some factory everyone worked at boarded up or government investment ran dry. Where people put down roots and built homes and schools and churches. Lives dependent on work.

An economy dependent on work.

Most of these kinds of towns eventually died. The young moved away, the elderly expired, and the wind turned their houses into wood and stone sculptures.

That was the best-case scenario.

The worst-case scenario was a town full of hungry people. Parents driving hours to other cities for work, paint peeling and metal rusting, time slowing and slowing until it stood still.

Good enough to keep things going. Not enough to ease anyone's suffering.

Just enough that people refused to move away.

They stayed, caught. They *died* there.

Hollis understood why it chilled the sweat on James's back.

BROAD

Hollis peeled himself out of bed and wandered downstairs. He could smell spaghetti sauce from his room and now he was hungrier than he felt hurt.

His ma was on the couch burning through another episode of *The King of Queens*. Mrs. Brown was red-haired, broad-shouldered, and fine-boned like a bird. Pretty in a way that time couldn't snatch, and Hollis looked too much like her.

She caught his eye as he passed through the living room to the kitchen and whistled low.

"You're not staying home tomorrow."

"Yeah, yeah," Hollis mumbled. "I gotta bake Yulia some bread later; she handled my copay. You need the oven?"

"What flavor are you doing?"

Hollis opened the pantry and scanned their jars and packages.

"We have a lot of sweet potatoes this year. Do you mind if I use cinnamon?"

"Do two loaves. One for her and one for us, then you can use as much cinnamon as you need."

Hollis could hear the grin in his mother's voice.

"Who was it this time? Someone strong, looks like. You gotta stop pissing off football players. Their love for me can only go so far to protect you, june bug."

Mrs. Brown was a PE teacher, and kids who played sports did tend to go a bit soft on Hollis because of it. Embarrassing as that was.

"It wasn't— Ugh. It was James Miller."

11

"Holly, leave that kid alone. Don't you think he's dealing with enough? His pa's been using the computer lab like an internet café, so his job search can't be going well. And Hannah can only pick up so many hours at the diner before she's working a twenty-four-hour shift."

Hollis pressed his forehead against the refrigerator.

"Okay." He couldn't apologize. He didn't feel like he had the right to cry.

Instead, he reheated his dinner and settled down next to his ma to eat it. She brushed a hand through his hair and rubbed his back.

BRUSH

Hollis woke up painless, so he got ready and left.

The trains ran mostly on time, and he knew he wasn't late. He'd have heard the whistle from his house on the way over. The wind blew hard, cutting through his down overcoat to chill his bones. Under his mittens he knew his hands were turning blue, but he stayed rooted to the spot.

Nothing else seemed to work.

Hollis's uncle used to do this too, so maybe it was a family thing. A gambling-with-death thing. Waiting for the train like this.

The dry leaves whispered against each other; Hollis curled his hands into fists and closed his eyes.

Freight trains were faster than commuter trains when they needed to be. You can't jump on them; they'll break your legs. If you stumble, the wheels are like surgical knives. They could fill graveyards with the people who have tried.

Whistle and the light. Steel against steel, the warmth of sparks and gravity: relentless as the tide. Hollis leaned forward to taste that speed at the front of his teeth.

The gust tossed his thin brown hair into tangles as the cars rushed past, scented his clothes oily with smoke, and beckoned him forward lover-soft. Even as he stepped back, heart aching.

Annie asked him once why he didn't just jump, when she was mad at him for doing something so dangerous.

He didn't answer her.

GROW

The walk back took longer than he hoped. The cold made Hollis's bones creak, and the air was heavy and wet in the morning dew.

Annie was waiting for him. Her wide face was pinched in disapproval. She always waited, no matter how long it took him to get back or if he got up early and didn't go at all.

"Don't even bother denying it, I can smell it on your clothes," she snapped.

Hollis shrugged; he closed the gate behind Annie. "You're not my ma; you can't tell me what to do."

"You're gonna get torn to pieces, you masochist."

Hollis laughed. Annie pushed him hard from behind.

"You're laughing now, but we're going to be late, and Yulia isn't going to be happy."

Was she ever?

Yulia was waiting for them again. Her buzzed head covered in a fluffy fur hat, puffer coat down to her ankles, in gold eyeliner and a sneer.

"We're late," she drawled.

It would never have occurred to her to go in without them.

Yulia hugged Annie hello and palmed the back of Hollis's head, pushing him through the door.

"We're going to Pino's for lunch. I'll see you both out front, don't be late or you'll have to play catch-up."

"Noted," Hollis mumbled.

Yulia stopped to stare at him. Then she scrunched her nose and reached out to pinch his earlobe.

"You need earmuffs."

"You buy them, I'll wear them," Hollis shot back immediately.

Yulia grinned.

STRANGE

Hollis's pa was in construction. A lot of men were.

Hollis had his eyes and his dishwater dusty brown hair. He was the source of all of Hollis's blunt edges: heavy brows, stubby fingers, knobby knees, overbite, nervousness.

Mr. Brown left them on Monday mornings for the city and came back home on Fridays. He didn't like to talk about where he slept when he was away, but the money was good enough to bear it.

He was a quiet man.

When he was home, he eyed Hollis with disappointment. He didn't say a word of criticism, but Hollis could just feel him wishing for more. You don't work as hard as Mr. Brown did and *not* look at your son and wish he could be better. That your sacrifices were going somewhere meaningful.

The promise of upward mobility.

Sports were a ticket out, and Hollis wasn't good at any of them. He had average grades no matter how much he studied. He wasn't good at painting, photography, history, or anything else, really.

He baked, but it wasn't a hobby. Most people around town made a lot of their own stuff. Bread, jams, pickles, preserves of all kinds. Powdered eggs, canned chicken, penny-pinching, crust-saving. Real rural shit.

The only reason Yulia thought his bread had any value was because she was too rich to have learned how to make her own.

Hollis glanced up at the group of kids in the middle of the classroom, snickering and whispering. Their history teacher always ignored them and kept going. Everyone knew senior year was a waste of time for some people, so why yell at them to pay attention?

Everyone who was going to college already had been admitted. As for the rest, factories and construction sites were full of guys like them.

Guys like him.

BONE

They caught up with Annie out front, and Yulia drove them both out to Pino's for lunch.

It was a horrible family-owned Italian American greasy spoon, with only two seats inside and an owner who yelled if you asked for substitutions.

Annie got marinara chicken fries, Yulia went for an eggplant parm burger, Hollis ordered mozzarella sticks, and they parked in a lot nearby.

Annie rolled down the window and flopped her legs out the door.

"I'm breaking up with Jorge," she announced.

"What did he do? Breathe wrong?" Yulia didn't like Jorge. She didn't like any of Annie's boyfriends; Hollis wasn't sure if she liked guys at all. They didn't talk about it.

"He's too possessive," Annie continued, biting a fry ferociously. "He keeps wanting me to go places with him that are clearly group hangouts and not talk to anyone else but him. What's the point of going to a party if you only get to talk to one person?"

"That sounds like regular boyfriend stuff," Yulia said. "That's what having a boyfriend is like, probably."

Annie groaned and kicked her toes a bit. "Why can't a guy just act normal and hang out normally?"

Hollis gazed at the back of Annie's neck through the slats in the car seat headrest.

He could act normal and hang out normally. But if Annie had wanted him, she would have done something about it. She'd asked out every boy she ever dated, and they'd already known each other for nine years.

It wasn't going to happen.

"Did you try telling him to calm the fuck down?" he offered instead.

Annie scoffed. "Boys don't listen to girls when we do that. Give me a mozzarella stick. Let's trade."

Hollis handed over one of his and took a chicken fry.

"Jorge was going to take me to Rose Town for that overnight sleep-in thing. But he had all these weird rules he wanted me to follow." Annie put on a deep voice. *"Don't go anywhere without me. You can't be in a room with too many other guys. We've gotta be sleeping together alone. You can't wear a nightgown.* It's fucking ridiculous."

Hollis perked up. "I didn't know they were doing that again this year. Last year was so crazy I figured the police would shut anything down."

Yulia laughed. "The police haven't gone into Rose Town after sundown since the 1970s. They're not 'equipped for haunted shit.'"

"They're not equipped for regular shit either," Hollis muttered.

Annie turned around in her seat to face him. "Why do you ask, Hollis? Do you want to go with me? I won't be going with Jorge, and Yulia is too superstitious."

"I don't do ghosts and witches, anything spooky," Yulia said, crumpling her empty takeout bag and tossing it into the back seat. "I'm avoiding the family business. You guys are on your own."

Hollis didn't know much about it, but Yulia's father had deep tribal marks—slashes on his face—and was very tight-lipped regarding anything magic. Yulia followed suit. Hollis respected it.

Annie shrugged. "Figured as much. Anyway, it's this Friday night, Hollis. My parents don't own any sleeping bags—do you have some?"

Hollis felt his back prick with nervous sweat. "We only have one."

Yulia pushed her seat back until her head was in Hollis's lap.

"Bring that and some comforters," she said, closing her eyes. "Use the sleeping bag like a bed and put the covers on top. I'm sure Jorge will love walking in on that."

Annie laughed, but Hollis couldn't bring himself to.

Yulia opened one eye and looked up at him. "Be careful. Don't treat that place like a game."

"I wouldn't."

Yulia opened her other eye.

"I won't," Hollis corrected.

FLUSH

It was a baby crush. A thing he hadn't fed or watered in years.

Hollis wasn't a creep.

He knew it was probably proximity more than anything. He could have imprinted on Yulia just as much, if she wasn't so out of his league and probably a lesbian.

Hollis still remembered what it felt like to be in elementary school and look at Annie with rose-colored glasses. To feel nervous when she put her grubby hands on him, to feel his heart jump when she giggled.

None of that happened anymore.

But there were Moments: When Annie fell asleep on his shoulder during a field trip bus ride. Or that one time they had to share an umbrella and she clung to him the whole walk home. When she said things like "I wish guys would—" and then described him perfectly. Which was so . . . stereotypical that it made him feel sick to even imagine volunteering.

Only the *worst* guys did that. Ones who lied about friendship so they could wait for a good time to pounce.

Hollis wasn't like that. If Annie asked him out, he would have to ask her for time to think about it. Decide if it was worth destroying one of the best things he's ever had. He might even say no, in spite of everything.

But Rose Town was . . . Hollis knew there would be a Moment.

TIME

Every rural locality has legends and spooky circumstances. It comes with the territory.

Rumors get out of control; there's never enough police presence to figure out mysterious deaths; farmers and churches often cook up lies to keep curious teenagers off their properties. There were lots of rotting houses, abandoned ranches, people building weird things in the woods.

But Rose Town was something else.

It was a settlement about two miles away. Half of it was ancient industrial-era buildings and tenements, the other half was aborted construction projects. It was a much bigger place than where everyone lived, with better land, closer to fresh water, and shady trees up and down the streets that grew fruit free for the taking.

The steel mill was there. Had been bought and paid for four times over since Rose Town had been abandoned back in the 1940s.

But no one could live in a place like that.

It takes a lot to get investors to agree that a location is haunted. Being afraid of ghosts and ghouls was for wary townspeople, not suits from the city. So it meant something for a place so valuable to sit uninhabited. For a mill full of machinery to lie coated in dust.

ROAN

People joked about it and laughed in a way that didn't exactly reach their eyes.

Everyone was too young to remember the many deaths in the 1930s. But enough of the adults were around during construction accidents through the 1950s, the disappearances in the 1970s, the terrible fire in the 1980s, and the group of kids sent to the madhouse in the 1990s.

You couldn't just stay scared though—life blunted the edges. It was like the Sanderson sisters in *Hocus Pocus*, which Hollis's ma made them all watch last Halloween.

No one would build in Rose Town or buy a house there, and everyone was poor because of Rose Town. But kids still went over to dare each other to cross the city line. Or went into the houses during the daytime and tried to stay until sundown without pissing their pants.

Occasionally, Hollis would sneak over in the morning and pick as much fruit as he could to save on grocery money. Nothing ever seemed to happen when it was bright outside. He didn't go when it was overcast or too close to sundown.

Last year a group of popular kids went to stay overnight and managed to make it to 10:00 p.m. before someone got too freaked out hearing noises and they all fled.

Brandon Finnegan broke his leg, and Stephanie Moore got a concussion from falling down some stairs. But no one died, so they were doing it again this year.

In two days.

DUST

Hollis went home alone. Annie had band practice, and Yulia was in study club.

He swung by the market to pick up some baking powder and allspice for Yulia's bread.

Everyone had a patch of land to work here and people were generous to their neighbors if the soil yielded. The previous year Hollis planted sweet potatoes, onions, garlic, peanuts, carrots, turnips, and ginger. In the summer he did zucchini, tomatoes, basil, and cucumbers. Stuff that was easy to plant and had a high yield. They dried the garlic, onions, basil, peanuts, and potatoes. Pickled the cucumbers and turnips; canned the zucchini, tomatoes, and ginger.

His pa dug out an underground cellar a while ago to keep everything. It would be a year before the family went hungry. Hollis wasn't the main cook, his ma was, but it was the only skill he'd been able to pick up easily. He spent most of his time with her anyway.

Hollis made the batter extra sweet for Yulia, sprinkled it with a little of their precious stock of pecans, but left the one for him and his ma plain. She wouldn't mind.

He wrapped it in wax paper, walked it over to the nicer part of town, and stuffed it in Yulia's mailbox so the crows couldn't get to it.

SWEET POTATO BREAD

Ingredients

½ cup granulated sugar

½ cup brown sugar, light or dark

2 large eggs

½ cup vegetable oil, or sunflower or corn oil

⅓ cup water

1 cup cooked and mashed sweet potato

1¾ cups all-purpose flour, sifted

1 teaspoon baking soda

¼ teaspoon salt

½ teaspoon ground cinnamon

½ teaspoon ground nutmeg

½ cup pecans, roughly chopped

Instructions

Preheat your oven to 350°F/180°C.

In a large bowl, whisk together the sugars, eggs, oil, water, and the mashed sweet potato.

In a separate bowl, combine the dry ingredients (flour, baking soda, salt, cinnamon, and nutmeg).

Add the dry ingredients to the wet ingredients; mix until there are no dry patches of flour, but do not overmix (this is very important).

Fold in the chopped pecans.

Pour batter into a greased 8.5 x 4.5–inch loaf pan and bake for 50 to 60 minutes, or until a toothpick inserted into the center of the bread comes out clean.

Allow the sweet potato bread to cool completely on a rack before removing from the pan and serving.

START

Friday came fast.

Hollis spent all night struggling over what to wear before settling on a soft brown sweater and black trousers.

He thought about stealing his pa's cologne but got too anxious at the last minute.

Hollis took their sleeping bag to the laundromat, and even skipped visiting the train that morning so that everything would stay fresh and good smelling.

He stumbled through the school day distracted—even lunch was a blur. Yulia watched him with sharp eyes until the bell rang. Then she tossed him her keys.

"Don't make mistakes," she warned.

"I'd rather die than owe you a new car." Hollis opened the trunk and stuffed his sleeping bag inside.

Yulia folded her arms. "I'll hold you to that."

Annie wriggled underneath them to force Yulia into a hug, then slid into the passenger seat.

"Bye! We love you," she shouted.

Yulia nodded sharply, then turned and started her long walk home.

BRIEF

It was so much.

To have Annie beside him in the quiet like this. One hand on the wheel, one hand sweating on his knee.

Annie could tell he was nervous.

"No one is going to mess with you, I'll be there the whole time. You can hang out with me and the rest of the girls."

"I don't think the girls like me either," Hollis mumbled as they turned onto the highway.

"Dude, they don't know you. Worst-case scenario, they know their boyfriends don't like you, and for some of them that might even be a good thing," Annie said. "The one thing they *do* know is that me and Yulia like you, and that counts for something."

"What do you mean?"

Annie glanced over at him. "Well. Your reputation rides on ours in its own way. . . . People think, '*They wouldn't hang out with him for no reason.*' They don't know you, Hollis."

Hollis smirked. "They think there must be something worthwhile going on with me since you and Yulia waste all your time with me?"

Annie huffed. "They don't deserve to know you if they think that. I told them you're our mascot."

"You can tell them whatever you like," Hollis said, fond and indulgent.

Annie grinned.

BEGIN

Rose Town was beautiful in the summer. A city in a garden, trees down every street, shade for a hot summer, birdsong.

But in the cold, with brown leaves cluttering the roads, there was nothing to obscure the decay.

Someone had set up a garbage can fire, and people from school were gathered around it. Hollis could see candlelight brightening the windows of the buildings closest to the city line. They were in the town, but just barely.

He pulled the car onto the gravel, far from where the others were parked. In a better position to drive off if anything happened.

"You come here more often than most people do," Annie said. "Any of the houses your favorite?"

"I don't go in the houses."

Annie sat there, worrying her lip between her teeth. She bounced her knee anxiously but didn't get out.

"It'll be fine."

"You don't know that," Annie said quietly.

Hollis reached over and tugged the sleeves of her thick sweater down over her hands.

"We'll take care of each other," he promised. "No matter what happens, I'm getting you home."

Annie took a deep breath.

"My pa will kill you if I die here." She laughed dryly.

Hollis reached across her lap and opened her door. "Let's get this over with."

RED

By the time they made it to the others, Annie was confident again, walking quick and sure.

Jorge was by the fire, predictably. Surrounded by the rest of the guys Hollis would prefer to avoid: James Miller, Brandon Finnegan—leg healed of course—Liam O'Malley, Alex Stevenson, and Timothy Reid. There were a couple of girls who looked like sophomores too, braving the cold to flirt with seniors.

"Where are the rest of the girls?" Annie called.

Liam pointed at the building next to them.

"Not even a hello?" Jorge yelled.

Annie ignored him. She curled her hand around Hollis's bicep and tugged him toward the light.

It was a three-story row house, formerly red paint faded pale pink and flaking in the sun. The wood beneath had turned gray from years of rain. Hollis's heart jolted in his chest the instant his shoe touched the first step, but Annie drove forward, relentless and brave.

The door slammed open against the side of the house and everyone inside screamed, startled.

Hollis closed the door gently behind them as Annie's other friends rushed up to hug her hello.

"Hey, Hollis," Lisa Damone said warily.

Hollis smiled.

Lisa grimaced back at him. She turned to Annie and said, "This floor is full unfortunately. There's a room or two available upstairs, so feel free to set up there if you want. Right now, we're playing truth or drink until the boys come in."

"There are some other houses lit. Are people just exploring?" Hollis asked.

Lisa seemed surprised that he was speaking to her, but she answered anyway. "There are a few sophomores and juniors here, and they wanted to do their own thing. Stephanie's boyfriend is with them. Technically you can go into any house you want, you guys don't have to stay here with us if you don't want to."

Annie nodded up at the stairs and started heading off without him.

"We'll sleep here," Hollis said. "I'll see you later."

ODE

They walked gently on the wood. Rose Town didn't stay dry long enough for it to get brittle, or wet long enough for it to rot. But it would be stupid not to be careful.

There was a room upstairs with a bed and dresser, everything set up like the owner would be home any minute. Hollis and Annie shut that door tight and instead chose a room that was completely empty. Judging by the scratches and staining on the floor, it had been a formal dining room at some point. Probably looted decades ago before everyone was too scared to take things.

Hollis unfolded the sleeping bag while Annie tested the windows and the floors for soft spots. She propped up a flashlight and two packs of batteries by the head of their makeshift bed.

Hollis unpacked the candle his ma let him bring. It was the gingerbread-scented one she bought the previous year and hated the smell of, but Hollis didn't mind.

Annie was doing something by the door.

"What's that?"

"I'm taping across the lock, so it won't stick. I'm not getting trapped in this room by anyone, ghosts or otherwise."

"Smart."

Annie grinned. "I do my best. Anyway, do you want to play with the girls downstairs or go on a walk? Lisa was kind of a bitch to you."

Hollis didn't mind.

Lisa didn't know him; she didn't have to be nice to him.

"Let's walk. I could show you some stuff."

BOW

Hollis knew it had been a mistake to come back outside the instant they opened the door.

Jorge had clearly spent the time they took to get unpacked getting worked up. He pushed away from his friends and charged up the porch.

"So you're staying with him?!" he shouted.

"Dude, calm down," James interjected, to Hollis's surprise. Their eyes met, and James looked away quickly, but he didn't back down. "It's not that serious, Jorge."

Timothy Reid, James's best friend, also looked very concerned. Tim was tough, and played soccer just a bit better than Jorge did. Hollis knew the taste of his fist just as much as he did James's. Tim ignored Hollis completely.

Jorge pushed Hollis hard. He banged against the door behind them, painfully. "What's he got that I don't got?!"

"Leave him alone, Jorge!" Annie cried.

Hollis's face still throbbed from James's blows from less than a week earlier, so, quite frankly, he was in shock. He caught James's eye, and for the first time ever James looked helpless. Like he wanted to say something to Hollis but couldn't.

"I'm just sick of this, man. Tired of being disrespected," Jorge was ranting.

Idiot.

"No one's disrespecting you," Hollis snapped. "But it doesn't look like anyone respects you either, to be honest."

"Hollis, shut up," Annie hissed. "Jorge, Hollis is just a friend. Me staying in a room with him is none of your business. We're not dating anymore."

Jorge twisted and pushed Annie too. "How could you say that in front of my boys, man?"

"Hey!" Timothy yelled. "Don't touch her! You can't hit girls!"

Jorge's face went frighteningly blank. Then without another word, he turned away from Annie and slugged Hollis in the stomach *hard*.

Hollis dropped to his knees and heaved. He rested his forehead on the ground. This wasn't anything like the fights he picked himself. There was no adrenaline to save him. There was no joy in this violence, just pain and humiliation.

"No! Fucking stop!" Timothy yelled, and Annie screamed.

Hollis could hear the sound of a struggle, then a large hand clamped around his arm and yanked him off the ground.

"Go," James said, thrusting him toward Annie.

"What—?"

It was strange to see James like this. Like he was scared for him, face pinched and upset.

"Get her out of here, Hollis!" he said, pushing Hollis's shoulder hard, knocking him out of the shock of it all.

Annie grabbed his hand and dragged him off the porch and out into the night. They fled down the street until the light from the fire faded and everything was winter blue.

Annie stopped. She leaned against a rusted streetlight, panting hard to catch her breath.

"What . . . is Jorge's fucking problem?" Hollis gasped. "Did he just hit you?"

"No, he was about to stomp on your head," Annie said. "Tim pushed him before he could, and they started fighting."

Hollis laughed; he couldn't help it. What a miracle. He felt around his stomach for tender spots. It was a solid blow, but nothing seemed to be damaged.

"Definitely didn't think *James Miller* and *Timothy Reid* would come to our rescue. Feels like some sort of miracle." Hollis rubbed his new bruise and looked up at the stars. "You remember when Tim broke my nose freshman year?"

Annie shrugged. "Who knows why people do what they do."

"Ugh, whatever. We can't let Jorge ruin our night. Come on, we're near the pond. You'll like it there."

KNIFE

The pond at the back of Rose Town was the rainwater-filled aftermath of some kind of explosion. Near enough to the factory that you could guess how it happened but deep enough that it filled anyone who saw it with unease. It was starting to ice over in spots, the ground at its edge was hard and dry.

The area around this industrial zone didn't have any of the trees that choked light out of the rest of the city. Out here, the moonlight was bright enough to read by.

"There are wild cherry trees on the other side of the pond, but the ground is soft and loose. It's dangerous to pick over there," Hollis said quietly.

Annie sat at the water's edge and pulled her winter hat down over her face.

"I'm sorry about Jorge," she said.

Annie wouldn't meet his gaze. Hollis stayed quiet, expecting her to elaborate, but when she didn't, he had to ask.

"Why did you like him in the first place?"

Annie sighed. "I don't think I did? He just . . . He showed interest and . . . I don't know. Saying yes seemed like the thing to do at the time."

Hollis crouched down next to her. "It's okay."

He picked up a piece of gravel and tossed it in the water. Annie sat back so she could watch him throw another.

"I thought you would have more to say about it," she said eventually.

Hollis stopped and took her in. Her face was splotchy and red, eyelashes spiky, wet: ready for tears. Her big wool coat covered her knees, and her arms were shoved inside the torso with them, leaving her sleeves deflated and empty.

"Why?"

Annie met his gaze. "I *know* you like me."

Hollis froze.

There was a version of him that was screaming, horrified and embarrassed. But it was younger than he was, and so far away.

He tossed another rock into the pond. "What does that have to do with you and Jorge?"

Annie shook her head and pulled her hat down. "Nothing, I guess."

Hollis pressed his lips together tight, now that Annie couldn't see him, and swallowed until his chest hurt a bit less.

"I know what it feels like to want to be seen," he continued. "You shouldn't have to feel bad for liking to be wanted."

Annie sniffled.

"'Liking to be wanted . . . ,'" she echoed.

Hollis smiled despite himself.

"What about you? Do *you* like being wanted?" Annie asked.

Hollis chucked another rock, hard this time.

"I can't even begin to imagine what that feels like," he said. "I'm still focused on wanting to be *seen*."

Annie frowned and pulled her hat all the way up.

"Do you know if Yulia . . ." She paused and swallowed hard.

"What about Yulia?"

Annie glanced at him, cheeks pinking, but Hollis just waited. He knew when Annie needed time.

Finally, Annie opened her mouth to start. But blocks up the street, from where they came, there was a scream.

Hollis scrambled to his feet.

Someone yelled again louder, and there was the sound of frantic footsteps on gravel. Hollis's heart slammed in his chest.

"We can talk about that later. Let's go."

STRIKE

By the time they reached the group, cars were already speeding off and the garbage fire had been put out.

Annie grabbed the sleeve of a sophomore girl running past. "What happened?" she shouted.

"Let go of me!" The girl tore her sleeve out of Annie's grip and sprinted off into the night.

Hollis burst into the house where most of the noise was coming from and nearly tripped over someone running out into the dark.

"What's going on!" he yelled.

Stephanie was tugging something down the hall.

"Shit! Hollis! Help me, I'm not strong enough to pick him up!" She dragged a body into the candlelight.

It was Jorge.

"Jesus fucking Christ! What happened?!"

"I don't know! He just went downstairs and . . . and . . . and . . . ," Stephanie started hysterically.

Jorge was a mess of red and black, sliced all over, deep gouges on his face, arms, chest, and legs bleeding freely. Unconscious and deadweight. Hollis froze, staring at him in horror, until Stephanie yanked him back to reality with another cry.

"Okay. Get the blanket from upstairs," Hollis said. "We've gotta take him to the hospital. He can ride in the back with us." He turned to Stephanie. "Where are the rest of the guys? How come they're not helping you?"

"I . . . I . . ." Stephanie was in shock, her eyes glassy and wide.

She tugged Jorge again, but she was clearly losing strength.

Hollis grabbed her arm and shook her a bit. "Go blow out those candles," he said gently.

She blinked at the order, then rushed across the living room to comply.

Annie flew back down the staircase with their backpacks and sleeping bag.

"Give those to Stephanie; help me with Jorge."

"What the fuck . . . What the fuck . . . ?!" Annie stammered.

"I don't know, we'll ask Stephanie later. Steph, I need you to come with us."

Jorge was shorter than Hollis, but he was heavy; he was an *athlete*. Hollis could barely manage him with Annie helping. But adrenaline was enough to get them out of the building, down the stairs, and to Yulia's car.

Stephanie threw the blanket and sleeping bag down on the back seat to protect it from bloodstains and then got in to help Hollis and Annie pull Jorge inside.

"God, I hope he doesn't wake up before we get there. He is *not* going to be happy to learn that we were the ones who helped him," Annie said.

But that didn't matter.

Hollis peeled out of the lot and left Rose Town behind.

HUSH

It was 3:00 a.m. when Hollis got home.

He immediately got into the shower to wash Jorge's blood off his skin, used his toothbrush to get the red from beneath his fingernails.

Then he lay in bed awake until morning, hearing the echo of everyone's screams.

DAWN

On Saturday, Hollis's father was home.

Usually, Hollis had to take care not to wake him up on Saturday mornings. After a hard work week Mr. Brown liked to sleep in as late as he could.

But that day Hollis woke up last.

He rolled over and looked at his phone. Two texts, one from Annie and one from Yulia.

Yulia: You didn't have to drop the car off that early, damn!

Annie: Heard through the grapevine Jorge's parents are pissed as fuck.

Hollis grinned. He texted Yulia first.

Hollis: At your service princess, lmk if it needs more cleaning.

To Annie, he sent:

Hollis: U traumatized? I'm traumatized.

Annie responded right away.

Annie: I've never seen so much blood. That was extremely fucked up.

Hollis: U wanna come over? Hash out the circumstances?

Annie: I woke up both my parents coming inside. I'm grounded for the whole weekend. :/

Hollis: :/

Annie started typing, then stopped. Then started again.

Annie: Are you going to make me talk about the pond thing?

Hollis frowned. He never made Annie do anything.

Hollis: We don't have to.

Annie: :/

Hollis: Like ever.

Annie: :////

Hollis: We can talk about it when you're ready. I don't mind having to wait.

RUSSET

Mr. Brown was in the backyard harvesting onions before the next frost.

Hollis's ma was in the kitchen washing the dishes and watching him. She looked happy.

Things were always lighter on the weekends, warmer when his father was home.

Hollis sliced a thick piece of sweet potato bread for himself and spread it with fresh rosemary butter. He settled in at the kitchen table and rested his head on his elbow as he chewed.

"I'm going to roast a few onions when he's finished," Mrs. Brown said. "Mr. Allen gave us a chicken. Two of his got out and froze in the night."

Hollis hummed. The weather got like this when fall was almost over—warm one day, freezing the next.

"I've gotta make some cheese before this milk sours," she continued, scrubbing hard at the pan in the sink.

"I'll do it," Hollis murmured. He tried to pick up more chores when Mr. Brown was home so that his parents could spend time together. Forty-eight hours a week didn't seem long enough to him.

Hollis's ma wiped her hands on a dish towel, then crossed the kitchen to give Hollis a kiss on the top of his head.

"Sweet boy."

GHOST

Hollis prepared the rennet and citric acid, then set the milk up to boil. Cheesemaking wasn't his favorite, it was more of his ma's thing. But he could make mozzarella, cream cheese, and ricotta if they wanted to have lasagna.

Mrs. Brown could stretch milk and cream out into yogurt and sour cream, buttermilk, farmer's wheel cheese, and that bitter white cheddar his father liked to open on New Year's Eve every year. There was even an experimental Parmesan moldering away in the root cellar.

But mozzarella was easy; anyone could make it.

They had onion soup with firm white slices of it for dinner, and he shredded a bit of it to make a cheese pizza with store-bought sauce the next day. Mr. Brown packed some of it to take with him wherever he went during the week. He pressed his big hand onto Hollis's shoulder as he passed through the room.

Hollis went to bed Sunday night warm and full.

MOZZARELLA

Ingredients

1¼ cup water

1½ teaspoon citric acid

¼ rennet tablet or ¼ teaspoon liquid rennet *(not Junket rennet*)*

1 gallon milk, whole or 2 percent, *not* ultrapasteurized**

1 teaspoon kosher salt

Equipment

5-quart or larger *nonreactive* pot

Cooking thermometer

8-inch knife, offset spatula, or similar slim instrument for cutting
the curds

Microwavable bowl

Rubber gloves

Slotted spoon

Instructions

Prepare the citric acid and rennet: Measure out 1 cup of water. Stir
in the citric acid until dissolved. Measure out ¼ cup of water in a
separate bowl. Stir in the rennet until dissolved.

Warm the milk: Pour the milk into the pot. Stir in the citric acid
solution. Set the pot over medium-high heat and warm to 90°F,
stirring gently.

Add the rennet: Remove the pot from the heat and gently stir in the
rennet solution. Count to thirty. Stop stirring, cover the pot, and

let it sit undisturbed for 5 minutes.

Cut the curds: After 5 minutes, the milk should have set, and it should look and feel like soft silken tofu. If it is still liquidy, re-cover the pot and let it sit for another 5 minutes. Once the milk has set, cut it into uniform curds: make several parallel cuts vertically through the curds and then several parallel cuts horizontally, creating a grid-like pattern. Make sure your knife reaches all the way to the bottom of the pan.

Cook the curds: Place the pot back on the stove over medium heat and warm the curds to 105°F. Stir slowly as the curds warm, but try not to break them up too much. The curds will eventually clump together and separate more completely from the yellow whey.

Remove the curds from heat and stir: Remove the pan from the heat and continue stirring gently for another 5 minutes.

Separate the curds from the whey: Ladle the curds into a microwave-safe bowl with the slotted spoon.

Microwave the curds: Microwave the curds for 1 minute. Drain off the whey. Put on your rubber gloves and fold the curds over on themselves a few times. At this point, the curds will still be very loose and cottage cheese–like.

Microwave the curds to 135°F: Microwave the curds for another thirty seconds and check their internal temperature. If the temperature has reached 135°F, continue with stretching the curds. If not, continue microwaving in thirty-second bursts until they reach temperature. The curds need to reach this temperature in order to stretch properly.

Stretch and shape the mozzarella: Sprinkle the salt over the cheese and squish it with your fingers to incorporate. Using both hands, stretch and fold the curds repeatedly. It will start to tighten, become firm, and take on a glossy sheen. When this happens, you are ready to shape the mozzarella. Make one large ball, two smaller balls, or several bite-size bocconcini. Try not to overwork the mozzarella.

Using and storing your mozzarella: The mozzarella can be used immediately or kept refrigerated for a week. To refrigerate, place the mozzarella in a small container. Mix a teaspoon of salt with a cup of cool whey and pour this over the mozzarella. Cover and refrigerate.

*Junket rennet is less concentrated than other kinds of rennet and isn't ideal for making cheese. If this is all you have access to, try using 1-2 whole tablets to achieve a curd.

**Almost any milk can be used for making mozzarella: whole, 2 percent, skim, cow, goat, raw, organic, or pasteurized. Pasteurized milk is fine to use, but make sure that it is not ultra high temperature (UHT) pasteurized. The proteins in UHT milk have lost their ability to set into curds.

RAIN

Hollis took a deep breath.

The train slammed past, loud enough to set his ears ringing.

He tasted that velocity he needed, soft and strong as the tide.

It was cold that morning.

By the time the caboose flew by, pulling hard enough for him to stumble, the tears that leaked out of the corners of his eyes had turned to ice.

CRACK

It was quiet and strange when Annie and Hollis made it to school on Monday. Yulia didn't seem in on whatever it was that was making people in the hallway stare at Hollis warily, so they couldn't even get any intel from her.

Timothy was in his English class, and while Hollis didn't usually talk to him, it was a good opportunity for a debriefing. But when he arrived, Timothy's seat was empty.

Nothing happened until after lunch, when the intercom finally called him into the principal's office. As Hollis headed down the hallway, he saw Stephanie walking quickly. Arms wrapped around her stomach, face red and wet.

When she saw him, she startled, then walked faster.

"Sorry," she said as she passed. "I tried my best."

Hollis's heart sank.

He made his way to the administrative wing and sat down in one of the waiting chairs until the assistant principal called his name.

STORM

Hollis was so surprised to see everyone gathered in there that he stood in the doorway for longer than was probably polite.

To the left of the principal's desk was Timothy and James. To his right were the younger girls he'd vaguely remembered being around the fire, as well as two adults who looked enough like Jorge that Hollis could comfortably assume they were his parents.

They looked furious.

"Sit."

Hollis made his way to the only empty chair next to Tim and James and sat down.

The principal, Mr. Feehan, was the sort of man who got angrier at being bothered than he did about actual problems. He was sweaty and balding, but younger than most principals usually were. Hollis knew him to be fair, and kind more often than not.

So it was jarring to see him with this expression, like Hollis had done something very wrong.

"Do you know why you're here?"

"This is about Rose Town . . . ?" Hollis asked, purposefully vague.

Mr. Feehan took off his glasses and folded his hands.

"Can you give me your account of Friday night?"

Hollis glanced over at Timothy and James. They seemed annoyed.

"Annie Watanabe and I got there around nine," Hollis started. "We went in to set up a place to sleep, then came back outside. Jorge had an argument with Annie because they just broke up. So, Annie and I decided to take a walk away from the group. We went off on our own for a while, then came back when we heard screaming. Something happened to Jorge that got him all cut up, and no one was waiting around to help, so Annie, Stephanie, and I took him to the hospital. Then we all went home."

Mr. Feehan flicked his eyes over to Jorge's parents, then back to Hollis.

"So, you agree that you and Jorge fought before he got hurt?" he asked.

Timothy sighed loudly and muttered something Hollis didn't catch.

"Uh . . . not really? He punched me in the stomach, and then I left. Annie and I didn't show up to the house until *after* whatever happened to him happened," Hollis clarified. "They were playing truth or dare or something, I don't know."

"He's lying," Jorge's father cried.

That pissed him off. Hollis turned around in his chair to face the man directly.

"I spent most of Saturday morning scrubbing Jorge's blood out of the seat of my friend's car because me and Annie and Stephanie were the only people who cared enough to stick around to help him," Hollis said bluntly.

Jorge's father ignored Hollis completely. "What if he just did that to cover up what he did?!"

To Hollis's surprise Timothy spoke up. "He didn't. Look, I don't like this guy as much as anyone, but he quite literally wasn't there when Jorge went into the basement. I don't know how many times we have to say it. Hollis and Annie were blocks away."

52

Hollis's blood went cold, and the hairs rose on the back of his neck.

So *that's* why it had taken so long for them to call him: Jorge was pinning this on him.

Mr. Feehan held up a hand, and the room went quiet. He nodded over at the sophomore girls.

"They say Tim and James came to your defense during the fight you had with Jorge, so I'm having a hard time believing they aren't on your side. Stephanie went with you to the hospital, so there's a chance she was an accomplice."

Hollis leaned forward and drove the heels of his hands into his eyes and rubbed hard, trying to get his heart rate down.

Everyone knew Rose Town was "haunted," but it's one thing to make spooky jokes and another to try to wiggle out of assault charges by claiming that "a ghost did it."

"I barely know Stephanie, and Timothy and James aren't my friends," Hollis said, sitting back up. "Tim broke my nose freshman year, and we haven't exchanged a single word since, until Friday."

He glanced over at James. "James beat me up so bad last week I had to go to urgent care myself. To be honest, I'm shocked they aren't joining Jorge in whatever the fuck this is."

Mr. Feehan leaned forward, curious. "Will urgent care have a record of this?"

"Urgent care has cameras in their parking lot. You can literally watch Annie and Yulia dragging me in there. Hospitals should have cameras too."

Hollis turned to Jorge's parents, then stood up and peeled off his sweater. The bruise on his stomach from Jorge's fist was still purple and green. James's marks were also there but fading yellow.

One of the sophomore girls gasped and turned away quickly.

"Jorge punched me so hard I almost threw up because he thought I stole his girlfriend and I still carried him on my back out of that house and into the hospital." Hollis seethed. "He's a fucking dickhead, but I'm not going to just let another kid bleed out in a filthy basement. Why don't you start asking everyone who *was* there why they didn't stay to help?"

Jorge's mom started crying, but Hollis didn't care.

"We stuck around the hospital until two a.m., checking to make sure he was all right." He continued louder. "Stephanie spent an hour calling people, trying to get your phone number, so that you'd know where he was. I can't believe I have to sit around defending myself. That Tim and James, who *truly* don't care whether I live or die, have somehow decided to defend me too. But it's still easier for you to believe I sprinted to the pond and back to stab Jorge and then felt bad enough to take care of him. It's fucking insane."

"*Hollis!*" Mr. Feehan yelled. "Put on your shirt and sit down."

Hollis wrestled his sweater back over his head but didn't stop talking.

"Also, Jorge punched me only once. James punched me like eight times into a brick wall, and he's sitting there extremely unstabbed," he spat.

"Maybe if you weren't a bitch, people would punch you less," James muttered.

"Exactly!" Hollis cried. "I get punched way too often for that to even be considered a viable motive for anything." He folded his arms. "Besides, Annie and I aren't dating, and Jorge probably would have figured that out in about forty-eight hours. He was just mad and confused. It wasn't even a punch with intention, unlike James, who was punching me for a reason."

"And what reason was that?" the principal asked.

Hollis paused in his rant, deflating a bit.

He didn't know how to articulate what happened between him and James without making himself look bad.

James rescued him again. "He called me stupid. Don't like being called stupid."

"And I feel worse about that now that you're . . . here and all," Hollis admitted.

Mr. Feehan held up a hand. "Jesus. Give me a second to think."

Hollis glanced back over at James, who rolled his eyes and shifted his chair to face away from him. Timothy was staring at his shoes, hands clasped beneath his chin. Jorge's parents seethed at him from across the room. Jorge's ma was still crying quietly.

"All right. It will take a bit of time for the authorities to corroborate your story. The police will need to pull the security tapes from the hospital and urgent care, as well as probably send some officers to the scene to check for footprints around the pond. But in the meantime, the school can't move forward without disciplinary action of some kind. Two days in-school suspension for you, James and Timothy. Stephanie and Annie will be receiving the same." Mr. Feehan paused and looked at Hollis. "A week's suspension for you, Hollis. Out of school. We can't have you on the school grounds during an investigation."

"*What?*" Hollis stood up fast.

"And—" Mr. Feehan continued, undeterred. "I highly suggest you don't leave town. If your claims are verified by the police, we'll have the suspension scrubbed from your permanent record. You'll have a week to make up any classwork or tests you may have missed.

It's the best I can do, under the circumstances."

Jorge's parents looked smug, but Mr. Feehan wasn't finished.

"And you two. If it comes back that this child had nothing to do with your son's injuries, I would strongly suggest giving him and his family some sort of apology. Because if this situation happened as he described, it would be a considerable wickedness to pin your own child's foolishness on the only person who was brave enough to save him. Now get out of my office."

RAGE

Hollis pushed through the door and walked quickly down the hall to the exit.

"Hey, where are you going?" Timothy called. "We have to sign some shit with the front desk."

Hollis disregarded that and stepped outside.

If he stayed in that room any longer, something bad was going to happen. When Hollis got this angry, he got reckless, and he was smart enough to try to avoid that.

The blood was pounding in his head. He felt like he was looking down at himself from above. Hollis didn't get his books from his locker or tell Annie and Yulia he was leaving.

He walked straight into the woods.

WHITE

It took Hollis a while to process big emotions. There was no one in his life to model that for him.

He came from hard people. You took what you were given, and you swallowed it. Fought when it was time to fight, lay down when it was time for that too. Mrs. Brown was calm as a stream in spring; Mr. Brown absorbed rage like damp earth.

But the unfairness of this was raw and red. It felt like being slapped and then held underwater.

Hollis didn't know Jorge from Adam. They didn't have history like he did with Timothy; Hollis didn't provoke him on purpose like he did with James. When he and Annie headed off toward the pond, Hollis fully expected Jorge to show up at school on Monday, give him a hard time, cool off by Tuesday, and then quite literally never speak to him again.

He'd have no reason to.

Now Hollis was facing down assault charges, maybe even attempted murder—and for what?

He marched far into the woods, until the sky was darkened with branches and his voice no longer echoed. Until there was a body's space between trees and the quiet felt like a threat.

Then he sank to his knees and screamed.

Hollis dug his hands deep into the cold soil to stop them from shaking.

He rocked back and forth, head pressed against the ground.

When the heat of anger faded, it took everything else with it.

Hollis pulled his hands from the dirt, curled them around his chest, and lay on his side. Then he drew his knees up close and shut his eyes.

BLOOM

His phone was ringing.

Hollis scrubbed his hand across his face, then sat up, pulling the phone out of his pocket.

It was Yulia.

"What do you want?"

"Where are you?" she snapped. "We've been calling for hours."

Hollis checked the time—11:39 p.m. Twelve calls from Annie, seven from Yulia, and two from his ma at around 11:00 p.m.

Shit.

"I'm sorry. I'm fine, I'm out in the woods just . . . being a baby, I guess."

Yulia scoffed. "What the fuck are you doing?"

Hollis sighed and stood up to stretch. "Trying to have a nervous breakdown in peace. I fell asleep. You know, like, *everyone* got suspended because of Friday, right?"

"Yeah, it's pretty bad. Worse for you though."

Hollis chuckled and looked up. The woods were so dark, he couldn't even see the moon.

"How much trouble do you think I'll be in if they clear my name and then I stab Jorge for real the instant the charges are dropped?"

"Too much. Don't be an idiot. And don't sleep in the woods in winter unless you want to die."

Hollis's throat tightened. A fresh wave of pain swept over him, and he was quiet until it ended.

"You don't want to die, Hollis," Yulia said after a minute. "You're just very sad right now, you know that."

"Yeah." He looked down at his shoes. "Yeah . . ."

Yulia was always soft toward his sadness. She knew what he needed to hear, they'd been through this already in his darker years.

"Call your ma, she loves you," she said.

Hollis turned toward where he came from and squinted at the light.

"Okay. Can you tell Annie I'm all right? I don't want to talk to her right now because I don't want to make this whole thing about me. I'm sure she's already feeling fucked-up enough."

Yulia sighed hard.

"Tell her yourself," she said, and then hung up on him.

Hollis rolled his eyes and put his phone back in his pocket.

BITE

Hollis brushed the frost from his coat, wiped his nose, and started heading back toward town. It had begun to snow. He wiggled his feet in his shoes to make sure he still could. He should have been more careful.

At the edge of the woods, at the tree line before grass and sidewalk began, there was another person. It was . . . some guy.

Maybe a little younger than him.

He was standing so still.

Before Hollis could try to hide, slow down, or move quieter than he already was, the boy turned and looked at him.

Hollis stopped and stared right back.

"What are you doing in there?" the boy asked.

He was . . . His face was sharp, like an owl's. He had blond hair, nearly white, and his cheeks were bright red with cold. Everything of his was red with cold. He wasn't wearing gloves, wasn't wearing a winter coat; he looked like he'd fallen out of a portal to spring and been abandoned on the side of the road.

Hollis opened his mouth and closed it, then opened it again. "Are you okay?"

The boy frowned in surprise, then looked very annoyed.

"Are *you*? I'm not the one with ice tracks on my face, pal. You been crying?" he replied mercilessly. "Why are y'crying in the woods? Are you lost or whatever? You look a bit old to be lost."

Rude. Hollis scowled back.

"I'm not lost. Why aren't you wearing a coat?"

The boy folded his arms tight. "Because I don't got one, obviously. If I had one, I'd be in it."

Hollis rubbed a hand over his face, knocking off some of the ice crystals roughly.

"Whatever, man, but fucking Christ, you scared the hell out of me."

"I scared *you*? All I've been doing is standing here. You're the one emerging from the forest like a jackal. What are the waterworks about anyway? How warm you are in your winter clothes?"

Hollis sighed really loudly and began unzipping his coat. It was thirty degrees outside and about to get colder. This was obviously some kind of drifter in an emergency—regardless of his terrible personality. Hollis's house was close enough that he could make it all the way in his sweatshirt.

Plus, he still had last year's coat in a closet somewhere. . . .

"Here."

The boy stared at it. "For free?" he asked.

Hollis immediately felt sad. The kind of sad that has nothing to do with yourself.

"Yeah. I can . . . get another one."

The boy took the coat and put it on slowly, staring at Hollis, wary and defensive.

"Something happened to me at school today. I wasn't crying on purpose; I was trying not to."

STRUM

Walt was walking with him now. That was his name.

He'd held up a hand to pause Hollis in the middle of his explanation and demanded they exchange names because he "wasn't going to stand around wearing stranger clothes, listening to stranger problems," unless he had something to call him.

He was extremely rude about Hollis's situation, but he was listening to it. He seemed to care.

Hollis couldn't blame him for that anyway. Whatever Walt had going on was so much more traumatizing than being briefly accused of an assault he didn't commit and "suspended from school for a few days" that Hollis was almost humiliated to even be talking about it.

But Walt just gazed up at him and grimaced. Listened.

He had brown eyes, a strange thing for someone so blond.

ACHE

"Things would be easier if people liked you more."

"I am absolutely not in control of that," Hollis said immediately. "Also, that was a fucked-up thing to say. I need you to know that was fucked-up to say to someone."

Walt didn't seem bothered. He stopped walking and tilted his head to the side.

"It's really not that hard. Have you tried being nice and interesting? Or being real straightforward, but not in a bastard way?"

"What?"

Walt clicked his tongue, annoyed. "I said, have you ever given up your own ego and submitted to the horror of being known, or did you just shrug your shoulders and assume the whole world's filled with people full of talent who all got lucky while you got the short end of the stick of life? The whole world can't be filled only with people who hate you for no reason."

"I have friends, just not a lot of them," Hollis shot back. "And what do you even know about it? If you were so good at being liked, why don't you 'being liked' yourself out of your own fucked-up situation?"

Walt covered his eyes in frustration. "Jesus H. Roosevelt Christ," he muttered. "Look, pal. All I'm saying is that your opinion that everyone around you is running on full cylinders from birth is hooey. And that you could stand to work on yourself a bit before throwing yourself away. This Jorge guy is only pinning this on you because he knows you're disliked enough that he'll get away with it. . . ."

Walt paused. "And 'cause he's more scared of his parents than he is of you. Which is something you could change."

Hollis scoffed. "Hooey? Who even says that?"

"Me, you asshole. If I'd half the opportunity you got in life, I sure as hell wouldn't waste it crying in the woods. Look at you. You've got everything!" Walt threw his arms out wide. "You've got all your arms and legs, strong heart, strong lungs; you're tall; you're not ugly; you've got friends, a family, a place to live—"

"And what do you have?" Hollis asked meanly.

Walt stopped and let his arms fall to his sides. "All the answers, apparently." He grinned. It didn't reach his eyes.

"And my coat."

"And . . . your coat." Walt shook his head and started unzipping it.

Hollis immediately felt bad. "No, dude. I'm sorry, I didn't mean that. You can keep it. I'm just . . . frustrated."

Walt grimaced but stopped unzipping. He brushed his fingers through his hair and looked up at the night sky.

"My life ain't been easy," he said softly. "But I like to think I've learned a lot. We might be able to help each other out."

"How?" Hollis was certain that this guy was either about to skip town or be found in the woods frozen to death.

Walt met his gaze again. "Well, you wouldn't be talking to me if you had anyone else to talk to. So, I think at bare minimum, I can give you that."

"And what can *I* give *you*?" Hollis asked.

Walt smiled.

A real one this time, with all his teeth showing. It transformed his face, in a way that made Hollis immediately want to look away. Eyes squinted into half-moons, canines sharp in the late-fall starlight.

"You're enough as you are," Walt said.

Hollis huffed humorlessly. "Is that your way of saying that you're lonely?"

Walt shrugged. "Aren't we all?"

And that was the rub.

As terrible as it was to admit, this guy was quite literally doing exactly what Hollis claimed he couldn't: making someone like him enough to offer to save him. Walt had even talked himself into a way out of standing half-dressed in the cold.

Hollis looked down at his shoes. At the edges of Walt's beat-up Chuck Taylors across from his. This . . . felt so easy.

Hollis loved Annie and Yulia, but he couldn't remember the last time it was this easy to talk about his feelings with another guy. He felt seen, even though it was clear Walt didn't exactly like what he was seeing.

Walking away from this felt like a missed opportunity. It was unhinged to even think of this as an opportunity. He'd known this guy for thirty minutes and most of those they had spent arguing.

But Hollis already felt lighter inside, better than he had going into the woods.

Walt waited for him patiently. Steady and still. Not eerie still, like he'd been the first time Hollis saw him. Quiet still. The way old people did when they were waiting for the bus without a cell phone to look at, or on a bench while they were feeding the birds.

"Where do you live?" Hollis asked.

Walt's gaze sharpened. "I don't sleep far from here. It's nowhere you'd want to visit, that's for sure. But I can meet you tomorrow at the corner of Ridge and Greenway. Near where we met today."

"What time?"

"Fifteen to midnight, I gotta work during the day," Walt said immediately.

"That's so late—"

"It's later than that right now," Walt pointed out. "I'm sure you don't want people to see us hanging out or whatever. I'm not exactly polite company."

Hollis huffed. "Fine. Eleven forty-five at Ridge and Greenway. You better be there."

Walt grinned again. "You've got it."

Hollis looked over his shoulder at his house. "I'm . . . gonna leave now. Have a good night, I guess."

"Stay safe," Walt said.

"It's like twelve feet away, dude." Hollis laughed. "You stay safe. Don't freeze to death."

Walt laughed back, soft and deep. "No promises."

When Hollis put his key in the door, Walt gave him a sloppy salute, then turned and left.

GREEN

His ma was asleep at the kitchen table.

Hollis took the empty mug and plate from in front of her and put them away.

Then he wrapped his arms around her shoulders and stayed still until she woke up.

"You're cold."

"I was outside. Sorry for worrying you."

Mrs. Brown sighed and looked at him with dark eyes.

"Did you do it?" she asked. They must have called home about him.

She asked it plain: without judgment, resignation, disappointment, or anger.

Hollis came from hard people.

"No."

His ma believed him.

"Okay."

DRUG

Hollis went to sleep and dreamed of blood tacky on his hands.
When he woke, he remembered bright eyes and sharp teeth.

TIPTOE

Annie called him again, and this time he answered. He listened to her sniffle through an apology she didn't have to give.

"Robin says James vouched for you publicly, so at least when you come back people won't think that we're murderers."

Hollis stared up at the ceiling in his room. At the chipping paint and water damage.

"Why does he care so much?" he mumbled.

Annie paused before answering. "He thinks you're pathetic and doesn't like the idea of people believing guys like him and Jorge can't handle you."

That made sense.

Hollis was tired of people thinking that of him.

"They letting you come back on Thursday?" he asked.

"Yeah. Stephanie managed to wriggle out of her own suspension because she was able to gather enough witnesses to place her in the living room instead of the basement," Annie explained. "The rest of us are out till Thursday. They said they'll let you back next Monday, unless the cops show up at your place with cuffs."

Hollis closed his eyes and willed the anger back before the tide pulled him under again. "Sure."

"I'm even more grounded now though," Annie said softly. "But after Thursday I should be able to visit. Yulia too."

"Fine."

"Okay, Hollis. I'm sorry again. I didn't mean for this to happen."

She sounded so small.

"It's fine, Annie. I'll talk to you later." He hung up.

DELICATE

It was cold. True winter.

The air couldn't hold moisture at this temperature; snow swirled on the ground like dust.

Hollis was wearing his coat from two years ago. It was plaid, knit, and ugly as sin. He had the mittens Annie made and the hat Yulia bought him just after they met, and they just barely kept him from shivering.

The streetlights stretched his shadow in shades of orange and gray.

Hollis saw Walt from a distance.

He was six blocks down, directly in the center of the road. His blond hair white in the dark. He was staring up at the sky, head tilted back far enough that he had his arms out for balance.

It felt still, like it did when they first met.

The wind grew quiet. The whole neighborhood was frozen.

Hollis's heart slammed against his ribs as he gazed at Walt, and he thought—for just a second—about turning around and running back home.

As if Walt could hear the moment Hollis's brain produced that thought, his head turned quick.

Hollis stopped walking.

Walt grinned at him.

RUN

"I was sure you weren't gonna show!" Walt shouted down the street.

Hollis couldn't help but look around quickly before picking up speed. It was late; people were sleeping.

"That should be my line," Hollis said when he got close enough to not have to yell it.

Walt laughed and shrugged.

He was still wearing Hollis's coat, and for a moment Hollis envied him. His newer coat was a lot warmer than the one he was wearing. But that feeling didn't last long. Walt looked bad.

Not the way someone did when they were sleeping outside, or if they got in a fight. He looked . . . sick.

Like someone who had been ill for a long time. Definitely more than twenty-four hours' worth of illness. His hair was lank at the roots, his skin was papery and dry. He even looked thinner, though Hollis knew that shouldn't be possible.

It had been only one day.

"I know, I know," Walt said. "I swear to God I clean up well."

Walt's eyes were shiny, burning with energy he didn't look like he could afford. He raised an eyebrow playfully, then shrugged as if to say, *What else can we do?*

"Yeah, I guess," Hollis said dubiously.

"Don't stare, you're making me bashful."

Hollis looked away.

"So, what's the story, morning glory? Did the black-and-whites catch up with you yet?"

"What?"

"The fuzz. Police. They clear your name?" Walt clarified, rubbing his hands together and blowing on them.

"No, I have to wait until Friday. In the meantime, I'm stuck at home. Anyone can say anything about me at school, and I won't even be able to defend myself."

"Ya do that often? You seem like you might have a viper's tongue."

"If you want to call it that, yeah," Hollis said, folding his arms.

Walt nodded. He seemed pleased. "Good to know. At least you got that going for you."

"What do you mean by that?" Hollis asked.

Hollis thought they were about to go on a walk or something, but instead they were just lingering there in the center of the road. Walt hadn't moved an inch from where he stood. Sure, his feet turned to face Hollis as he walked closer, but Walt seemed comfortable where they were.

Maybe Walt was just tired. He *looked* tired.

"Some people start with nothing. I gotta really build them up to be something better, solve their problems with nothing but wit," Walt explained. "But, if you're clever and everyone already knows that, it's not hard to be charming. Being charming is just being clever without being a dick. Everything's easier when you're charming."

"So, this is something you do often. . . . Is it, like, your job or whatever?" Hollis asked.

Walt grimaced. "Kind of? It's basically the only thing I'm good at. Pays well too, sometimes."

Hollis gave him A Look.

"I mean *clearly* not *right now*," Walt said, "but that's how freelancing works. Some days are cream and caviar, others are sleeping in a hole I dug over a buried thermal spring so I don't freeze to death. You win some, you lose some."

"You should get a real job. How old are you?"

Walt's face did something complicated. "Seventeen. But I've been on my own for a while."

Ah. "Foster kid?"

"Sure, let's go with that." Walt shook his head. "It is *not* my favorite thing to talk about."

Hollis smirked. He liked Walt. He was weird and kind of unnerving, but he was always funny.

"So, matchmaker. What would you do with me?" Hollis spun in a circle so Walt could see the full picture, throwing his arms out wide.

Walt put a hand on his chin theatrically and peered close.

"Well, for starters, you dress kind of bad, so I'd work on that first—and *don't* start with me, I am literally homeless. You have no idea how I dressed when I could wear what I want."

Hollis laughed. "Okay. What else?"

"Your haircut is bad; men today have no understanding of the impact of a good haircut," Walt griped. "After that I'll need to know more about your social situation so I can slow-burn a meteoric rise of some kind. You going to college?"

Hollis shook his head. "It's the factory or construction out here for most of us."

"Still?" Walt said, disgusted. "Small towns. Things never change."

City people, Hollis thought meanly. *They don't change either.*

"Whatever, I'll figure out something. We can talk about it

down the line," Walt was saying, to himself it seemed. "It's October, so there should be about eight months of schooling left. That's enough time—"

"You sure you'll still be here in eight months?" Hollis interrupted.

Walt looked up, startled, like he forgot Hollis could hear him. Then he grinned.

"Aw, baby, for you? I'll stick around," he murmured.

Walt was flirting with him, Hollis realized. He was *flirting*.

Hollis didn't know how that made him feel. It was one thing to be flirted with in the hallways at school, by a girl who was confusing his standoffishness with being mysterious.

It was another to be looked at—beneath hungry lowered eyelids—by a boy who was visibly running out of options.

Accepting affections like that was for bad people.

Hollis wasn't a bad person.

"You don't have to do that," he said.

Walt immediately rearranged his face. "I thought I might," he admitted, wary.

Hollis frowned. "Not with me. You want something from me, you just ask."

"Okay," Walt said, his eyes darting to the ground. "Okay, fine."

He looked up quick—so quick it startled Hollis a bit. Then he stuck out his hand.

"I'll stick around and put you on the straight and narrow. All you gotta do is feed me and find me shelter. Six months and I'm out of your hair. Permanently, if that's what suits you."

Hollis looked at Walt's palm.

He was just another kid out in the snow. Desperate.

Hollis could bring Walt home; his ma would know what to do. If that didn't work, there were houses, abandoned and viable. He'd have to suss out the extended family of the people who once owned them, but they'd do. Food he had plenty of; he could swing by in the mornings and after dinner. An extra portion wasn't going to break the bank.

It was fine. It was going to be fine. He even had a week to work on it.

"Okay."

Walt grabbed his hand tight before Hollis could finish offering it.

FLINT

It was like falling down a hole.

The vertigo was there, the overwhelming and immediate awareness that he'd made a terrible mistake was there. The dark rushing up at him, warm and quick.

The echo of his own scream.

Light, limited.

And there was despair.

Deep as genetic memory: Paleolithic.

Human beings had been afraid of falling in holes for as long as there had been holes and human beings.

GORGEOUS

Hollis saw Walt in front of him. His eyes rolled back in his head and the color drained from his face completely. He saw Walt's body fall to the ground and it was suddenly so obvious that this body had been dead all along.

His vision was . . . disorienting. It felt like he was looking through holes in a mask instead of through his own eyes. Black and fuzzy around the edges. It took even longer to figure out what that meant.

Because of the *body*.

Hollis couldn't stop staring.

Its hair was so brittle now that the wind was starting to blow it clean off Walt's skull. And suddenly Hollis was close enough to see pores, even though he didn't feel himself moving.

He couldn't even scream. He wanted to throw up.

"—favorite part. But it shouldn't be a problem by tomorrow," Hollis heard his own voice saying.

What?

"I said it shouldn't be a problem by tomorrow."

And Hollis knew he'd *never* sounded like that. Exasperated and casual in the face of something horrible.

He wanted to run, but his legs weren't listening to him. Then his arms began doing the unthinkable:

Pushing the grate off the street drain. Yanking the body closer. Peeling off his coat, then tipping the boy into the darkness with a hideous splash. One of Walt's feet was in the way of the lip of the drain, and it hit the metal hard with a crack.

It fell clean off with a puff of dust and lay there on the sidewalk.

Hollis felt the urge to heave so hard that it translated externally, and he doubled over. But his arm continued moving without him. It slapped the foot into the drain.

"You're quieter than most. Anyway, don't worry. He's not from anywhere remotely close to here, and his body will dissolve after an hour or so. He's not wearing your coat anymore either, which is cracker, forensics-wise. This coat you have on now sucks; I can't believe you just gave me your good coat like it was nothing."

Hollis had murdered someone. In the middle of the street where everyone could see.

"There's no one here for at least two blocks down. You've got a ton of abandoned buildings, which is . . . so convenient. Besides, I can smell pretty well; people have a stink. Unless Google Earth narcs on us, we're good," Walt said.

We.

Hollis finally began screaming.

SWEET

Walt's voice echoed like it came from above, and it made the hairs on the back of his neck rise. When Walt spoke out loud, Hollis heard his own mouth speaking, of course, but internally it was all Walt.

He had an accent, but Hollis couldn't place it.

You focus on the strangest things when time slows for a panic attack.

Every sensation was new and different. Layered in a way that was almost impossible to describe.

He was aware of the scrape of the denim on his legs, the itch of his sweater, the shock of cold as Walt took off Hollis's old coat and shrugged on his new one. His bones felt a bit long, and his shoulders were tight. His shoes were too light for the weather.

His skin was taut, full to bursting the way it had been during the growth spurt that left Hollis tall enough to duck doorways. Walt was running his tongue over his teeth, blunt blunt blunt. In comparison to the other boy's, Hollis realized.

Walt was adjusting to his body.

It was a new jolt of horror, but Hollis was already screaming. He couldn't double scream. He couldn't even struggle.

He remembered when he had almost thrown up—when it somehow overrode this for a bit—and tried to replicate that sensation. If he remembered how he felt just before, he might be able to wrestle back control.

Hollis strained and twisted.

Walt stopped mid-stride and put Hollis's foot down.

You need to stop doing that right now or you're going to give yourself a stroke, he said, very serious. **If you're patient, I'll teach you how we can share, but you need to calm down first.**

Share? Share?!

It's too late at this point.

Walt continued walking.

Screaming isn't going to do anything. I'm used to it.

LUSH

Ten years ago, Hollis had broken his arm. He'd been climbing a tree, stepped on a dead branch, and fell like a comet to the ground. He could still hear the echo of the crack.

There he lay on his back in the grass, in an agony so sharp that his brain filled with static. He knew he must be seeing the trees above him, blue sky, white clouds. But the pain was so large he was blind with it. Only red, orange, and black remained as he was pulled from the ground and rolled into his father's truck.

Horror was the same.

Intellectually, he knew he was screaming. He could surmise what had happened and guess at what sort of creature "Walt" was. He could see the world lurching forward as they jolted toward his house. Spared a bit of scientific curiosity about what sort of thing had happened with the very human body Walt had previously been wearing.

But at the front, drowning out everything, was fear.

Animal and instinctive. Gnaw-your-arm-off-to-free-yourself sort of stuff.

But Hollis couldn't even gnaw. He couldn't do anything but scream and think.

Walt had walked him home that first night. Waited until he put his key in the door to make sure it was his house.

Asked about his friends, family, and behavior. Said, *"That's good to know."*

Food and shelter. Hollis had never asked what kind. He never thought he needed to.

Maybe Walt was going to eat his body, maybe that was what he did to that other guy. Sucked him dry until he was so brittle. Hollis remembered the foot and the crisp sound of its separation. Another wave of nausea hit him so bad that it made Walt stop and lean against a fence to catch his breath.

"I eat normal food, Hollis. That other thing had nothing to do with eating." Walt panted. "Quit trying to make us throw up."

Hollis *hated* that Walt was using his voice. It made him roar in anger and beat against the inside of himself.

Walt sank to the ground and wrapped his arms around his chest. He took a deep breath and closed his eyes. A feeling of calm settled over them, disorienting and unwanted.

Furious, Hollis twisted in the exact way Walt told him not to, and Walt stopped what he was doing immediately.

Fine.

Walt's inside-voice again, and that accent.

Walt picked up the pace. He walked up Hollis's stairs like he did this every day and rummaged Hollis's keys out of his pocket. He opened the door and closed it sharply behind him.

"Where did you go?" Hollis's mother called.

To Hollis's despair she was waiting up for him again at the kitchen table.

Walt turned Hollis's body and walked it inside.

TAKE OFF YOUR SHOES! Hollis howled.

Walt bent and began undoing Hollis's laces.

"I felt a bit stir-crazy," Walt said. "So I just went around the neighborhood. It's only been about twenty minutes."

Hollis's ma got up and opened the cabinet. She pulled out a mug and filled it from the pot sitting on the stove.

"Here, take some milk with you to bed. It's too cold to be wandering around so late," she said softly.

Hollis flinched as his mother kissed Walt on the side of the head and placed the mug in his hands. He wanted to push her away, warn her, shout, fight, anything. But he couldn't. He *couldn't*.

Walt took the mug and used Hollis's face to smile.

ONEROUS

The disgust was too overwhelming for Hollis to continue his instinctual scream; he was shocked into silence as Walt walked his body up the stairs.

Walt took a few steps toward Hollis's parents' bedroom, then paused, turned Hollis's body around, and chose the correct door. He shut it behind them, placed the mug on Hollis's desk, and took off his coat.

Then Walt closed Hollis's eyes and breathed in deeply.

This room doesn't smell nearly as rank as most other guys' rooms. Could be cleaner though. Your ma seems nice.

Spend a lot of time in teenage boys' rooms, you pedo? Hollis couldn't control his mouth.

I'm seventeen, Walt replied. **Kind of. Choosing people around the age I feel is more comfortable. So yeah, I've endured a lot of rank-smelling rooms. And I can't just immediately clean them; people get suspicious.**

Walt took a sip of the hot sweet milk and ran a curious finger over some of the books in Hollis's cheap Walmart bookshelf.

You seem calmer. That's good.

It will pass, Hollis snapped.

Hollis could feel the muscles of his face shifting into a smile again, and it made his skin crawl.

I hate you. I hate you I hate you I hate you I hate you.

Walt scrubbed a hand over the back of Hollis's neck and stopped talking to him. He just sat in Hollis's desk chair and finished his milk as Hollis shouted obscenities at him inside.

Then he stood up and took a deep breath.

"Here we go."

He left Hollis's room and headed for the bathroom.

GRUNT

Walt shut the bathroom door, turned on the light, then looked in the mirror.

He ran his hands over every inch of Hollis's face. Touched his bushy eyebrows, the freckles that covered his cheeks and chin, ran his fingertip down the curve of his nose, tapped the bump on its slope gently.

He pressed a thumb to Hollis's lips, dragged across them in a burst of sensation. Hollis began to weep, overwhelmed.

Walt made a soft hush noise, but Hollis cried harder. He couldn't help it.

Walt looked inside Hollis's mouth at his teeth, lifted his tongue, fingered the back of his throat to test his gag reflex. He swiped along the edge of Hollis's ear—a thing Hollis had never done on purpose—and his knees involuntarily buckled. Walt caught him and stood again.

He tilted Hollis's head back and clasped the full arch of his neck, drummed against the jut of his collarbone, then dragged his hands through Hollis's thin, limp brown hair.

Everything about this was so horrifying and intense that it took Hollis a moment to notice that his eyes were the wrong color.

They were brown.

Walt's eyes.

Hollis's had always been *green*.

Hollis stared at them, hard. He had only ever seen Walt at night, by streetlamp, with winter shadows crossing his face. Or whoever's face that was.

He'd thought it was strange for someone who was colored so light in every other way to have such dark eyes.

In a wave of despair, he knew it would take a while for anyone in his life to notice: his green wasn't bright; it was close enough to brown. But Hollis knew his own face, and a change was a change. Mercifully, Walt let him lean them a bit closer to look.

Walt's eyes were honey brown, had a dark ring around the outside and a yellow one around the pupil. They made Hollis's face look sleepier, more serious and less fresh. The outside hadn't changed shape, Hollis couldn't tell what Walt looked like from this, how old he really was or whether he had crow's-feet . . .

Hollis was so engrossed in this that he didn't realize Walt was stripping off his clothes until his pants were on the ground and Walt was using his arms to roll up his shirt.

STOP! he shrieked.

If you think I'm not taking a shower, you've got another think coming, Walt hissed.

STOP, PLEASE.

Walt ignored him and wrestled the shirt off his head.

DON'T LOOK AT ME.

Walt stopped.

Everyone has a body, Hollis. Yours is fine. I won't look at it if you don't want me to, but I haven't showered in three weeks, I just want to feel the water on my face.

Hollis was so panicked he could feel his ears getting hot and red. No one had seen him naked before. Not even his parents after

90

he was done being a kid. He didn't want this. He didn't want the first time someone saw him to be like this.

But Walt was already facing away from the mirror, gaze locked on the ocean-themed shower curtain, obeying.

FUCKING FINE. PLEASE, JUST CLOSE YOUR EYES.

BLUE

Walt didn't shower with his eyes closed.

Instead, he turned off the light.

The crack under the door broke the darkness enough that Walt could locate the soap and shampoo, but he couldn't see Hollis's body, not even accidentally.

He washed it quick and mechanical, "a military shower," Walt supplied. Then the invader in Hollis's body just stood there under the spray. Head tilted back the way he'd been when Hollis had seen him standing in the street.

Hollis didn't know how to feel anymore. He'd felt too much in too short of a time, it was exhausting. He started to cry again, softly.

Walt put some of Hollis's ma's conditioner in his hands and rubbed it together. Then he smoothed it into Hollis's hair and scrubbed his scalp in soothing circles. Dipped his fingers behind Hollis's ears and down the nape of his neck, then back up to the crown.

It felt . . . nice, in spite of all things, and that only made him want to cry harder.

Walt sighed.

He leaned them against the wall, forehead and hands touching the tile, and let Hollis weep.

APPLE

Hollis jolted from the darkness to find himself already dressed and in bed. A spike of terror gripped him, but Walt was talking.

You cried yourself to sleep. It's okay, nothing happened, Walt whispered. **I didn't look.**

He put a hand in Hollis's hair and petted it gently, like it wasn't attached to him. Like he was gentling a horse or quieting a child.

Go back to sleep. It will be easier in the morning. I won't get up without you.

Without you. Without you. It echoed in the darkness of this place where Hollis now lived, behind his own eyes. Lapping like waves against his feet.

And something in him just . . . surrendered.

He drifted.

ELEVATOR DOOR

Hollis woke up still in bed. Walt was sitting cross-legged in the center of it, already awake, sewing a hole in a pair of Hollis's pants.

Hollis didn't know how to sew, and it was unnerving to see his hands doing it. He watched Walt close the hole quick and efficient, then test his mending by pulling the fabric taut.

I have questions, Hollis said, calm.

Walt grimaced, then let out a sharp breath.

Before we start, I need to make some things clear, he said. **First, I'll never lie to you. If I don't want to tell you something, I'll just say that or be vague. But I don't lie. It complicates things.**

You already lied to me— Hollis started, but Walt cut him off.

No. I didn't, he said firmly. **I didn't, Hollis. I was vague and I was clever, but I didn't lie.**

Walt tossed the pants to the side and picked up a shirt from the pile he'd made beside them and turned it over to find the hole that needed fixing.

Second, you can't ask them all at once and constantly or we'll never have any time for anything else. Let's pick a time, and when I say we're done, we have to stop. You don't have hours to lie around picking my brain all the time. You have school, and I have our deal.

Speaking of that—

You should ask important questions first, Walt snapped.

Hollis paused. He had a lot of . . . complaints about what

happened the day before, but there were much scarier implications that needed defusing.

So, he began:

What did you do to me?

Walt answered, short and perfunctory as he stretched out a length of thread to start sewing again.

We're sharing. Everyone has a little wiggle room between *them* and the rest of them. Enough to sneak into. It's a tight squeeze, of course, but not much worse than a packed elevator.

What are you?

Walt laughed, but he didn't sound happy. **I'm . . . just a guy. An unlucky one. I'm not a demon; I can't do magic, can't grant wishes. The only thing I can do is this. The jumping in. The rest of it is just manpower.**

Hollis relaxed a bit. Not completely, but enough to ask:

What happened to that other guy?

Walt shook his head. **His name was Sam. That wasn't my fault.**

What the fuck do you mean that wasn't your fault?! Are you doing that to me right now? Are you fucking sucking me dry or whatever the fuck—

Sam did that to himself!

Walt squeezed Hollis's eyes shut hard until they hurt, then opened them again, calmer this time.

It's . . . There are other options. This . . .

He gestured between the air and his chest like Hollis was standing in front of him.

This could have been an option. Bodies don't like being

stressed like that all day and night. Sam wouldn't let us sleep; we could never rest. He just screamed and screamed. He wore himself out so fast he didn't last three months. I couldn't even concentrate on our deal, and of course I couldn't leave—

Walt paused. He'd clearly said something he hadn't intended to, but it was too late.

You're only the fifth person who calmed down enough to even ask me something like that, he admitted.

The next question was obviously *How many people had it been?* It was on the tip of Hollis's tongue, but he could tell Walt was braced for it. Hollis didn't have much power in his body, but he could be clever.

Cleverer than Walt, if he was lucky.

Why do we wake up at different times? he asked instead.

Actually, this is a good question. We have separate consciousnesses, obviously. You think things and I think things; you feel emotions and I have my own—even though it's harder for you to feel mine than for me to feel yours.

Hollis remembered that moment outside, when Walt was forcing him to feel calm when he wanted to be angry.

You can think things that I can't hear unless you think them loud enough. I'm sure you can grasp at this point that I haven't had much time to play around with this, but that's all I know. I can't tell you why because I'm not a fucking scientist. I can just tell you what I've experienced.

Could you sleep while I'm awake? Hollis asked, feeling a glimmer of hope.

Walt paused, and Hollis could feel his face twisting into an unusual expression.

Yes, but I try not to. You wouldn't like it.

That sounded like a threat.

It's not a threat. It would be like having locked-in syndrome. I'll let you read a bit about that later today if you want.

Okay.

Is . . . there a way to undo this? Hollis asked.

Walt stopped sewing and put the shirt down. He was thinking, Hollis could feel it. It was like hearing neighbors walking around upstairs, muffled, echoed.

He waited patiently until Walt felt ready.

Everything wants to survive, Walt said quietly. **Is it so bad that I wanted to as well? Everything has a house. Is it so bad if mine is made of flesh? If I've . . . kept them clean and tidy, made them better, treated them kind. Grew roses in the garden, kept the fence painted white.**

Walt picked up Hollis's hand and held it to the sunny window. Hollis had a hangnail, and if he focused, he could still feel it smarting.

There are natural rules you have to follow to be safe, healthy, and alive. Eating, sleeping, whatever. Being me has rules too. There was no one to tell me what they were, so I had to learn them the hard, slow way, and it cost me more than you'd think.

He put Hollis's hand down.

No, Hollis, there isn't a way to undo this until it's finished. But I can tell you that it doesn't have to be terrible. It can be good if we try. It's been good before.

He sounded wistful.

Hollis didn't like that. It pissed him off.

Get up and take us downstairs, I'm hungry.

Walt stood and tossed the shirt to the side.

Finished with your questions?

Hollis refused to respond.

BRAG

Walt was . . . hm. It vacillated wildly between *horrifying* and *interesting* watching Walt pilot his body. If Hollis pushed aside his genuine concern about Walt's long-term intentions, his fear of becoming a Sam-husk, and the disorienting experience of watching Walt do things he couldn't, it was starting to feel more educational than anything.

Walt ignored his demands for sweet potato bread and instead forced him to eat boiled eggs, muttering something internally about increasing Hollis's protein intake. Walt used some of their preciously guarded olive oil in the boiled egg water and the peel came off easier than Hollis had ever seen in his entire life.

Then Walt scanned his entire house for things that needed repair. The screen door was squeaky, their carbon monoxide detector had been beeping for months, one of the legs on their kitchen table was loose. Hollis's father didn't want to spend the precious time he had with his family doing chores, and Hollis's ma was busy living. Walt set upon fixing what he could with what they had.

Why are you doing this stuff? Hollis asked after a silent hour of work.

He got back a frisson of an emotion from Walt that he couldn't name. Frustration and something else.

All you people love doing is buying new things. People used to fix what they owned, maintained it. We worked longer hours too.

Walt tightened a screw on their kitchen cabinet, then shook it to make sure it stuck.

You need to start mending your clothes when they tear or get worn.

I don't know how to sew. You have no idea how creepy it was watching you do that.

You should learn. It's not hard. Everyone should know how to sew, knit, or crochet, darn, and do some basic tailoring. How can you look your best without it? What if you couldn't afford warm things for the winter? A few balls of yarn are cheap in the summer but priceless in the winter months.

I'm not fucking . . . Laura Ingalls Wilder, Hollis spat.

Walt laughed dryly.

I'm surprised you even know who that is.

HUM

Walt stopped working whenever Hollis's ma appeared. He didn't seem to want her to know what he was doing. As if she would just not notice that her house was cleaner and better than it was earlier in the day.

Walt opened their kitchen pantry and just stared at it.

What now? Not organized well enough for His Royal Highness?

If Hollis could feel his arms well enough to fold them, he would.

Walt reached out and dragged his fingers across the labels, then picked up a jar of pickled asparagus.

You're still doing this here . . . ? he said.

Everyone does it. We have a supermarket, of course, but who wants to rely on that all the time? It's cheaper to make and grow stuff and share with each other. Should be familiar to an ancient demon like yourself.

Walt was using Hollis's face to frown. He made a soft mournful sound and hung his head.

Don't worry. Along with Little House on the Prairie, *I've also read* The Jungle. *You can close the pantry and walk away if it's too traumatizing for you to look at,* Hollis said meanly.

Walt gripped the side of the pantry hard enough to hurt, then he put the asparagus back down.

You don't know what it was like. If you did, it would never occur to you to be cruel.

Walt closed the pantry doors like he was closing the doors to a church.

TORN

After dinner, Yulia came by.

Walt had cooked. Focused on Hollis's apparently "insufficient protein intake," he made some rice-and-beans concoction with dried peppers and onions. He'd started back up the tedious work of fixing Hollis's clothes when she rang their doorbell.

Neither Yulia nor Annie texted before they came over most of the time, so it wasn't entirely surprising.

But Hollis had been so tied up in all of *t h i s* that it hadn't occurred to him to talk to Walt about how to act around his friends. If he didn't have the power to grab his body back and beg for help, at least he could have come up with some kind of contingency plan. But between arguing with Walt internally, and the six hours of manual labor Walt had forced them into, Hollis had completely forgotten.

Hollis begged, screaming, for Walt to just ignore her, but Walt walked them downstairs and opened the door anyway.

Yulia didn't wait to say hi. She immediately pulled them into a tight hug, rocking them back and forth the way she liked to after it had been too long since they'd seen each other.

DO YOU HAVE A GIRLFRIEND? Walt shouted, alarmed.

No, this is just Yulia, act normal, for the love of God, Hollis begged.

Yulia pulled back and held both his hands in hers.

"Are you all right? I'm so sorry about what happened—" Yulia was saying, but Hollis could barely focus on her because Walt wouldn't stop talking.

Jesus. She's so hot. Gals never used to shave their heads back in the day, it looks so swell on her. She smells real good too, like caramel and lemon. Like a lemon pound cake.

SHUT THE FUCK UP, Hollis shrieked.

"—gonna go by Annie's, but her parents are really mad, and they might ground her more if they catch us outside," Yulia was saying.

How did you manage to get a girl this fine to pay attention to you at all? Walt asked. **Her hands are really soft.**

Externally, Walt said, "That makes sense. Hey, do you want to go for a walk?"

Tell her we're busy, don't try to talk to her more. You don't even know her— Hollis hissed.

You do. Walt was slipping on Hollis's shoes and pulling his coat out of the coat closet. **It would have been convenient to know about this earlier. But you wanted to talk about how I need to stop changing out flickering light bulbs and cleaning all day.**

Please, Walt, please, Hollis begged.

Walt shut the door behind them.

"I have to get back soon though," he was saying to Yulia. "My ma wants me to help her with something."

"Oh? What's she working on?"

Walt paused, and Hollis panicked.

Tell her Christmas stuff.

"We're working on something for Christmas." Walt smiled. "It's a surprise."

"Mine better not be something other than plans for more bread," Yulia was saying.

Your parents bake too? Walt asked him.

No, I bake, you asshole, take us back home now.

"What else do I make that you like?" Walt asked Yulia.

Hollis couldn't tell what expression Walt was making with his face, but he didn't like it.

Yulia gave him a double take. "Are you fishing for compliments?"

Please tell me you've at least kissed this woman once. Walt groaned. **Looking into her face is like looking into a morning glory at dawn.**

I swear to God, if you don't stop talking about the way she looks I'll do that twisting thing you hate. I'll kill us both this instant.

"That rice bread you made that one time, and rhubarb jam, but if you didn't get some in the summer, it might be too late for that."

I won't die if you die, Walt replied smugly.

Sure, but you'll be trapped in my stroked-out body for a few decades, fucking locked in it, unable to charm your way into freedom. Don't fucking test me.

Walt stopped talking.

"Ha ha, I'll keep that in mind," Walt said to them both. His cleverness pissed Hollis off more.

"You seem to be taking this whole school situation a lot better than I thought," she said. They rounded the corner of the block and headed down one of the darker streets.

Walt shrugged. "I just . . . realized that I can't fight it, so why should I be upset? I know what I did and what I didn't do. No one here has enough money to bribe the police, and it's easier for them to pressure Jorge's family into leaving them alone than it would be to process the paperwork to frame me well enough to charge me. I'm not the only one suspended, so it doesn't feel as bad."

Yulia looked pensive.

They walked in silence for a while, all three of them.

"Well," Yulia finished. "At least you're confident. What are you gonna do if they decide to press charges?"

Run.

It was immediate and instinctive.

No. We're going to jail for like five months or paying a fine.

I'm not going back to jail for anything, Hollis.

Back?!

"I'll figure it out." Walt replied. "What else can I do?"

How old are you?

You don't know? You riffled through my wallet earlier.

Answer.

Seventeen, I'll be eighteen in January.

"If they book me in before the New Year, it won't even be on my record when I get out," Walt said. "I'll miss graduation though."

"And I'll be off to college. Annie too," Yulia reminded him as they turned the block again and headed back down his street.

"I'll find a way to visit," Walt said at the same time Hollis thought it.

We're getting better at this.

STARVING

Hollis wanted to scream at Walt as soon as they got inside, but he didn't.

He knew two things about Walt so far: yelling didn't have any effect on him, and he was vulnerable to surprises. He knew Walt would be waiting for some diatribe about Yulia. So, instead, Hollis waited until Walt had comfortably folded up his mended clothes and placed them back in his drawers to say:

Tell me about some of your other rides. The people you've possessed.

Walt paused, then shut Hollis's drawer.

Why?

You know more about me than I know about you, and I don't like it, Hollis said honestly.

He could feel his own eyes rolling.

Okay, but can I get in the bathtub? My back hurts because you don't exercise enough.

Keep the lights off.

Walt did. He even came in the bathroom every morning and evening to get dressed in the dark, faithful to Hollis's first-night request even though Hollis didn't ask.

Walt sat on the edge of the toilet, waited for the tub to fill, then turned off the lights to get in.

Hollis wasn't sure if it was the dark or the possession that made things feel . . . like more. He would never have taken a bath in the dark before this, so he couldn't tell if—

There's a feedback loop. You feel things and I feel things, mostly at the same time. But if something is really good or really bad, your sensations and emotions spur on mine until they double. Like nausea that first night.

Walt let his head thunk back onto the lip of the tub and closed their eyes.

I wish I had a cigarette.

Hollis waited him out, listening to the dripping of the faucet and the sound of the TV blaring downstairs. Walt draped an arm over their face and took a breath.

Before Sam, I was in a man called Ernest. The deal I made with him was about making women like him. He had a wife, but he wasn't talking about her; he was talking about the girls at his office. When he cooled off, I started doing things. Helping around the house, cooking dinner, going to bed earlier and earlier. Changed his hair and clothes, of course, people always need that.

Walt drummed his fingers on the tile.

Then I brought his wife flowers. They were an older couple, fifties. I think he forgot that she was beautiful.

He shook his head.

You can't do that, as a man. Treat your best gal like she's cold cuts. It ain't right. I tried to make him see that. Got her eyes following him all around the house. Instead of being thankful, he got jealous. Started screaming and never stopped. Poof. A Sam situation again. Had to find someone new with no time and resources so Georgia's husband didn't wear himself out and crumble. Couldn't do that to her.

Did you kiss her?

Walt grinned.

> You *would* ask that. A few times. It's just . . . love, you
> know? I've been a lot of people—men, women, old, young,
> whatever. Used to try to pick people I admired. Strong
> men, rich men. But their lives were . . . Well, everyone is
> complicated. Everyone is . . . sad in their own way.

Walt bit his lip.

> **God, I wish I had a cigarette,** he repeated.

You have about three months until we're old enough to buy them,
Hollis said dryly.

> **You'd do that for me? Let me dirty up your clean lungs to**
> **feed my habit?**

Who were you in before Ernest? Hollis asked instead.

> **Dina, a retired social worker. I didn't stay in her for long**
> **either. We got on like a house on fire though. She was**
> **funny and bright. Kept calling me** *kid* **in her head, which**
> **was really something,** Walt said. **With her, it was good.**

If you liked her so much, why did you jump into Ernest?

> **She wanted to travel the world in a camper van. I don't like**
> **being alone like that.**

What **do** *you like?*

Walt closed his eyes again.

> **Cigarettes. Especially in the bath or after dinner or in the**
> **morning. Peace and quiet. Tomato sandwiches, strong**
> **coffee. Dice. Dance halls. Playing music.**

Walt let their fingers tread across the surface of the water.

> **Being warm. Being useful. Talking to people. You?**

Hollis thought about lying.

Annie and Yulia. Reading. Baking, sometimes. Video games.

Who is Annie?

Walt didn't even wait for him to answer.

A girl, the one you like. Not that pretty one we just talked to, which is wild to me. How much of a looker can Annie be to turn your head like that? Annie, Annie, Annie. She makes your blood pressure spike, you horndog. You're making our face red.

My face. And she lives next door. I've known her since I was, like, nine. It wouldn't matter what she looked like, Hollis said hotly. And don't tease me about it; this isn't a game.

Walt laughed softly. **Yeah, yeah. She like you back?**

No. I don't want her to either; everything is fine as it is. You don't have to do anything to Annie, just be nice to her.

Walt made an unusual noise. A purr that warmed the back of Hollis's throat.

You got it.

ROAD

On Thursday, the police came. Mrs. Brown got to the door before Hollis could, and they lumbered inside.

Hollis could feel Walt's hackles rising and it was . . .

Hollis realized that he hadn't felt Walt feeling anything bad before. Walt's emotions were muted at the best of times, like being touched through a blanket. It was only now that Hollis realized how careful Walt had been to keep things light and give Hollis a blank tapestry to project his own feelings of terror and anger.

But now he was anxious and irritated. Frightened in a way that felt old.

Calm down.

Don't tell me what to do, Walt snapped.

Cute. Let me handle this. I can talk to cops.

We don't have time for lessons about that, just . . . hush up and let me think.

"Hollis?" Mrs. Brown called. "Can you come here, please?"

Walt's panic was sharp and involuntary. Hollis tried something new.

Go downstairs. I'm not asking, Hollis barked, authoritative.

Despair washed over them like a wave, but Walt obeyed and opened Hollis's bedroom door.

The police didn't look impressed at the wait. They were older men, hands around the mugs of coffee Mrs. Brown had poured them, a stack of documents in the center of the table.

"Man of the hour," one of them said sarcastically. He was short and had a thick mustache.

"What do you want?" Walt snapped.

"Hollis," Mrs. Brown hissed.

The taller officer raised an eyebrow but didn't take the bait.

"We need you to sign off on these forms. Tracks were found at the Rose Town pond and the back door to the property was inaccessible due to significant rusting. Nothing came in or out of that basement that didn't make it in through the front door," he said. "Not even you."

Walt snatched up the paper and read it quickly.

"Don't know what that kid did down there, who he pissed off, but it certainly wasn't your boy, Sheila," the man was saying.

Walt leaned over the table and picked up the pen.

Sign.

Suddenly Hollis had access to his fingers. Not even the entire hand, just the fingers.

What the fuck . . . ?

There had to be some sort of leverage Hollis could get out of this. He thought quickly.

"Right there, boy, we don't have all day," the officer barked.

If I sign this, you have to promise not to hit on Yulia. Ever again. Any of my friends actually.

Done, Walt said without hesitation. **Do it.**

It was hard to write; it felt like he had a plaster cast on the rest of his arm, but Hollis managed.

The officers picked up the paperwork and drained the rest of the coffee from their cups.

"Thank you for the coffee, hon," the tall officer said as he rested a hand on Mrs. Brown's shoulder, familiar and imposing. "You tell that man of yours I said hi."

Mrs. Brown was standing stiff, but she nodded and found her smile.

Their shoes tracked soil and grit across Walt's freshly washed floors.

"And, Hollis? Get your ass back in school." The door shut crisp. "Bright and early, Monday morning!"

Mrs. Brown flinched at the sound of their car door slamming before they peeled out of the road.

Hug her. Can't you see she's upset? You can't just leave her like that.

Walt folded Hollis's mother into his arms.

BIRTH

Let me show you something, Walt said.

He dressed them warmly and headed out. It was 1:00 p.m., too early for kids to be out of school, but late enough that most people were at work.

He took them to the bus stop and used some of Hollis's hard-earned money to ride to the edge of the community, in the opposite direction of Rose Town, close to where they met. Until the abandoned houses crowded out the full ones, getting shabbier and shabbier.

Then they walked for another mile, until the green crowded out man-made things and trees grew tall and the shadows beneath them dark.

Walt stopped in front of a small hill with dark green grass, strange for this time of year. He rounded the side of the hill, and Hollis was faced with a hole.

It was half the size of a man and dug deep enough to climb into.

This used to be a place that you could bathe in. Stayed warm all year.

Walt crouched to his knees and pulled them into the hollow, ducking Hollis's frame until it fit, curled up like a child.

Heat radiated from the soil in wisps of steam. Enough of it to feel like he was sitting by a radiator. Enough to not feel winter chill.

You slept here?

Before you.

Hollis didn't know what to say.

Walt closed their eyes and leaned back into the grass.

Walt.

Hmm?

Why did you come here? There are a million towns like this all over America. This isn't a place one finds themselves on accident. We can barely get one bus route down here. What are you doing here?

Walt bit his lip.

I can't tell you yet. It's personal. I don't know you well enough.

Oh, fuck you. You know me more than I know you, and you know that shit's not fair, so give me something. Anything.

Walt tapped their fingers against their knee, a nervous habit that Hollis didn't have, and sat silently. Hollis waited him out.

I . . . I think you're my last ride.

You thinking of dropping the habit? Hollis asked, cruel.

Walt laughed.

No, I'm just . . . I think you're it. For me. So, I have to do the best I can, try to make amends, give you the best of me while I'm still around.

What about that other guy . . . Why couldn't he be your last?

Walt shook their head, tapped their fingers.

Don't compare yourself to him. You're . . . more.

What does that even mean?

It means I'm glad it's you, in the end. Even if you're angry, even though you don't know me, I don't mind it being you.

114

GORE

Walt didn't like Annie. He didn't say anything about it, but Hollis could feel him stewing. Thinking. Upstairs-neighbor noises.

He was keeping his promise—he wasn't flirting with her or saying anything that spun Hollis into a panic attack—but he flinched when Annie first hugged him.

Walt kept her at a distance. Didn't talk to Hollis at all while Annie was talking to him, didn't push back on anything Hollis wanted him to say.

It was eerie and a bit frustrating.

Hollis waited until Annie settled in to watch a movie with them to say something about it.

What's your problem? Hollis snapped.

Nothing. It's fine, Walt said.

It's not fine, I can hear you fucking . . . deliberating or something. What are you thinking about?

Annie laughed at the movie and glanced over at Hollis to make sure he was enjoying it. Walt grinned back at her and stopped answering Hollis completely.

Things continued like this until she left, demanding another hug of Walt, which he reluctantly gave.

What the hell is wrong with you? Hollis yelled as soon as the door shut behind her.

Leave it be.

SOIL

Walt gave him a haircut.

He spent an alarming amount of time online looking at what was fashionable before deciding on layers in the front and shorter in the back. He parted Hollis's hair an inch from the middle and blow-dried it until it gleamed, bouncy and sleek.

Hollis didn't even know his hair could look like that.

Everyone you see who looks good puts in effort. Most people act like they don't, but they do. You don't have to be tall and strong to catch eyes. Just dress like you're paying attention. The guys have their shirts a bit tighter and their jeans a bit looser than what you've got. We can fix that.

Why does this matter so much to you?

Being square isn't a terminal illness, it's a default setting. This stuff you don't care about has impact and value. You'll see on Monday.

Walt rubbed a bit of Hollis's mom's jealously guarded hair dye into his eyebrows to darken them a little.

This one's a trade trick. I was in a man with a model girlfriend a while back, Walt said. **She was educational, among other things.**

So she was hot.

Walt grinned. **Among other things. She dressed like a concept. Taking in the whole picture instead of throwing together a bunch of stuff you like individually. Once you get it, it's hard to unlearn.**

If she was a model, she was probably hot enough to wear whatever.

Walt blew air out of Hollis's nose, annoyed. A weird thing that Hollis never did.

> **Doesn't mean she wasn't *right*. Take you, for example. Tall as a beanpole and just as skinny, no money for threads or shoes. Prettier than handsome, which ain't a disadvantage. The way you are, y'look like you just rolled off someone's farm. But with my owl eyes in your head, the right cut of fabric, better hair and posture, you could look like . . . well. Like a liability.**

Do you look like a liability? Hollis asked dryly. He knew Walt wanted him to.

Walt smiled fully this time, the way he did on the night they first met.

> **A liability is only halfway there. I was full-time trouble, sweetheart.**

GREED

Arrogance.

That was Walt's weakness.

It was not difficult to figure out how to stay awake while Walt fell asleep.

Hollis let Walt babble about fashion and women as he got them ready for bed. Asked the sort of questions that made Walt feel good and knowledgeable until Walt's fondness welled up in their chest like a summer sunrise.

Then, when it was time to sleep, Hollis let himself drift to a place that was quiet and calm, and stayed there. Like lying in bed for a few hazy minutes before getting up.

It was strange to hear his mouth begin to snore, when he had nothing to do with it.

REM sleep is deep, and Walt had said he needed that, so Hollis waited longer. Until his body stopped tossing and turning and a whisper didn't change the pattern of his breaths.

Hollis wasn't stupid.

He was younger than Walt and absolutely less conniving, but he wasn't so stupid he would forget the way it felt when Walt gave him access to his fingers.

It was a pulling feeling, from somewhere between his bones and the top of his skin. It didn't hurt. It was like spending a few hours with someone's hand lying on top of yours until you got so used to the weight and the temperature that you forgot it was there.

Then, when they lift off you for a few seconds and cool air rushes in, you remember what it is to be free.

It took until the dawn began to light the world beyond his eyelids.

But Hollis moved his own fingers himself—*just a twitch*—once again.

WILD

After a stressful week, Hollis would have headed straight to the train to get his fix of violence, but Walt didn't know he did that, and Hollis wasn't about to tell him.

Walt got up an hour before they had to leave, showered in the dark, blew his hair dry, and dressed him. Walt favored blue, gray, and brown, tossing Hollis's yellow, orange, and red clothes in a pile in the corner.

He'd promised Hollis he wouldn't throw them away, but Hollis was wary anyway.

Walt forced Hollis to eat more rice and beans, this time with a side of sweet potato toast because Hollis threw a fit, then he pushed them outside into the cold world.

We walk with Annie, Hollis announced in the voice Walt seem to take as a command.

He could still feel how much Walt didn't want to.

"Holy shit!"

Before Walt could jerk away, Annie's hands were in his hair, flowing like water, scraping past his ears. There was a helpless noise welling up Hollis's throat that Walt forcefully suppressed.

"This looks so hot, Hollis, what the fuck?" Annie laughed. "Did your mom do this?"

Walt moved politely out of her grasp.

"Felt like something different, that's all. If I have to walk back into everyone gossiping, might as well give them something to gossip about."

Annie's eyes narrowed mischievously. "They'll *definitely* talk."

Walt endured until they met Yulia in the parking lot, then his mood lifted.

This pissed Hollis off, of course, but Walt kept his promise and didn't say anything strange.

Yulia squeezed Hollis's face between her mittened hands and nodded sagely.

"It's armor. I get it."

Walt sighed inside with such longing that it made Hollis scream.

RUSH

It was a strange thing, being *seen.*

Giggling has a different tone when it's not mocking him.

Hollis could feel Walt preening inside him, but he was polite enough not to put words to it.

He sat Hollis closer to the front in most of his classes. Next to Timothy in English, and the other boy gave him a double take.

"We're not friends now."

Walt barely glanced at him. "I don't need to be your friend to want to see the board better."

Timothy sneered. "Strange timing for seat change is all."

That's one of Jorge's friends, but he provided my alibi, Hollis explained quickly.

Walt raised an eyebrow at Timothy and turned away so Timothy would have to say his next line to Hollis's shoulder.

"You're still a freak."

He sounds worried. Is being associated with you that much of an issue? Walt asked instead of responding.

Yes. Kind of.

Walt paused, and something twisted in their chest.

I'm sorry.

Why? For what?

That it's been this hard to be you.

Hollis frowned.

I'm okay. I have Annie and Yulia, and it's fine. You don't have to apologize for it.

All the same.

Hollis didn't know what to say to that, so he just stayed quiet. Walt let Timothy's comment slide until right before the bell rang, then he faced him directly.

"We're fine, Tim. Nothing is going to change. I didn't want this any more than you do, and I wasn't joking about the board," he said, quiet enough for the rustling of papers and backpack zipping to drown out any eavesdropping. "Don't talk to me unless you want me to talk back. But otherwise, we're square."

Timothy shook his head sharply and snatched his bag up. He turned toward the door, then paused and looked back.

"Jorge is out in three weeks. You gotta figure out what to do about that."

HUH

I think he likes you, Walt said.

Timothy Reid? Are you high?

Walt drummed his fingers against the edge of the desk and looked out the window instead of at the slideshow they were being made to watch.

> **I think he feels bad for you and that's closer to liking you than you'd think,** Walt explained. **He didn't have to give you an alibi, and he didn't have to warn you about Jorge, and he absolutely could have made a bigger deal about you sitting next to him.**

He called me a freak.

> **He was reminding you of your place. Try thinking about why people might do things before reacting. What would Timothy have to gain from warning you about Jorge? What would he have to lose by allowing people to think you're close?** Walt said. **Maybe this is less about you and more about *him*.**

Hollis shouldn't have to think about Timothy at all. He never had before then.

We eat lunch with Yulia and Annie. Sometimes Yulia drives.

Walt let him change the subject, humming quietly.

> **I'll eat anything except bananas. I don't like the ones from now.**

ANTHROPOCENE

Walt held his body differently.

Hollis liked to stoop a bit, but Walt stood tall, with his feet planted firmly on the ground. He tilted Hollis's chin up and looked down with his eyes instead of crouching to talk to smaller people. He walked like he was used to people darting out of his way. Eyes followed them, scraping over places they usually didn't. Shoulders, jaw, hands.

Walt's original body must be shorter than Hollis's. Taller than Annie, but probably not as tall as Yulia.

Walt seemed to think about looks the way someone average did, so he probably hadn't been crazy hot or anything either. Hot people didn't think of ways to make up for lacking anything, they didn't think about colors or sharp haircuts or talking to women in a softer, slower voice.

Walt had been a guy who *worked* to be liked.

Hollis was getting closer to guessing his age, too. Gros Michel bananas were from the 1950s, but Hollis was already sure he was from earlier than that. The 1930s was a good bet, but *The Jungle* was set in the early 1900s and he clearly recognized that, so Walt could be from as early as 1905.

Hollis had heard music from the early 1900s, and Walt's accent wasn't that old. Unless it was somehow older and he'd been referring to agrarian life, not postindustrial hardiness.

So, he was either some 1920s–1930s hotshot, only as spooky

as a haunted house, or two-hundred-plus years old, which was vampire territory.

Neither was good. But the latter was definitely worse, so Hollis gritted his teeth and hoped.

BLIND

Yulia had her head in his lap, and Walt was tracing the curve of her eyebrow.

This was normal for them, Hollis insisted, but Walt was in wonder by it.

Annie brought her lunch from home, and the smell of noodle soup was chasing out the grease in the air from Yulia's and Hollis's food. Yulia tapped Annie's knee to the sound of the music.

Walt was thinking loud enough for Hollis to catch some snatches of words.

Feedback loop, fragile, soft, and *wish* were the loudest.

What does this mean to you? Hollis asked.

Walt paused, thinking quieter before answering.

This is the sort of thing I would do with my sisters. Just lying on the floor together after church.

Listening to the radio? Hollis fished for information.

He felt Walt's amusement inside like a sprinkle of rain.

Sometimes. It's not a thing to do with people you aren't related to. Single gals most of all. Boys though, sometimes. If the mood was right.

There was a story there. More important though, the radio had been invented when Walt was young and it was old enough for him to have one in his home. So the preindustrial option was canceled.

Yulia reached up and fingered Hollis's bangs.

"You should keep it like this, after everything settles," she said. "It's beautiful."

Tell her thank you normally.

"Thanks. I didn't know people would care so much."

Ugh.

Yulia closed her eyes and smiled. "I did this too, when I first came here. It's a part of me now, but I thought really hard about what I wanted people to think of me and then went shopping."

"It's hard to imagine you any less glamorous," Annie said. She touched the very tip of her pointer finger to Yulia's, and Yulia scrunched up her nose.

"What do you think of it? The hair and everything," Hollis forced Walt to ask Annie.

Annie looked at him hard. Her pink curls fluttering in the wind, bright and brilliant.

"I think that they don't know you like we do," she said.

Hollis felt a stab of pain and a wave of revulsion from Walt so abrupt that Walt lost control over his face. Hollis took over and stopped them from vomiting on Yulia's head from pure horrified reflex.

It was only for a second, and Walt seized back control immediately.

"I just meant that whatever they're seeing in you now, they should have seen in you before!" Annie cried.

Hollis hadn't been fast enough, Annie looked very worried.

Walt laughed for them and it settled rancid in their throat. "It's nothing. I think maybe something I ate just didn't settle right. I think I've got heartburn."

"TUMS in the glove compartment," Yulia said, eyes still closed.

Annie dug them out for him.

What happens if we eat those for no reason?

Walt didn't answer him and popped one into his mouth.

"Thanks."

Annie laughed nervously. "Anyway, I'm sure they'll adjust. We only have a semester of school left."

"Yeah," Walt said. "It shouldn't be a big deal."

SICK

It was.

People started talking to him more as the week went on. Clementine asked him if he was interested in helping with the school paper. Joe picked up his sweatshirt when he dropped it in the hall and jogged over to hand it back to him. Marika said, "You're good at this, huh?" when Walt raised his hand to answer a question correctly.

Some part of it made Hollis angry. He didn't like the idea that Walt could do more with the raw material of his body and face than he could. Other parts of this just filled him with wonder.

The amount of times people smiled at him or held the doors open for him was baffling. Even teachers were being a little different. It was confusing and sad.

It made him want to pull deeper into himself. Hide more, even though he knew this was better than what would have happened if he came back without Walt at the wheel. He thought about what Annie said.

"They don't know you like we do."

He thought about Walt's reaction to it. Walt had refused to explain himself, shutting Hollis out for a full hour of silence when he pressed too hard. Even pointing out that he'd been given back control for a bit didn't faze Walt.

Walt just said, **Thank you for saving us**.

Then went back to bleaching and dyeing all Hollis's red, orange, and yellow clothes the "appropriate" colors, since they couldn't afford new ones.

WIND

By Friday night, Hollis could open and close his own hand.

TENEMENT

Saturday morning came soft. The air was warm, and it was raining.

Walt was awake before him, but he wasn't up doing chores like usual. He was lying on his side, staring at the wall, quiet.

What are we doing?

I'm just . . . tired, Walt said.

Hollis felt a thrill of alarm; he'd been up most nights this week learning to move. He'd waited for Walt to fall asleep, but maybe that wasn't enough.

Walt was still talking.

Not an effortless job. Sometimes it's good to just *be* for a while.

Oh. Like, existential tired, not sleepy tired. Like . . . depressed.

Walt shrugged and turned over onto their back.

I didn't spend a lot of time in school growing up. We are both seventeen, but seventeen was a man back home. I was already working.

There was an ache in their chest and their head felt fuzzy like a slow drowning. Hollis had been depressed before, but this was different. This was worse.

Tell me something good about back then.

Walt huffed.

Fishing for facts, huh? You don't have to try so hard; you could have just asked. I was killed in 1931.

Killed?

So you're 109.

Walt shook his head.

> It's not the same. I never . . . grew or changed. If a ghost haunts a house . . . a *child's ghost* haunts a house for one hundred years, that kid isn't a man after that one hundred years. They're still . . . running around its walls, asking for someone to play with them. Missing their mom.

*But you're not in a house, you're in **people**.*

Walt clenched his hands into tight fists, then let them go.

> Playing pretend in other people's lives isn't living and aging. It's acting in a shifting playhouse. Waking up to each day your own, making choices and having responsibilities, growing—truly growing old, getting tired and brittle and having your face reflect that in lines that are yours. Watching everyone you know grow beside you, die beside you. This is not the same. You're just a house I'm haunting. You're a house, Hollis.

And you're a ghost, not a demon after all, huh.

Walt turned back over to face the wall.

> There's no such thing as demons and ghosts, there's just me.

Walt closed their eyes, and a wave of anguish swept through them, so sharp and discordant that all Hollis could do was sit in awe of it. He had never felt like this, ever. Not once in his entire life. It was a pain that left him breathless, grand and wide as a cloudless summer sky.

Then Walt dampened it, and he received a burst of embarrassment before it faded away. Walt hadn't meant to share that.

> I don't like Annie because she's related to someone I knew, Walt said. She looks like him.

EXCUSE ME?

She's the age we were when I last saw him. Being with her is . . . difficult. Thought you should know why.

You can't just SAY THAT and not elaborate on it. What the fuck, Walt?

I can and I will. Just don't think I don't feel like she's a swell gal. How I feel's got nothing to do with her.

Hollis yelled, furious. But Walt refused to answer.

Just, leave me alone for a bit. I'm tired, Walt said, and even though it was already 11:00 a.m., Walt forced them both back to sleep.

RING

If Walt knew someone who was related to Annie, then he had to be from here. Or near to here.

Annie's family had been in this valley for as long as Hollis's had. Her grandparents had lived in the area of abandoned properties and died when Annie and Hollis were in middle school. They hadn't been super old either, so it wasn't silly to think that her great-grandparents were the ones who settled in Michigan.

It would be quicker if he could just ask Annie about this, but he couldn't.

He wasn't even able to look up information about it himself yet.

It did make a few things about Walt clearer though. Like how he knew where the thermal springs were, why he seemed very comfortable getting around in general. Maybe even his skittishness about local cops.

He was making bread now, in a way Hollis never would. Quick and sloppy with just flour, yeast, and water.

That's going to be tough, Hollis said.

Walt didn't respond. Instead he sent a frisson of irritation Hollis's way and continued kneading.

Hollis didn't know what to do when Walt was sad. He shouldn't care, but he *did* because Walt was using his body to feel things, and it was making him upset by default.

Had Walt been sad this whole time? It didn't seem like it at first, but Walt had a lot of reasons to be unhappy. Hollis had more, considering the circumstances, but still.

Hollis watched him put the loaves in the oven and then tidy up the kitchen.

HOW

They were strangers, he realized.

This experience was different, knowing Walt was a person.

The horror of his intrusion was disturbing enough to feel demonic at the time. A spirit playing some sort of game that Hollis had lost. Every instance of Walt's amusement felt like being taunted, his irritation like a threat, his ennui an insult.

Watching him talk to people Hollis knew was so dark that it tripped him into hysteria. Even now, after a month of Walt being somewhat normal, he still couldn't control how it made his heart race with panic.

Yeah, he could joke around with Walt, but it never stopped feeling like a survival tactic. The chasm of the unknown behind Walt's intentions was at the edge of his feet.

Hollis wasn't a religious guy. He wasn't scared of Walt because of hell or whatever, the supernatural existing at all was very much enough of a motivator. As was being a puppet of sorts.

But it was . . . different knowing Walt used to have a home. Had . . . sisters.

Knew another seventeen-year-old well enough to create the sort of revulsion Annie inspired in him.

That he went to dance halls and smoked and probably made the same food he cooked for his own family for Hollis's. Even if his bread was about to be so dry and tough it would shock Hollis's ma into disgust.

He was a *person*.

There was a feeling in Hollis's belly that he couldn't name, at bearing witness to Walt's depression. Hollis wanted to be angry, he had the right to spit at Walt, *You're the one hijacking my life, why do you also get to be the one who's sad?* But it didn't feel . . . right.

He didn't feel sorry for him, and he was absolutely still going to try to figure out how to get Walt out of him. But he just couldn't yell at him.

Not about this.

EAT

Walt's bread turned out fine. It wasn't pillowy and delicious with yeasty holes like Hollis's was. It was dense and almost like cake, but it soaked up his ma's white gravy well enough that no one made them answer any hard questions.

Mr. and Mrs. Brown were watching a black-and-white movie, and Walt lingered on his way up to Hollis's room.

I saw this in theaters, he said.

I figured. What's it called?

***The Third Man.* It's funny how well it's held up. You never really know what things people will latch on to in the long run. This wasn't even the most popular movie of that year. *Samson and Delilah* and *Pinky* were the ticket. No one mentions those now.**

"You want to sit down? Casting a long shadow, june bug." Mrs. Brown tilted her head backward to smile at Hollis upside down.

"Nah," Walt said. "Some other time."

Walt walked them up the stairs in the dark, and Hollis tasted his loneliness.

WALT'S BREAD

Ingredients

4½ cups all-purpose flour

1½ teaspoons salt

4½ teaspoons yeast

1½ cups warm water (110°F/45°C)

About 1 tablespoon olive oil (or some cooking spray—I like coconut
  oil cooking spray)

Instructions

In a bowl, stir together flour and salt.

Make a small hole in the middle of the flour mixture and pour the
  yeast in the hole.

Pour warm water in the hole with the yeast and mix with your finger to dissolve.

Continue mixing/kneading until there is no more loose flour in the
  bowl (or until you have a dough ball). If you need to add a little
  more warm water than the 1½ cups, then go ahead and do it just
  a little bit at a time until you have enough.

Remove the dough ball from the bowl. Wash and dry the bowl, then
  spread the olive oil on the bottom and sides of the bowl.

Place the dough ball back into the oiled bowl. Flip it over once.
  Cover the top of the bowl with a dishcloth and place the bowl in
  a warm area.

Wait about one hour for the dough to rise.

Punch down the dough, then divide it into two sections (shaped somewhat like a mini loaf of French bread).

Place each section on a lightly floured cookie sheet or in a bread pan. Cover with a cloth and let rise about a half hour more.

Preheat the oven to 350°F/180°C.

Remove cloth and cook on the center rack in the oven for about 30 minutes.

HEART

What kind of music do you like?

They hadn't listened to any at all since Walt had arrived.

Yacht rock is my favorite. The Doobie Brothers, Steely Dan, the Eagles, Hall and Oates. Walt licked his finger and turned a page of the book he was reading. **Why?**

No reason, I'm just surprised it's not like . . . swing . . . jazz—

Walt snorted.

There was more than just swing and jazz around. Besides, yacht rock is a combination of a lot of things. It reminds me of jazz, but it has stories like country, a sarcasm to it like big band; it's got folk guitar. It's not chintzy or over-produced like stuff from the nineties. Smoother on the ears than things from now.

Like all the genres between then and now, just . . . averaged out.

Walt shrugged. **You could put it that way.**

He said he liked "playing music" that night in the bath. Maybe this would stop him from filling their head with wool and rain.

Can you play some? Like, make a playlist?

Walt sent Hollis a spark of annoyance but closed his book and pulled out Hollis's phone. He spent about twenty minutes arranging something to his liking, then put Hollis's phone in a mug by the side of their bed and pressed play.

It was . . . not exactly Hollis's cup of tea, but it was certainly something.

It took about a half hour for Walt to begin tapping his fingers against the sides of the book. An hour for him to start singing along quietly, like he'd forgotten Hollis was even there.

Hollis didn't sing. Hearing his own voice wielded with skill was . . .

There wasn't a name for this emotion. He didn't have words for the way the notes buzzed in his throat, slipped like honey through his teeth. The way his ears rang with it, pleasure unformed and indistinct.

Sitting in the dark of himself, both a witness and a hostage, violently aware that his heart picking up speed had nothing to do with how Walt was feeling.

And Walt himself wasn't sad anymore, he was comfortable. The way they'd felt in that warm hollow, without that layer of despair over it.

Warm and pleased, and Hollis shook with it.

He watched and listened and shook.

PLAYLIST

"Ventura Highway"—America

"Old Man"—Neil Young

"Brandy (You're a Fine Girl)"—Looking Glass

"Summer Breeze"—Seals & Crofts

"Kid Charlemagne"—Steely Dan

"Doctor My Eyes"—Jackson Browne

"Long Train Runnin'"—The Doobie Brothers

"25 or 6 to 4"—Chicago

"Use Me"—Bill Withers

"Take It Easy"—The Eagles

"Sara Smile"—Daryl Hall & John Oates

"Your Song"—Elton John

"Year of the Cat"—Al Stewart

"Wild Night"—Van Morrison

"Free Ride"—The Edgar Winter Group

"Let It Ride"—Bachman–Turner Overdrive

"Peg"—Steely Dan

THREE

As the weeks passed, more people kept talking to him, and Walt was nice to them. He wasn't charming like he'd bragged about in the earlier days.

He was just *nice* in a way Hollis wasn't.

Walt shared their homework with a shrug. He answered when people asked him for the time. He held doors open for people, said excuse me when he passed them.

There was always this look of shock and defense on people's faces, but it was starting to melt away. People were starting to expect this of him, and it had been only two and a half weeks.

He sat next to Timothy every day now, and Tim hadn't changed seats. The sneer he gave when he handed papers to Hollis on the first day had mellowed into a neutral expression. Walt had kept his own promise and didn't talk to Timothy at all. Didn't ask him for anything or look at him more than anyone else.

There was another girl in chemistry who had started talking to him more too. Clementine. She was blond with big watery blue eyes. She kept giggling at him and forced them into being partners for most situations when they needed one.

Hollis thought she was annoying, but Walt insisted that it was good to have at least one person other than Yulia and Annie who other people consistently saw him being nice to.

PE was also different.

Walt was athletic. He was using Hollis's body, but he had the muscle memory to sew and the muscle memory for softball too apparently. Hollis didn't say anything to him about it, but his heart burned with jealousy and sorrow.

Walt did not ignore it.

You could have been good at this.

TUESDAY

It was easier to hold his hand open now, to curl his fingers closed and back open again.

But in order to reach his phone, Hollis had to have more control than that. He needed be able to turn his hand over and walk it across the mattress, use the muscles in his arm to reach to his desk and pull the phone across the space.

He needed to figure out a way to open his eyes. Not so much that he'd wake Walt up, but just enough that he could see a sliver of light.

Then he could do two things: he could text Annie and Yulia for help, or he could spend some time doing his own research.

There was always the threat of Walt waking up and getting very angry, but there was no way in hell Hollis wasn't about to try.

Sometimes, he fantasized about beating the shit out of Walt after he died. Exorcizing him out of his body, living out the rest of his life, passing surrounded by his loved ones, arriving at the pearly gates, hunting down this son of a bitch, and just tearing him to pieces.

The indignity of not going to the toilet alone was worth several elbows to the neck.

There were just some things about being a person that didn't require a witness, much less the experience of sharing.

Walt acted like he didn't care, but Hollis knew he would. If this were his body, Walt would *care*.

SWEAT

Hollis wondered if Walt knew what it felt like to be on the other end.

Human beings were adaptable by nature. You got used to things; Hollis got used to this. It hadn't even taken long, maybe a day or two.

Did Walt know that for an instant, when he poured himself into the space between Hollis's body and his soul, it felt good? Shocky, like the relief after being electrocuted, deeply psychologically horrifying, but good all the same.

Was he aware of how light Hollis felt now? When they lifted his arms and legs it was like two people working together to pick up a heavy box. His own hand was so heavy when Hollis moved it by himself in the dark of night. He had forgotten the real weight of his own bone and meat.

Did he know Hollis could feel his feelings too? Not just the ones he sent on purpose either. That craving Hollis didn't have a name for at first was Walt's addiction to nicotine. He claimed to eat everything except bananas, but Hollis knew Walt didn't like celery, and there was discord when they ate it because *Hollis* liked it.

Walt was ticklish, and that thing about not being able to tickle yourself was out the window. His own elbows had grazed his side during one of the reluctant hugs Annie forced upon them and Walt had to grit his teeth hard to avoid making a sound.

Did Walt know that walking felt like being carried? The jolt of each step, present and real, but the work of it all held at a distance.

How familiar was Walt with this? Did his other "rides" tell him? How being possessed didn't feel like being puppeteered from above, or remote-controlled.

That it felt like having someone stand behind you while showing you how to play pool or golf or wheel-throw clay.

Their heat at your back.

Their breath on your neck.

BLUSH

Yulia was drawing on Hollis's palm. They were watching a movie in class, and no one was really paying attention to them.

The glide of the pen made Walt want to shiver, but Hollis made it very clear what he thought about *that*, so they were suppressing it.

I had tattoos once, Walt supplied, apropos of nothing.

Okay, Hollis said. He didn't care.

It was less common then than it is now. People thought things of you, so I used to hide them, Walt explained. **I'm still not used to seeing so many people with them. It's like being in the navy.**

That was interesting.

You were in the military?

For as short a time as I could manage. I don't like being in organizations anymore. Also the food blows.

"I know you're not going to the actual Homecoming dance, but Clementine wanted to know if you'll come to the Homecoming after-party, but she's afraid to ask," Yulia whispered.

Ew, why?

"Who else is going?" Walt asked instead.

Yulia pursed her lips. "It's actually kind of a bigger thing. Will R.'s parents are out of town, so everyone is going over. Saturday night from ten until whenever."

"Are you going?"

Yulia smirked. "I might swing by. I know you don't like this

150

stuff, and normally I wouldn't even ask, but Clementine looked so hopeful. She doesn't know you like I do."

I do not want to go with Clementine.

But you *do* want to go.

This is the first party I've ever been invited to directly; I'm not just going to say no.

"I'll be there," Walt said. "Not with her, you know. But I'll show up."

Yulia's smirk curled into a smile.

"You surprise me often, lately," she said.

Before Hollis could stop him, Walt sucked his teeth intimate and animal.

"Happy to."

BRIGHT

"Are you on drugs?" Annie asked.

Walt turned Hollis around so quick they almost knocked into a door.

"What? No. Where would I even find drugs?" Walt said immediately.

Everywhere, idiot, this is a small American town.

"Uhhhh, everywhere. You're, like . . . weirdly happy these days," Annie said. "Too alert to be opiates, not cuddly enough for ecstasy; if it was weed you'd absolutely reek. You're doing better in school though, not worse."

I'm smarter than you.

You're like one thousand years old, you've had more time.

Yeah yeah yeah, I was a good student too before all this.

It's an original quality.

"—th to Hollis. Earth to Hollis," Annie was shouting. "See, this is what I'm talking about."

Walt shook Hollis's head. "Annie, I'm not on drugs, I'm just trying harder. I don't understand why you'd think that's a bad thing."

Annie narrowed her eyes at him, then crossed her arms tight over her honeycomb-yellow sweater.

"I'm going to practice, but when I see you next, we're having words." She flounced away.

Hollis watched her go; he missed her. Walt only let them hang out with her when he had to.

What kind of practice? Walt asked with a frown.

Band, she plays snare drum.

Walt brightened a bit. **They got violins in there?**

Kind of? They're not the expensive kind; they're plastic. Most people buy their own after a year. Why? Do you play?

When I can. Fiddle, some songs for temple, Walt explained. He pushed through the school doors and started walking them home.

You're Jewish? I thought you were Catholic or something.

I'm half. The rest is Irish Catholic on my mom's side. So I didn't worship, just played and went home. It paid a little here and there. Always a good thing to be on the good side of a house of God.

Do you even believe in God?

Walt looked up at the sky. It was gray, getting ready to snow again.

I don't know. Would you? If you were me?

That was . . . depressing. Hollis tried something, pushed a softer feeling Walt's way. Concern.

Walt stopped walking in the middle of the sidewalk and said a quiet **Oh** and pressed a hand against Hollis's chest. Where that feeling ended and began.

I . . . Walt blinked their eyes hard and fast. **Thank you, Hollis, I'll be all right. We ought to focus on this party you have coming. We should focus on that.**

CORINTHIAN

Hollis felt . . .

Never mind, it didn't matter.

Walt made his family eat chipped beef on toast, something so archaic his ma stared at it for a minute, then stared at Hollis too, before mumbling something about eating this once when she was a little girl.

Hollis's ma was from Georgia, and he hadn't met his grandma. Walt quickly lied about finding the recipe in that old dusty cookbook from the corner of the kitchen counter. But Mrs. Brown's eyes were a little wet. She ate and went straight up to her room instead of watching TV.

Walt took them to bed early after a quiet shower, quick as usual in the dark.

Hollis lay awake for long hours until Walt fell asleep, then waited longer than that.

Walt had placed his phone on the desk, closer than ever before. Hollis flipped his hand over and scraped it across the sheets. Slow and careful. Even though Walt's eyes were closed, Hollis could feel the cool wood and the edge of the bed in his ocean of darkness.

By the time he was able to get there, it was long past midnight.

Hollis took a moment to catch his breath and rest, then he stretched his fingers out until they touched the edge of the desk.

Their heart picked up speed.

Suddenly, his hand was light again.

It reached out for his phone and closed around it and, to Hollis's horror, their eyes opened just a crack.

Walt watched him. Quiet and awake, bleary with the warm weight of sleep.

Then, without speaking or acknowledging Hollis's terror and their racing heart, Walt gave Hollis control over his own fingers again.

DROWN

There they sat, in the halo of light from the screen. Waiting.

Hollis wasn't sure what Walt wanted him to do. Walt wasn't saying anything, and he wasn't projecting any feelings at all.

Hollis called his bluff and opened Google.

He typed: *crossroads demon rules.*

All of it was . . . just nonsense.

Book recommendations, top ten demon movies. Fan fiction. Christian conspiracy theories. Walt let him scroll for at least an hour, searching variations of *demon removal, ghost exorcism,* to similarly disappointing results.

Walt was fully awake now, but silent as the grave.

Hollis was starting to feel bad and get frustrated. He'd prepared for how to react if Walt had woken up furious, but he didn't even have the grace to give Hollis that.

Slowly, Walt gave Hollis more control. He opened up access to his palm, wrist, and then all the way up to his elbow. Hollis felt a spike of anger. Why now?

Immediately Hollis used his new freedom for retribution. He grabbed himself around the throat and squeezed.

Walt let him.

Is this what you wanted?

Hollis pushed his palm down harder until his breath caught and his heart pounded in his head.

WHAT DO YOU WANT FROM ME? Hollis roared, helpless.

Then, *WHAT IS THE POINT OF THIS?*

Walt just closed their eyes. He leaned into the pressure like it was an embrace.

Hollis didn't expect that. *"You're my last ride."* Walt had said a few weeks ago. Without hesitation, like he knew. Like he was going to make sure of it.

Hollis let go.

Afraid of Walt. Afraid to die.

If he could breathe on his own, he would be panting; if he wasn't so angry, he would be sobbing.

Walt gently took back control of Hollis's hand. Slow, like a poison in the veins. He rubbed Hollis's throat and took deep calm breaths until nothing hurt. Then he turned over and faced the wall.

Go to sleep, Hollis. Tomorrow is just another day.

WEEP

Annie made fun of the scarf around Hollis's throat.

Said it made him look French. Yulia dragged her fingertips across the edge of the fabric and smirked at him.

"Clementine?" she whispered in the back of geology, and Walt shrugged for them. Let her believe that.

Hollis let Walt autopilot, and instead he ran the image of Walt arching in surrender to the violence of his hand in his mind over and over from every angle.

It reminded him of Walt standing in the snow, in Sam's body, arched against the night. There was despair in it. He recognized the recklessness.

"*You don't want to die,*" Yulia reminded him when he'd struggled with this, too often for Hollis to forget. "*You're just very sad right now.*"

He thought about ninety years. How sad could one get, given that amount of time? How many flavors of fucked up could one learn about sitting in the wreckage of other people's lives? He was still angry, by God, Hollis was still very *angry,* but . . .

At night, hours later in the blackness of the shower, water beating at the nape of their neck, Hollis asked:

Do you want to die?

Because it was cruel, and because he could.

Walt just tipped his head beneath the spray and let the soap glide down their back.

SIN

Hollis had to get Will R.'s address from Yulia. Walt spent Saturday watching TV and napping off and on. Mr. and Mrs. Brown had gone to the city for a romantic day together, and Walt wanted to take advantage of the emptiness in the house to be lazy in the common areas.

He hadn't answered Hollis's question the other night, but he seemed happier now, or at least more content.

Currently, they were eating olives Mrs. Brown canned two years ago like they were potato chips.

What are you going to dress me in for the party? Hollis asked over *I Dream of Jeannie.*

Black, Walt answered immediately. **You don't wear much of it for school, so it'll make an impact.**

He rustled up one of Hollis's ma's sweaters and some black dickies from a couple of years ago that he'd let out during the first week. Instead of borrowing Hollis's pa's cologne, he rifled through Mrs. Brown's dresser to find a perfume that suited him better.

Scents don't have gender. Your pa's stuff is too metallic for you.

Hollis watched while Walt iced beneath his eyes and brushed out his hair. He eyed the purpling marks around his throat.

Are you going to cover that?

Walt paused mid-brush.

You gonna need me to?

He looked Hollis dead in the mirror, then raised a single brow.

Hollis wasn't sure what Walt wanted him to say to that.

Walt went back to brushing.

"I gave you the scarf on the first day, but we're done with that now. Don't do things you're ashamed to show," he said out loud. "You're gonna treat me reckless from now on? People are gonna look at it."

You didn't have to give me control. What did you think I was going to do with it? Hold your hand?

Walt huffed. **You could, if you wanted.**

What the hell is that supposed to mean? You're lucky I didn't gouge our eyes out, Hollis snapped.

Walt put the brush down on the sink. **You wanna try it?**

What?!

Walt sighed.

He laced Hollis's hands together, resting his elbows on the porcelain, then deliberately locked his gaze on them in the mirror. The closest they could get to looking back at each other.

It chilled Hollis to the marrow.

His palms felt warm, there was stickiness from the pomade. Walt gave him his arms back, made it his choice to keep their hands locked together. Hollis could control his own face now too. His neck.

At all the points where he and Walt touched, it felt strange. It itched at first but rapidly escalated to something violent and electric.

Hollis looked between their embrace and himself in the mirror frantically, seeking explanation, but Walt said nothing. Their fingers twitched against the sensation, but Walt didn't let go.

Instead, Walt slid his right hand up, and Hollis's nerves jangled sweet and discordant. This touching and being touched and touching all at once meant something, but Hollis didn't know what. It scared him and made their breath come fast and hot. Hollis tightened their grip with a gasp, like grabbing a branch while falling from a tree.

He stared into the mirror at his own face, cheeks burning, eyebrows twisted in confusion. Walt's sad brown eyes that no one had noticed—not even his ma—gazed back at him. Old and sure.

Walt separated their fingers but kept their palms close, then delicately touched their fingertips together. Each ridge of Hollis's fingerprints scraped harmonious like angels screaming, and Hollis's knees failed him.

Their hands separated to catch them, slamming to the tile floor. Walt picked them up off the ground.

What was that?

It was us.

What do you mean it was us? Why did it feel like that? Why doesn't it feel like that all the time? What did you do to me?

Walt pressed Hollis's lips together, tight and unhappy. He went back to getting ready like he hadn't just rocked Hollis's world. Finished brushing their hair, then checked the time on Hollis's phone. But Hollis could feel him turning over inside, like a dog in a crate that was way too small. The panic of it.

Walt, stop. What was that? How, why—

Walt put Hollis's keys and wallet in his pocket and headed downstairs to get their coat.

I shouldn't have done that.

WALT, STOP.

*FUCKING **STOP!***

Walt shrugged on their coat and opened the door. It wasn't even close to the time the party was supposed to be. It was barely eight o'clock.

BLEED

Walt was walking them toward the bus stop, quick and silent.

Where are we going?

Walt didn't answer.

There was one last bus before the route was done for the night. Hollis knew that if they made it in time, Walt was going to catch it. And if he caught the bus, they would leave this town, and Hollis didn't know if they would ever come back.

I can't do this. I can't do this.

Walt was saying it over and over, and Hollis knew he wasn't talking to him.

This was ridiculous.

Hey, calm down, dude, Hollis begged. *I'm not mad, I just wanted to know what happened.*

Walt was shaking his head.

Please. Please. Take us home.

Walt kept walking.

Please.

Hollis reached out and tried to force calm into them the way Walt had the very first night. Tried to communicate his anxiety, wordless and tender, and the wish for understanding. He couldn't tell if it was working, but he tried.

Walt stopped in the middle of the street and closed his eyes. He tipped his head back, the way he always did when his heart was breaking. They were a half block from the bus stop. The sign bright and yellow, close.

Take us home, Walt, Hollis said, firm and sure.

Walt took a breath, shaky and wet. He covered their face with both hands.

Why, Hollis? What will that change?

It would never quit shaking him to hear his own name spoken in his own voice.

Give me our arms.

Hollis was a lot of things. Nice wasn't one of them. But he wasn't the sort of person who saw someone crying and did nothing about it. He wasn't the sort of person who was raised to feel nothing from something like this.

Give them to me.

Walt did, all at once. Let them fall to his sides and hang, as hot tears found themselves in the curves of their ears.

Hollis took his own arms and wrapped them around his middle, held tight. Walt startled.

Why are you doing that?

Shh.

Hollis used his hand to wipe his face, to gentle away Walt's crying.

Walt laughed, hysterical and joyless, but Hollis didn't let that push him into cruelty.

Do you still want to go to the party? Hollis asked. *Or do you need to stay home?*

Walt shook his head. **Why ask me that? It's your party; it's your life—**

You don't have to get all upset. Hollis wiped his face again. *I'm not mad, just confused. Did you do something to me or was that just . . . us? As we are supposed to be.*

None of this should be happening at all, Walt whispered.

I am an abomination.

Hollis thought for a bit. He wanted to do it again, whatever that was. He could still remember the shivery pleasure hidden in the pain of it. Felt muted shocks of it as he wiped their face.

So what? Hollis said finally. *I'm not that great of a person either.* More tears.

You don't *understand*.

There were years in those words. But Hollis didn't think that was important.

Why should I need to? We're both stuck here. You metaphysically and me because looking up exorcisms failed. Let's just make the best of it. So much of this experience is bad. This one thing is good! I don't understand why you're freaking out so much.

I could just jump into someone else.

Dude, I'm not letting you fuck up someone else in this town over this shit. If I saw your eyes in someone else's head I would feel so bad, I'd throw up immediately. It would feel like my fault, and I can't deal with the stress of that.

I...

Walt was shifting though emotions too quickly for Hollis to keep track. It was like standing in a river with a current rushing past, until Walt settled on that breathtaking anguish he'd shown Hollis on accident. Open and shocky, like a raw nerve. Too big to shove anywhere, to hide.

Hollis wondered if he was the first person Walt had ever shown this to. The first person who knew.

He remembered Walt making bread and flirting with Yulia

and laughing at him and taking a bath and getting ready for school, just smiling and talking like he wasn't a thing that hurt so bad it would drive a stronger man than Hollis to his knees.

Walt clenched their fists tight and breathed hard, a pitiful noise.

He was trying to force it back inside, but it wasn't working; Hollis didn't think Walt could while Hollis was looking at it so close like this.

Hollis pulled back the layers, crimson bright, until it was a shape that made sense. Until he understood what he hadn't before.

It's hard to be you, isn't it?

Walt flinched. He wiped their nose hard.

What does it matter? You shouldn't care. It's not your responsibility to care.

You don't control that, Hollis said firmly. *I do.*

The red got deeper, like someone was tugging out the bottom of their lungs, their heart.

*You can't decide whether someone cares. I care that you feel this way. I care. Don't think I don't know what loneliness feels like on you either. You make me hungry with your hungers. You're the one who said we'd be sharing, so **share.***

Walt covered their face, hid.

I feel like I'm bleeding all the time, Walt whispered, wet. **I'm sorry for scaring you, I just got frustrated.**

Hollis could understand that. Walt was a frustrating kind of guy; it was probably the most predictable thing about him, if he was being honest.

Hollis grinned.

Please don't laugh at me.

I'm not laughing at you, Walt. I'm laughing at me. I'm sorry for trying to choke us. And for being a pain in the ass.

Walt giggled softly, then took back control of Hollis's left arm, wiping their face as dry as he could manage.

All right . . .

Somehow it was easier to admit this to Walt than it was to himself. That Hollis didn't "like this" exactly, but he was dealing with it. Apparently better than most people. And it was strangely a bit of a relief to know that Walt was miserable too. It made them . . . equals in a way.

Just . . . stop crying in the street, Hollis said, kind. *You're making me look like a loser. Take us home.*

OUROBOROS

They splashed their face with cold water until it wasn't puffy anymore. Walt let Hollis have his own arms back so Hollis could make a snack for them for the first time in over a month, and Hollis almost wept again at how good fresh food was.

Walt never made salads or roasted vegetables, everything was just boiled and fried and creamed. They were going through lard faster than they had in years.

You could make this a career, Walt said as they washed the dishes. **You'd have to travel out to the city, but you could open up a place.**

No one would want to buy my stupid food.

Walt stacked a plate on the rack.

I would.

DRINK

Will R.'s house was close to where the abandoned neighborhood began. Hollis could understand why Yulia was excited. You could be as loud as you wanted over here and no one would complain.

It had two stories, and Hollis could see people's shadows through the window, lights strobing behind them. There were two people on Will's balcony, legs sticking out of the slats.

Brave. It didn't exactly look stable.

The door was already cracked open so Hollis slipped inside. The music was loud enough to hurt, rattling his teeth. Walt winced and took them deeper into the house away from it.

The living room was so closely packed he had to push his way through, but the kitchen was less crowded.

There were some people he'd seen around Rose Town in there, and they made eye contact with him in a way that didn't feel hostile. But Hollis was looking for Yulia, so he just waved.

A hand dropped on his shoulder, and Walt flinched.

"Hollis!"

It was Clementine. She'd taken her fluffy blond curls and flattened them straight; her eyes were ringed in liner. She looked a bit garish, but it was kind of interesting that she was trying so hard.

"Hey."

It was too loud for a conversation here. Clementine grabbed his hand and tugged him to the back of the house until the music was quieter.

"I'm glad you came!" she was saying.

Hollis scanned the crowd for Yulia's tall frame or Annie's pink hair and came back empty.

"Do you know where Annie and Yulia are?" Hollis asked.

Clementine looked a bit disappointed, but she shrugged. "I don't think they're here yet. . . . Do you want a drink?"

She took him outside, where there were a few coolers taking advantage of the cold weather.

The door closed behind them, and it was quiet. Clementine handed him a beer, then started looking for a bottle opener.

"Here, give it to me," Walt said.

He leaned Clementine's bottle against the brick of Will's house, smacked the top hard, then handed it back to her.

"Cool."

Walt reached for the door, but Clementine grabbed his arm.

"Wait, I thought we could . . ."

This is annoying, where's Yulia?

Clementine was looking up at him in a strange way.

Walt sighed. He took off Hollis's coat; he draped it around Clementine's shoulders.

"So, how are you?" she asked. "We don't get much time to talk outside of class."

Walt shrugged. "I'm not that interesting, Clementine. I'm just a guy."

She looked down at her shoes—red Converses with pen scribbled on them—and gathered more bravery.

"Yulia said you like to bake? I like to bake too. Do you do cakes and cookies or something else?"

UGH.

We're being *kind*, Hollis.

"I do. I mostly bake for her and for my family. She prefers my bread over anything, but I think she's just too lazy to try learning to make it herself." Walt smirked.

"You hang out with Yulia a lot," Clementine said, pulling Hollis's coat tighter.

"She's my best friend."

Clementine looked a bit relieved. "Oh."

"Did you. . . want something from me?" Walt asked. "People don't usually invite me to stuff, much less pull me out to stand in the cold like this."

She likes you, dumbass.

I know, simmer down.

Clementine shrugged. "I don't know. You seem . . . different. I always noticed you, but it didn't ever feel like you'd notice me back until recently. But I think maybe I might have . . . misunderstood that."

She did. Get us out of here and go find Yulia.

"Clementine, I—"

The back door opened, and Timothy Reid poked his head out.

"Hollis, get in here."

Walt gave Clementine a tight smile and gratefully seized the opportunity.

RIPE

Timothy grabbed Walt by the forearm as soon as he was fully inside the house and started pulling him deeper into the party.

They were dragged through the kitchen, to the front of the house, to the basement stairs, then down into the darkness.

It was quiet, dim with only one lamp. William's basement was finished; there was a couch, coffee table, and TV, all pushed against the walls so that the thirty or so guys in there could fit in the space, gathered in a circle. Timothy let go of his arm and pushed Hollis forward.

Hollis met James's gaze first. James looked tired and angry, like he didn't want to be there at all.

Everyone else in the room was a guy Hollis hadn't spoken to or didn't know in any real way. Some basketball guys, some baseball, more than a few on the football team, Stephanie's boyfriend, Tim and James, of course. None of them were speaking, and they all looked serious.

It was so confusing that it took a moment for him to recognize Jorge.

He was standing in the middle, waiting.

"Hey," Jorge said, sharp and loud.

"What is this?" Walt asked.

Jorge . . . didn't look good. His cuts had healed enough for him to be walking around, but he was crisscrossed in lines of pink. Coming back to school like that was going to be difficult. His whole life would probably be difficult, if Hollis was being honest.

But again, this *wasn't Hollis's fault.*

Timothy rubbed the back of his neck, agitated.

"He wants to fight you, man," he said, like it was embarrassing.

Walt looked back at the stairwell, then returned to the conversation.

"I assume I'm not going to be allowed to leave?"

"What do you think?" Jorge snapped.

Walt ignored him and looked to Timothy again.

"If I win, can I leave?"

Timothy glanced at Jorge, then shrugged.

"I don't . . . really see that happening," he said without an ounce of malice. "But, I guess."

Jorge turned on him quick. "That shouldn't be a question. You think I'm a worse fighter than James? James had him on the ground and you think I can't?"

Timothy put his hands up and took a step back, closer to James.

"I got him down here, what else you want from me?" he muttered. "Chill."

James sucked his teeth. He was chewing on a lollipop stick and sitting on the back of Will's sofa.

"You got a problem too?" Jorge snapped.

James tilted his chin up, looked at Jorge from under his lashes. "S'not a fair fight, is all."

You're really calm, Hollis said.

I think that guy has a pack of cigarettes in his left pocket, Walt said inexplicably. **Maybe a lighter too.**

What? Why does that matter? Do you think he'll share with us after he beats us half to death?

172

Hollis felt the thrill of Walt's amusement.

"I don't like people thinking you got the jump on me. You didn't," Jorge was saying.

"I know," Walt said. "The cops came to my house about it. Why do we have to do this? Can't you just leave me alone? I don't even care if you date Annie—"

"Oh, we're way past that now," Jorge said dangerously.

Timothy sighed loudly. "Can you guys just get this over with?"

"Shut the fuck up," Jorge snapped.

"Okay, fine, we'll fight," Walt said, eyes glued to Jorge's pockets. "But after this you have to stop bothering me. Completely. I've never had any problems with you, and technically you shouldn't have any problems with me. Half the people in this room have had good reason to beat my ass, and they did. But you're not one of them, Jorge. So, let's just get this over with."

There were a few laughs in the crowd, and Jorge did *not* like that.

He lunged at Hollis, but Walt moved back quick, faster than Hollis anticipated.

"Promise you'll leave me alone after this or there's no point to it." Walt looked back at the crowd and pulled a face that got a few more laughs.

"I'll leave you alone. After they scrape your ass off the floor," Jorge yelled.

"Great."

Walt snapped Hollis's arm out lightning quick. His fist was loose.

Hollis was sure he was about to slap Jorge, which would have been funny and probably hurt his hand a bit. A nice appetizer to a beating that was certain to land them in urgent care, yet again.

Instead, Walt's knuckles collided with the side of Jorge's head with a sickening crack, and Jorge fell like a sack of meat.

He didn't move.

The room was dead silent. *Hollis* was dead silent.

Walt rolled his shoulders, walked over to Jorge's unconscious body, and turned him over. He rummaged in Jorge's pocket and took out his cigarettes and lighter.

"Can I take this?" he asked Timothy.

Timothy took another step back.

"Do what you want, man." He sounded scared.

Walt flicked Jorge's lighter until he was sure it would light.

God, it's been months. I'm gonna have to do this in private.

What the fuck . . .

"What the fuck?" James said out loud.

"He'll be fine." Walt replied. "How much are these now . . . five, ten bucks?"

He pulled out Hollis's wallet and removed ten precious dollars and tossed them on top of Jorge's body.

"Not a thief," he muttered. "Anyway, see you guys later."

Walt walked them toward the stairs, and the crowd parted immediately to let them through.

PHILAUTIA

Jesus fucking Christ, you couldn't have let him whale on us for a few minutes? I'm not that good at fighting! Why did you do that?!

Not now, Hollis.

Walt was practically running for the front door. He pushed open the screen and stepped over to the side of the porch, Jorge's lighter already out, flicking it madly.

Hollis winced at the acrid smell of cigarette smoke. But Walt jammed the thing in his mouth.

Jesus, Mary, and Joseph.

Walt groaned shamelessly into the night. He let Hollis's head loll back on the house's siding, rolled his eyes back, euphoric.

Hollis was horrified.

Come on, man. Can't you be quieter?

No, I can't. Just let me enjoy this.

In the privacy granted by Walt's distraction, Hollis dug himself deep inside, into that dark place from when they first met and ran through the feeling of Walt punching Jorge. Over and over and over again.

The way Walt relaxed a bit before he did it, how he shook his hand off just once when it was done. The way he moved Hollis's body with casual violence, a natural threat, like it was common for him. Reconciling this moment with the one they had earlier, crying in the rain, made Hollis want to push his face against a wall and gasp for breath. He had never been this horny in his entire goddamn life.

Hollis used everything in him to make sure Walt couldn't feel what he was feeling right now. But he could still access the wave of joy Walt was getting from Jorge's stupid cigarettes, and it was making the situation worse.

It was easier when he'd thought Walt was a demon, but he was a *person*, and he was *spectacular*. Hollis thought, deliriously, about what Walt would have looked like if Hollis saw him from the outside. What it would feel like to see the curve of his shoulders as he bent down to rifle through Jorge's pockets.

Hollis muffled his emotions as best he could and then: he wondered if Walt's knuckles had calluses.

The door banged open.

"Not a good idea, bro. He looks like he wants to be alone," Timothy was saying.

James jogged down the porch stairs and stopped in front of Hollis, breathing hard.

"How did you do that?" he demanded.

Walt growled in irritation just for Hollis to hear, but externally he opened his eyes to slits and gazed back at James.

"I was well motivated," he said.

James seized Hollis's arms and pushed him back against the house. To Hollis's mounting horror, Walt breathed in, preparing to blow smoke directly into James's face.

GIVE ME MY MOUTH.

Hollis turned his head at the last minute and blew the smoke into the corner.

"Dude, stop."

James let go of him and backed away, eyes wide.

"Why didn't you do that to me?" James asked. "Why . . . didn't you do that to me . . . ?"

Hollis shook his head, while Walt folded their arms and tapped the ash off his cigarette.

"James, we don't have any problems with each other. It's fine. Just, I don't know, make sure Jorge keeps his promise."

"If we could do that, we woulda done it," Timothy said. "Jorge was our friend, but he's been acting out of hand. Has been for a while. We think he's on steroids or something."

Yikes.

Walt shrugged their shoulders.

"So. What now?" Hollis said.

James looked conflicted. He glanced over his shoulder at the party, then turned back.

"You're good," he said.

At Walt's blank expression he continued.

"Your form, I mean. Do you train anywhere? You move like someone who practices boxing or something like it. When you're being serious, I guess."

See! This is what I was talking about!

Walt took another drag and blew the smoke up at the moon.

"I don't like fighting," Walt said. "If it happens, it happens, but I don't like to do it on purpose—"

"And Jorge pushed you up against a wall," Timothy finished. "I get it. Makes sense."

It was quiet after that.

Neither Timothy nor James seemed to know what to say, but they weren't walking away either.

"Sorry for breaking your nose," Timothy mumbled eventually. Walt shrugged.

"Water under the bridge," Hollis said. "Wasn't even mad the day after you did it."

"You." James paused. He looked angry. "You shouldn't let people toss you around. Stop provoking people for a beating. That . . . that sounds like self-harm . . . to me."

Walt's fondness filled their chest with warmth. He shrugged again.

"I don't think anyone is going to try again after tonight, anyway."

"But don't do it after you leave here either," James said, and he was serious. "People are talking, yeah. Things might not be the same, and you might not be able to goad people at school into it anymore. But that's a habit you gotta break, and it's not going away when we graduate and you're not with us. You'll be surrounded by people who don't care. A lot of guys at the gym get into it for that reason. I'm not one of them, but I've seen it. If you don't practice or have a coach, there's probably no one around to tell you to stop. And Hollis, man, I know we're not fucking friends, but I'm telling you to stop."

Timothy looked down at James, pleased, then turned back to Hollis.

"You're an all right guy though, Hollis." Tim smirked. "Didn't expect to learn that today."

Walt put out his cigarette on the stairs.

"Well. I hope Jorge and steroids have a happy ending. He comes my way again, I'll knock him out flat again. He gives you guys trouble, send him to me. I don't have a scholarship to keep."

James opened his mouth to reply, but the door slammed wide. Clementine was standing in the rectangle of light. She threw Hollis's coat down at him hard and stormed back inside.

Timothy grimaced.

"Yeah, you should probably leave. Will's freaking out, and he probably told Clementine about the fight. You know that's his sister, right?"

Walt snorted; he pushed his arms into Hollis's coat. "No, I did not."

"You can't catch a break, man." Timothy laughed. He slapped Walt on the shoulder, friendly and rough. "Have a good night."

James nodded and followed Timothy back up the stairs.

"Hollis," he called.

Walt and Hollis looked up.

"You can change that, you know," he said.

Hollis had never seen James smile, but James's eyes crinkled at the sides like he wanted to. "Scholarship and all," James finished. "It's not hard if you try. See you around."

The door closed behind him.

STAY

Walt crouched down on his heels, then stretched up tall, cracking their back.

You gonna tell me how you learned to do that?

I was seventeen and broke in the twenties. Half of us fought for cash. You learned quick if you wanted to keep your teeth.

Hollis laughed. *Sometimes you say things and I just imagine Oliver Twist, or, like, Sherlock Holmes.*

Psh. That was a completely different time period and country.

Hollis turned over that thought in his head a few times until the edges softened, but the heart of it still pleased him. Walt punching someone for him. Effortless, practiced.

Walt lit another cigarette.

I'm gonna savor these, but I think I deserve another for the wait.

Fine. You fucking hedonist.

Walt sent Hollis a thrill of amusement, and Hollis soothed it back with bitter fondness.

Suddenly there was a tapping sound, like someone was banging glass.

I think that's coming from upstairs. . . .

Walt looked back at the house. Annie was standing at the top-floor window looking down at them. They waved at her. She didn't wave back.

Weird.

Well, we can't go back inside, just text her or something.

> **Walt:** Sorry I missed you. Things got out of hand. See you later.

> **Annie:** It's okay. See you later.

It doesn't sound okay.

Annie doesn't like it when I fight, is all. Take us home.

Walt didn't hurry, filling Hollis's lungs so slow and smooth that they ached unpleasantly, and Hollis let him.

DIONYSUS

It felt like a truce. Like something important had shifted.

It was eleven thirty when they made it home. The house was empty and dark. They got ready for bed, and it felt anticipatory. Downstairs- and upstairs-neighbor noises both until they were settled beneath the sheets.

I need to know.

What?

If you could be doing anything else, if you could choose not to do this, would you?

Walt took a moment to answer.

My first day like this was on purpose. I was desperate and childish and selfish back then, but no. Now, knowing all that I do, I wouldn't have chosen this, Hollis. If I knew you and understood who you were, I wouldn't have chosen you. You deserve more than this.

Walt sounded stubborn. Embarrassed. Also, he'd answered Hollis's question even though it had taken him a whole day, and with that, something settled.

Permanently and in every way that mattered. Hollis wasn't afraid of Walt anymore, and he wasn't angry.

Okay. Okay, we need some rules. Everything you've done so far has been mostly all right. But when I need to use my hands or mouth or whatever, you have to let me. Tonight was as close to a trial run of that as we could have had, and it worked. I liked it better.

All right.

You have to let me cook dinner and do food stuff. It's not that you're bad at it—your recipes are just . . . a bit out of date and you keep triggering my ma.

Walt laughed.

Last, if we fight—and I know we will—you can't just run off and start doing whatever. We have to resolve it. This can't be me versus you, it has to be me and you versus the problem.

You read that one in a book?

Heard it at a wedding, Hollis snapped. *Do we have a deal?*

Hollis, you could have whatever you wanted from me if you ever asked it, Walt said, rolling over on their back. **All I do, I do for you. I'm a guest in your house.**

Hmm.

Give me my arm.

And it was his. Hollis raised it high enough that the moonlight fell across his skin, then turned his hand around, stretched it.

It's dangerous for me to trust people, Walt admitted. **Early on, I used to just sit back and not touch anything. Explained stuff up front. It got real messy. Jail, hospitals, work camps. I've been murdered twice. Y'wait longer and the risk of the screaming sickness gets higher though. It's hard to find middle ground.**

Hollis understood.

Have you ever met anyone else doing this? Another ghost?

Walt shrugged their other shoulder.

I'm the only me I've ever known. Spirits are more common. They're less like a person and more like bad energy attached to a space where something bad happened.

So you've been alone. This whole time?

Ninety-two years?

Walt shrugged again.

Wasn't all bad.

Just most of it, huh?

Hollis placed his hand on his chest over their heart to cover Walt's aching.

It's not happening, that wild feeling.

> **It has to be skin to skin. You're the first person who actually likes it, you know. Dina said it felt like hitting her funny bone or sticking a fork in a socket.**

Walt sighed and closed their eyes.

> **We didn't do it often, and when it happened it was an accident. I did it to you because I thought it would scare you some, 'cause you scared *me* some. Wasn't sure what to do when it didn't.**

Hollis smirked, and Walt let him.

I'm an unusual guy.

It reminded him of standing in front of a train. The overstimulation of it, the rattling at the back of his teeth. He liked things like that. He wanted to do it again, now that he knew what Walt's tears tasted like, knew the speed of his fist.

Can I . . . ?

> **It's your body, Hollis.** Walt cracked their eyes open just a sliver.

But it isn't anymore, is it? Hollis thought soft, like a wish. Too quiet for Walt to hear.

You can't just touch people; you have to ask, Hollis insisted, louder. *Now I'm asking.*

Walt turned his face to the wall and shut their eyes tight.

ROME

Hollis thought about touching Walt's neck, but that seemed a bit too much to start with.

He reached over until Walt adjusted. Until they were settled firmly on their side, curved like a comma in the dark, back to the moonlight.

His fingers landing on his left wrist sparked enough that they both flinched, but Hollis didn't pull away.

Instead, Hollis pushed down the curve of their palm until the tips of him were nestled in the hollow of Walt's fingers. The shock rattled their bones and set their teeth on edge.

This was easier when they didn't have to stand.

They went nearly blind with it, tremors racking up their spine, light flashing behind their eyes. Walt threw their head back and made an incredible noise into the silence of their room.

Hollis didn't know he could sound like that. He was suddenly desperately thankful that they were home alone.

Walt closed their grip, pressed harder, held his hand, and the euphoria was terrible and grand.

Like Holst's Jupiter.

What?

Like original sin, like the bite of an apple, like staring into first sunrise before you learn to look away, like touching the hem of an angel, like milk hot from skin, like licking honey from the fingertips of God.

Walt.

Hollis slid their hands apart and clasped his wrist firm and grounding. They jackknifed, tangled in the sheets. Walt tried to tug away, almost like a reflex, but all that did was make them scrape together, flop sweat slicking, vulgar, luxuriant.

This is us, you said.

Hollis felt crazy; Walt was sobbing.

It has never been this long, Hollis, *please*.

How long has it been?

And he meant something else entirely.

Walt tried to hide from him deep inside, but Hollis pulled him back out, merciless. He was delirious; he didn't let go. The blood pounded in their head steady as the march of time.

This was easier for him, Hollis realized. Easier for him to bear this than it was for Walt, somehow, and he didn't know why.

TELL ME HOW YOU FEEL.

> **Like stealing from a rectory,** Walt was babbling, lost. **Holy sepulchre, sweet and terrible and sweet and sweet and sweet—**

Hollis released him, separated until they weren't skin to skin anymore.

> **Sweet like milk. Like honey from the hand of God.**

Their face was wet.

Hollis pulled up the sheet and wiped Walt's tears.

STRAP

We can't do that in public, not even accidentally.

I know. I'm not stupid.

> **I'm serious, Hollis, we gotta be vigilant. I . . . I can't handle it.**

Really? Why?

> **Stop mocking me. You know why.**

Hollis stared at Walt in the mirror.

Paused half shaven, razor against their cheek. He dragged the blade across the side of their jaw, then tilted his chin up and swiped to the tip without breaking his gaze.

And suddenly, Walt felt heavy with it, like lava flowing down his spine to pool at the bottom of his stomach. He was watching, riveted, clinging to the side of the sink with their other hand.

Hollis turned their face to the side and scraped it clean, clicking the razor against the basin out of habit before turning the water on, and gave their face to Walt. So he could see what he felt, look at him raw.

He was tired, expectant. Indolent, amused. Walt pulled the cloth from the bar beside the shower and wet it, squeezed it. Covered their mouth, slipped it down to their neck, then dropped it, soiled, onto the porcelain.

TOY

Contrary to popular belief, Hollis wasn't a stranger to this.

SPOILED

They didn't talk about the night after Homecoming the way they didn't talk about that night when Hollis had spent time learning how to get Walt out of him.

It was too much, it needed time to breathe.

Instead, Hollis bickered with Walt as they did the laundry, washed the dishes, and mopped the floor. Mr. and Mrs. Brown came back Sunday night to a clean house.

Annie hadn't texted them since Saturday night, but Hollis wasn't worried. He'd hear the music Monday morning; this experience wasn't new.

As the sun went down and it got closer to bedtime, Hollis could feel Walt getting nervous. He nearly spilled their water at dinner, and Hollis caught their cup at the last second. The upstairs-neighbor noises were relentless.

Walt waited for Hollis to overwhelm him again. To ask for it or do it unannounced, and it only made Hollis want to swoon and sigh. Made him want to use their face to grin.

And he didn't, because he could.

SPORK

Annie bounced out of her house and slapped Hollis on the arm.

"You ready?"

"Yup."

You said she'd be mad.

Give it some time.

Annie had dyed her hair light green over the weekend and cut the back very short. The rest of it she had tied into two space buns decorated with butterfly clips.

She had bright pink blush fluffed across her nose and eyeliner freckles; she looked like a sweet strawberry.

"Did you see Yulia at Will's?"

Annie shrugged. "Yeah, she came way after you left and stayed late. She's probably still hungover, to be honest. She was sad that she missed you."

Annie seemed too happy, and Walt was anxious about it. Hollis spent the majority of their walk to school soothing his worries while Walt tried to dual wield a conversation with his least-favorite person.

True to form, when they arrived, Yulia looked like she'd been through the wringer. But she was still well-dressed in matching cream-colored sweats and Birkenstocks in spite of the cold weather.

She pulled Hollis forward by the back of his neck and dropped a rare kiss on his forehead.

"We're going out for lunch, don't be late."

RUNE

Jorge wasn't at school yet—he had one more week.

That didn't stop familiar eyes from following them around the halls. It wasn't as bad as right after Rose Town. Only the people who had been at Will's seemed to be staring, but it was near enough.

Walt seemed pleased, but it was bothering Hollis.

Timothy looked over at him the minute he sat down.

"Hey."

"Hey," Walt replied.

Timothy said nothing to him until the end of class, while he was shoving his things in his backpack.

"James wants you to come by his gym. I know you said you weren't interested, but he's a hard guy to shake."

"He looking for a rematch?" Walt asked.

"Fuck no." Timothy smirked. "But he has a match and wants to let you know you're welcome to watch. See if you change your mind."

Timothy swung his bag over his shoulder.

"You can say yes or no."

I don't know if this is a good idea.

"Tell him I'm busy tonight, but I'm open to the next one."

Timothy nodded. He handed Walt his phone.

"Put your number in."

ANTIGONE

Yulia was playing with his hand. Dragging her fingers up and down the length of it, pinching the skin between his thumb and his pointer, digging circles into the center of his palm.

Walt was keenly aware of it, and Hollis was watching him.

As much as one could watch in this situation.

He cataloged what things made Walt want to twitch, the pressures that made him want to close their eyes. They sat unmoving, watching the whiteboard. Walt slid their gaze over the curve of Yulia's brow, the flick of her lashes.

I would love her, if I had the chance, Walt said.

Hmm. What would that look like? If you had your own body, I mean.

I'd be kind to her always. Work hard for her. Make myself good enough to introduce to her family. She likes bread, so I'd get her that instead of flowers. After we wed, I'd fill our house with it, make it fresh for her every day after work.

You're a romantic.

It was just the way.

Yulia doesn't like boys. But I'm sure if you were you, she wouldn't mind having you around the way she likes having me around. Hand?

Walt gave it to him, and Hollis curled his fingers until he and Yulia were holding hands properly.

She sighed, laid her head down on the desk, and closed her eyes.

HUNGERS

Hollis sat in the back of Yulia's car like he always did, but Annie kept looking at him in the rearview mirror. She was talking about a project she was working on. Something about armor made of resin.

"You could probably also do chain mail made of plastic as well. It wouldn't be the same as a full resin suit of arms, but you'd be able to retain the transparency," Yulia was saying.

"But the whole point is for the entire thing to be resin," Annie griped.

Mouth.

"If you change the entire project from resin to plastic, you'd have a lot more flexibility and it would be less toxic. And you could seamlessly recycle it when you're done with it," Hollis said.

Annie sighed loud and theatrical. "I guess."

They approached Pino's, but Yulia didn't turn down the driveway. That was okay. There were a few places to go, and no one had specified. Hollis was kind of ambivalent about where they ate, as long as he could get something for five dollars or less.

He didn't start to get concerned until at least three of the places they usually went to passed by.

Walt was very quiet.

"Where are we going?" Hollis asked.

Annie didn't respond.

"It's going to be okay," Yulia said.

Walt doused Hollis's brain in pure fear. He unlocked the door and tugged on the handle.

Dude, we're going like forty miles per hour!

The door didn't budge.

"What the fuck . . . fucking . . . child lock? . . . What the hell, Yulia?!"

They took a sharp turn and stopped in the familiar parking lot of the urgent care center.

Annie turned around and pushed her seat back so she was facing Hollis directly.

"Hollis, you know we love you, right?"

Walt instantly relaxed.

Oh, thank God.

Jesus fucking Christ.

"Yeah . . . that doesn't mean you can child-lock me in a car and take me random places," Hollis snapped.

Do you want to handle this?

Yeah, I've got it.

Yulia unbuckled her seat belt and craned over the seat. "Annie thinks you're on drugs, and I'm inclined to agree."

Hollis closed their eyes.

"I'm not on drugs, Yulia—"

"That's what everyone on drugs says." Annie interrupted. "But they're literally lying every time. We never see you anymore; you're acting weirdly pleasant all the time. You keep looking into the distance like you're dissociating. You've stopped texting us at night by such an intense degree that my sleep schedule has changed. You dress completely different—"

"That one's kind of an upgrade—" Yulia said.

Shut up, I can feel you smirking.

"THEY'RE ALL UPGRADES!" Annie shouted. "But they're not *him.*"

"So . . . you're mad that I'm nicer and spent some time on Google figuring out how to dress?" Hollis asked.

"Maybe James hit his head really hard that one time and knocked something loose," Yulia suggested to Annie.

But Annie was really upset; her face was red like she was about to cry.

"You haven't been . . . looking at me," she said.

That one hurt. Walt made them look at Yulia instead: at the worry in the tilt of her mouth. Thought about the kiss on his forehead, how long she'd held his hand.

You can tell them.

What, why?

I'm tired. They care about you. It's not like they can do anything about it anyway.

Walt, shut up. Just—

"Listen," Hollis said. "This year has been really hard. Things aren't getting better, and you guys are going to leave. I know I said I'd visit but, you know . . . things are going to change. You're going off to do really cool things, you're both going to be really successful. You're the most talented person I know, Annie, and Yulia . . . you have access to the whole world.

"But I belong here. I have a job waiting for me somewhere out there doing hard work, and that's fine."

"But—" Annie started, but Hollis put up a hand.

"I said it's FINE. But I can't just . . . I have to be a part of this community if I stay. I can't keep . . . being . . . the way I was being and be able to survive. People here survive because they work together, they know each other. They do each other favors because they like each other most of the time. It's important.

"And maybe it's stupid and too late, but I need to be a part of that. I need to try. And if that means I have to put in some extra effort, spend my nights doing research and work, think a bit harder about what I say to people, then that's what I've got to do."

The car was quiet. Yulia was gazing out the window at the urgent care center, and Annie was staring hard at him.

"James . . . James has been nice to me," Hollis said. "Timothy too. Seeing James get so fucked-up about staying here made me feel . . . made everything feel like it was an emergency. Changing, I mean, becoming a better person. I'm not on drugs, Annie. I'm fine."

Yulia pursed her lips. "Okay. That may be all well and good, but urgent care does same-day drug testing."

"If we let him out of the car, he's going to run," Annie replied.

Hollis rolled his eyes. "Run where? There's no bus stop out this far, and it's like a forty-five-minute hike back home."

Can we pass a drug test?

You shooting smack while I'm asleep?

What?! No. I'm just being careful. I don't know how this shit works.

"Just, let's go in and do the stupid test so we don't have to have this conversation again. I'll pay."

Annie and Yulia flanked him on both sides as they headed into the center. He slapped his credit card down on the counter and splurged on the more comprehensive one.

He could feel Yulia and Annie making eye contact with each other, but neither of them said a word.

HOLLOW

They got into the car hours later. Hollis slid into the back seat and closed his eyes.

"I . . . genuinely didn't think you'd pass," Yulia said.

"Thanks for that," Hollis said. "Thrilled with the way this lunch period went."

"Stop being a bitch about it, we just care about you," Annie snapped.

"I know. I'm sorry."

They rode back quietly, Yulia's acid jazz soaking up the tension.

Did you mean it?

What?

What you said to them earlier. You could've said anything, but you said that.

What we have together is our business. When they find out—if they find out—it's not going to be because I was too startled to think of something else, or because I was threatened into confessing. It will be on my own terms.

I told you it was all right.

Yeah. But also, if there's no way to make this stop, then it's mine. This secret belongs to me and I deserve to be able to guard it—

Hollis.

Jealously. I deserve to be able to guard it jealously, Walt. If this . . . thing we have is rare. If it's good, if it's mine, I should be able to share it when I feel ready to. Not when you're tired and not out of fucking . . . despair or whatever.

Walt was quiet.

And yeah, I did mean that stuff earlier. Loners don't survive well here. It's one thing to be edgy and isolated in high school and another to be kept out of food trades or resources because everyone thinks you're standoffish or a piece of shit. I've always known that, I just—I didn't notice that I was running out of time to figure out how to . . . not be like that, I guess.

You're not a bad person, Hollis.

And it was strange to hear it said like that. So plain, like it was obvious.

It wasn't that he thought he *was* or anything. It just . . . It was different hearing it from someone who knew him. Who watched him every day, saw the good parts, the bad parts, and the secret parts.

You're just *you* and that's crackerjack all by itself.

And Hollis didn't mean to, but he felt ashamed. He felt ashamed and relieved and seen, and he couldn't stop himself from crying if the world was going to end.

Oh, sweetheart.

Yulia put her right hand on the top of the wheel and silently reached back through the gap between the seat and the door.

Hollis threaded their fingers together.

STARS

Instead of going back to school, Yulia dropped him off at home. There was only one class period left anyway. She parked in front, and they both got out.

Hollis had long since dried his face, and Annie couldn't have seen him, she'd been facing the window the whole time. But Yulia cupped his cheek anyway and looked into his eyes.

"Are you all right?"

Hollis bit his lip.

"Yeah. I'm fine. I'll be fine, I think."

She stared at him hard, a small line of concern appearing between her eyebrows, but eventually let him go. Smiled, even.

"You'd better be," she said, then slapped at his face light and familiar.

Yulia kissed his forehead again, then messed up his hair.

"Text us later. Don't forget."

MELT

Hollis closed the door behind them. The house was silent and golden, warm the way it is when you stay home sick from school. Two hours before his ma was to be expected.

Hollis made a decision.

Go upstairs to our room.

Walt sent him curiosity but took them there as requested.

Hollis asked for their arms and opened the window, letting the cold air in.

You don't like flowers, do you?

I like 'em as much as any man, Hollis, why?

He'd never done this before, but it was easy to figure out. Hollis picked up Jorge's cigarettes that Walt had thrown onto the desk. Tapped one out.

He was faster with Jorge's lighter than Walt was, and he thanked a god that wasn't listening for making this smooth. Making him capable of cupping a hand round the flame as he lit it. Making sure he didn't fumble this.

Hollis wedged the cigarette between his fingers and with grace lifted it to Walt's mouth.

Placed it between Walt's teeth.

Hollis.

Quiet, just—

He couldn't feel whatever satisfaction Walt got from smoking. It tasted bad, made him want to cough and gave them a very slight headache. But that wasn't the point.

Walt made a soft sound. Blew hot air into the winter like a freight train. Followed Hollis's fingers as he pulled them away.

How do you flick the ash?

You . . . you . . . twitch your top finger. It's— Hollis? Why are you doing this?

I'm taking care of you.

"Jesus." Walt hissed it out loud into the stillness of their room, and Hollis knew Walt understood what he meant. Felt him circling the shape of it like a nervous cat. Cute.

Hollis laughed. *What about Mary and Joseph?*

Don't think I want them to see this.

Hollis brought the cigarette back to Walt's mouth, and this time scraped the edge of his thumb against their jaw. Savored the jolt that slid down their spine like a knife.

Walt fell forward, catching them on the window's edge. Leaned against it, breathing hard.

He snatched back ownership of Hollis's arms and used them to cover his face.

I don't even know what to say to this.

He took another shaky drag, then laughed anxiously.

You are a few bolts short of a Chevy, I'll tell you that. Bold as I've ever seen it. You woulda cleaned up in my day.

Hollis smirked, and he could feel Walt's annoyance at it.

I'm sure you were better.

Mmm, perhaps. But . . . let's. Pack this away a bit. I hear you loud and clear, don't think I don't. But I need a minute. There's not a lot new to me, but this? Hollis, you gotta understand, this is . . .

A liability.

Walt took one last drag, then chucked the cigarette out the window onto the road.

Some time, s'il vous plaît. Be kind and wait for me.

CORE

What do you think that feeling is, when we touch?

Don't know, don't care to know.

It's . . . I don't think it's supposed to feel good; I think it's supposed to just be "too much" because it isn't supposed to happen at all.

Hollis, it's 3 a.m.

Is it our souls scraping together, do you think? It's brittle, like charcoal, like it has a thousand holes and a thousand places for them to catch. It hurts, but hurt isn't exactly the right word because it's not painful, really. Just overwhelming.

Walt was quiet, and Hollis could feel him frowning.

What does it feel like for you?

Walt sighed angrily and opened their eyes.

I want to be asleep.

Like eating honey from the fingertips of God?

And there it was, the glow of Walt's humiliation, followed closely by frustration. Adorable.

God, Hollis, it's like being electrocuted, falling from a height and getting a massage all at once. It feels out of control, like trying to lasso a hurricane. It feels too small and too big, too hot and too cold, and I didn't even know that last one until you kept me there for more than five minutes.

That was certainly something to explore later.

Do you hate it? Hollis asked instead.

Walt sighed, still embarrassed.

No, I don't hate it, Hollis. I don't hate you being . . . being close. Now can we go to sleep?

NOVA

Annie eyed him sharp and keen the next day.

"You didn't used to smoke," she said. "I saw you yesterday, through the window."

Walt shrugged.

"This is a steel town. Almost everyone over forty does it. Plus, I got these off Jorge, so consider them victory cigs."

Annie pulled her backpack strap tight.

"They're saying you knocked him out in one hit. That's pretty wild."

Mouth.

"Pretty lucky." Hollis laughed. "It was a very 'knees weak, arms are heavy; there's vomit on his sweater already, Mom's spaghetti' sort of scenario, Annie. I didn't even go there to do that; I was looking for you the whole time, but Clementine distracted me and then Timothy manhandled me down the stairs."

Annie hummed, "I heard she's still pissed at you. She wanted to ask you out."

Gross.

Be kind.

"Yeah, that was never going to go the way she wanted. I'm not even slightly interested in her. Anyway, it's been days, why are you asking me about this now?"

Annie scraped the heels of her boots against the sidewalk as they walked, kicking up little puffs of ice dust.

"Someone recorded it. Didn't see it till now. You looked cool, Hollis, like someone in a movie."

"Thanks, I guess."

It felt strange thinking about that moment with Annie. It felt private now, like telling her about a hookup or something.

For the first time in over seven years, their walk to school was awkward.

Worse than the very first time, when they didn't know each other at all.

SPARE

Can we leave? Walt asked, in the middle of third period. **I don't want to be here anymore.**

Like leave school or just this room?

I want to take us somewhere.

They texted Annie, Yulia, and his ma that his stomach hurt and walked out the door.

They headed to the bus stop, and Walt wasted more of Hollis's money. Rode until the trees cleared and the air smelled like water and river greens. Got off at the last stop.

MICHIGAN

Lake Michigan didn't freeze all the way. It was too big.

The shards of ice drifted in dark soup, clinking against each other like bells, cracking sharp as a shotgun farther out. Colder than death.

But the sand held on to the sun, warm for the first few inches.

Walt laid them down, soft. Hoodie behind their head, they opened their eyes to the wide gray sky.

You're lucky you have a bus that goes to the beach, we used to have to walk. Do y'all still fish in here?

Not really. The big fish are closer to the middle of the lake, and only one guy has a fishing boat. The rest of us buy our fish from him.

Hmm.

You're from here, aren't you? This is where you grew up . . . ?

Born and raised.

Why did you bring us here, Walt?

He took a full minute to answer.

It's hard being close to home and not standing in it. Feels lonesome.

Walt gave Hollis his right arm without him having to ask. Hollis placed it over their chest, mitten, coat, and sweater keeping them apart, keeping them from bringing the burning.

Where did you live?

Rose Town.

He said it like it meant nothing, like it didn't grip Hollis by the throat. Make it hard to swallow.

> **This whole place used to be Rose Town, you know. You live in the newer part of it. They tore down some buildings between. It doesn't take long for grass to cover what's been left behind.**

It's fucked-up that you never told me that. You know that, right? It's fucked-up that I didn't know that this whole time.

Walt closed their eyes.

> **You asked that first week, but I couldn't tell you. I couldn't bring myself to . . . It was personal. We didn't know each other then.**

That's really not an excuse, you fucking asshole.

Walt huffed, irritated.

> **Do you know how many of my rides knew my name?**

Most of them?

> **Thirty. Only about fifteen got a good conversation out of me. Seven got to know what I liked and didn't like. Three got to know I had a sister. I've been in about two hundred people, give or take, and you know how many of them stopped cooking with celery without me asking?**

Five? They can tell you didn't like it. I could tell you—

> **Just you, Hollis,** Walt interrupted him, impatient.
>
> **Even Dina prioritized her needs and wants above mine, and it was fine of her to do that. Wouldn't have asked her for more than she gave, and every second with her was sweet, but you gotta understand why you frighten me sometimes.**

Oh.

This is more than I ever asked for. More than I hoped and more than I deserve. It doesn't help that you're a fella. I know myself and my proclivities, and times have changed, but even the angels couldn't have seen that coming.

Hollis understood, by God he did, but he could still feel Walt twisting inside. He took their hand and held his own face, tenderly. Mitten to skin.

Walt.

What?

What do you look like?

LICK

He was shorter than average, five foot six to Hollis's six foot one. He didn't have blond hair like Sam's; he was a brunet. Darker than Hollis's, he said. Curlier than Hollis's mom's but not as curly as Yulia's.

He was stronger than Hollis, and very sure he could pick him up. He had dimples.

He didn't get old enough to grow a beard or mustache, though he'd tried once apparently.

One of his fingers had been broken in an accident and was crooked. He had a scar across his eyebrow from a bottle thrown his way in a bar fight. Another across his knuckles from delinquent behavior, as he put it.

Walt traced the hills and valleys of Hollis's face as he talked. Got stuck drawing a finger down the hump on Hollis's nose over and over.

When I first saw you, I thought you were pretty.

I was disgusting, covered in tears and dirt.

All the same.

Did you pick me because you wanted to look like me?

I picked you because you were there. I was dying, again, and you were kind.

He rested their left hand, mittened, over Hollis's right.

Your coat smelled like dead leaves, aftershave, and your terrible shampoo. I was warmer than I'd been in weeks.

Yeah?

When I went to lie in the hollow, in your coat, I wondered if you'd be just as comfortable inside. Tall and thin as you are.

Hollis shivered, made them shiver.

I was going to clear out one of the abandoned houses for you. Cook you dinner and bring it every night, bread in the mornings. **Hollis.**

Tell my ma where to find you so that you could decide if you wanted to go to school. All that. I was willing to figure it out. Food and shelter.

It was a dirty trick, Walt admitted finally. **I'm sorry for it. I'm sorry, Hollis.**

Hollis shrugged his shoulder.

It suits you. But I forgive you. I like this.

Hollis petted them beneath the jaw, beneath the ear, where he knew his skin was thin and vulnerable, and Walt shuddered. He tipped their head back and leaked himself from the top down to right beneath their nose, so Walt could have their eyes. Then Hollis put his fingers in their mouth.

He touched their tongue like it wasn't his.

Rubbed it until their spine pooled liquid, and Walt's guilt swelled unbearable. Until Hollis taught him the meaning of need. Let spit run down their chin, gagged on it. Licked between their fingers, flicking between the webbing.

I wish I could kiss you, Walt confessed, breathless.

Is this not kissing? Hollis laughed, silent into the darkness in their chest. *Kissing can mean something different to us. We make the rules. We are a new thing.*

Hollis bit the meat of his palm, dragged their face across it, smearing wet and terrible over his jaw. Scraped his stubble until they shivered. Panted into the night where no one could hear them, no one could see them, hard and alive and spiraling.

Please, God.

I know.

Hollis took their face back and gave Walt their legs, everything from the chest down, then scraped his fingernails over their scalp. Dug in circles until Walt kicked out, helpless and twitching. Walt wanted to roll their eyes back, so Hollis did. He wanted to moan out into the darkness, so Hollis made that music and then laughed at him.

You're so easy.

No, I'm—

I know every inch of me, Walt. I was me before we were us.

Hollis spat on his hand, slid it slick up his neck and pinched his ear like teeth. Walt jerked them up so hard they tumbled over face-first in the sand and Hollis laughed again. Laughed until Walt's humiliation burned their cheeks red and made their heart race. Walt gritted his teeth to keep from admitting that he loved this. Like *that* could stop Hollis from feeling it in his silence.

But Hollis finally settled, merciful, and folded his arms over their chest, grinning.

Come on, man. Tell me. What are you so afraid of? You've never had a hookup? Never taken a dame up to make-out point and shown her some hospitality? Come on, Walt, you told me you were more than a liability.

Walt was still breathing hard and helpless, but Hollis could feel a spike of irritation at Hollis's mockery beneath it.

You're unholy.

I know. We suit each other.

213

DRY

The walk back was cold and exhausting, but Hollis still couldn't sleep. It was almost dawn now, and Walt was just lying with him in silence as the light from outside their room turned everything in it blue.

Hollis turned them onto their back and placed a hand over their chest.

You thinkin' about it?

Hmm?

Rose Town.

Hollis thumbed at the collar of the white T-shirt Walt had picked out for them.

No. I'm thinking about you and me. It's been almost three months of this. Early fall, Homecoming, beginning of winter . . . it's only going to get colder, you know.

I know.

Do you know what it feels like to have you inside? Any of your rides give you a good description?

I know, Hollis. The screaming gives that away pretty soundly. It's uncomfortable.

Hollis pulled their knees up and folded their arms behind their head.

It's nice. I don't think I'd like if it stopped.

You can't mean that.

Don't tell me what I can and can't mean. Did you know when you have the whole of us, it feels like you're carrying me? I've

214

never felt so . . . I didn't know that I didn't like being alone until it wasn't an option anymore.

It's not supposed to be like that.

Maybe it was supposed to be, for me at least. It feels like when you're a kid and you're playing hide-and-seek and you find a good spot—a small one—and you creep inside. Then your friend finds the same spot and there's just enough space for them to fit inside too. So you're both crammed in tight, and it's not comfortable, but it's not bad because it's them. And it's dark and you have to be quiet, but their breath is on your neck, and you don't know what it means yet to have your heart beat faster about it. That's what it feels like, Walt.

Oh.

Walt swallowed.

I like you. And I know you like me back, I can feel it.

How . . . how does it feel?

Hollis grinned, closed their eyes.

It's fast. You roll through emotions so quickly whenever I rile you up that it took a while for me to separate them. Terror, grief, longing, then back to grief and terror again. Like you think I'm going to notice and get angry, and get disgusted. But I'm not disgusted, and I'm braver than you, no offense.

He dragged their fingernails against the fabric, like a whisper.

I think I like you, Walt. I like you like I'd like you if we met in class or during a summer job, and it's not hard for me. The only difference is that everyone else doesn't get to walk around with knowing as much as I do about you. Did you think it would mean nothing to feel your smile before it hits our face? Or know that it twists your heart to see certain run-down

*things around here? What it would mean to feel you crying,
lonely, mad as a hornet, happy so big it feels like the sun is rising, all day every day until I look for it? Long for it? How could
anyone feel that and not eventually get a little sweet on you is
a mystery to me.*

Walt was quiet. He scraped his fingers through their hair, and
Hollis arched into it, pleased.

You're the strangest person I've ever met.

*I'm a country boy, Walt. You've spent too much time in the city.
This is still a place where people marry their high school sweet-
hearts.*

Walt snorted. **Don't remind me.**

*I'm not saying that it goes well; I'm saying people do it. Then they
figure things out and I'm not afraid to. Are you?*

I'm afraid of a lot of things.

*And I'm not afraid of anything. Maybe we were meant to teach
each other shit or something. I can teach you to face your fears,
and you can teach me to actually be nice to people.*

**You're already so kind. How could you think you're not
kind?**

"How could you think you're not brave?" Hollis said out loud,
and he felt Walt flinch and pull deeper inside.

Hollis dragged the comforter from the end of their bed up over
both of their heads so they were together in that dark place.

"Come on, admit it, it's just us. No one else can hear you," Hollis whispered.

Hollis.

"Say it with my mouth, use my lungs for the air for it. Say it,
Walt, I can feel it anyway, you can't hide from me."

"I . . . I *like* you."

"Yeah?"

"I like you, Hollis."

"You like me?"

"I *like* you."

TRACK

Hollis was smoking for Walt out the window in the early pink light when he remembered Yulia's request.

Hollis: You guys up?

Annie: You feel better, you big liar? You were fine this morning.

Hollis: I just went to the beach. I needed to think.

Yulia: It's so cold there, why would you want to be at the beach???

Hollis: Did you know the water is almost the same color as the sky when it's cloudy outside? You can't tell the difference unless you squint.

Annie: Hollis is smoking again. I can see him from my kitchen window.

Hollis: Narc.

Yulia: You're going to get lung cancer and die.

Hollis smirked.

You hear that? We have a limited time for this. Enjoy it while you can.

218

Walt rolled their eyes.

Hollis: Yeah yeah yeah.

Yulia: What are you doing this Friday?
I want to have a sleepover.

Hollis: It's been a while. What's the occasion?

Yulia: My daddy's heading to New York for work and
my mom is forcing him to bring her with so it can feel
like a vacation. They'll be gone Thursday.

Annie: Tomorrow! We can make it a four nighter?

Yulia: They're leaving at night unfortunately.

Hollis: Whatever. I'm in. Want me
to bring anything?

Yulia: Nope, just you and yourself.

Hollis: <3

She wants bread again. What should I make her?

**Something fancy, none of this peasant shit. Make her a
real loaf of French bread.**

I could do honey butter too.

**Then do it. She's your best gal; she deserves the fine
things.**

No, she's your best gal. Annie's supposed to be mine.

219

Annie hasn't made our heart race in a while.

Hollis exhaled into the cold and didn't deny it.

Do you miss it? Annie. Loving her, being in love with her.

Being normal. The way you should be.

It was comfortable. But there are other things.

WHEAT

He was halfway through kneading when Mrs. Brown settled at the kitchen table behind him.

"You worry me, june bug," she said. "You've been working hard doing extra chores, studying, and fixing things, and I don't know why."

"I'm fine, Ma." Hollis folded over the loaf and pressed into it again with his palms. "I'm trying French bread for Yulia. I know it's late, but I'll be done in a bit so this can rise overnight."

Mrs. Brown was quiet for a bit.

"You . . . worried about your old man and me?" She pressed. "We got a good thing going, and you can stay as long as you like when school ends. Or . . . Are things not going well at school with all your friends leaving?"

"It's . . . I mean, that's not the greatest. I'm just trying to take it seriously. Figure out what I want to do. Pay attention to the things I'm good at. There's nothing to worry about, I promise."

You're a good liar.

I'm not lying.

Walt turned their feet to face the kitchen table, so Hollis folded their arms and faced his ma. But Walt was yearning. So Hollis let him sit them down, he stretched out his hands so she could hold them gently.

It's okay to need this. Or want it, Walt.

"I'm sorry for making you worried about me," Walt said. "I didn't mean to."

Mrs. Brown shook her head. "Annie stopped by early today before you got home to check in on you. She seems like she's concerned, and seeing her all knotted up like that made me wonder how my boy was."

She squeezed his hands, and Walt ached.

"Sometimes good changes aren't always for good reasons," she said. "You smell like your father did when we first took up together. Never thought I'd have to warn you off smoking in the house, but here we are. He started for his anxiety; its a fool thing to assume it wouldn't be the same for you. We are family."

Walt shrugged. Hollis pulled himself from their hands and face and just watched.

"I know it's not . . . I can stop," Walt said.

Mrs. Brown smiled and kissed Hollis's knuckles.

"Make sure you do, eventually. There are many awful things you could be doing—I'm thankful it's just this. But it means more to me that my boy might be struggling than telling you what to do."

"Oh." Walt frowned.

"Did you think I wouldn't notice if my baby started smiling every day but seemed sad? You've had a little rain cloud over your head for a while. But this is the first big change, a meaningful one. You've seemed like you've been settling a bit lately, only in the last week or so. But I wouldn't be a good mama if I didn't ask. It could just be the eye of a hurricane."

Walt wanted to hide, wanted to put their hands over their face.

Do you still miss your own ma?

Please, just—

It's not embarrassing. It's okay.

Hollis shrugged their shoulders and smiled.

Sometimes I forget you're also seventeen.

Walt flinched inside, hid, and Hollis let him. How could he not? He wasn't made to ignore something like this.

"I'm thinking about things. Figuring out how to be happy, I guess." Hollis took over for them. "But things are going all right. My grades are better, I've made a few new friends. When you and Pa were out, I went to a party."

"Your first one!" She beamed.

"Yeah, I left early, but yeah. It was nice. I'm okay, I'm just figuring some stuff out, but I'm okay."

Hollis put himself somewhere small when Mrs. Brown hugged them. Curled up so Walt could have access to every bit of warmth. He was quiet when Walt leaned his head on Mrs. Brown's shoulder. Didn't say a word when Walt closed their eyes tight.

FRENCH BREAD

Ingredients

1 tablespoon cornmeal

6 cups all-purpose flour

2½ .25-ounce packages active dry yeast

1½ teaspoons salt

2 cups warm water (110°F/45°C)

1 egg white

1 tablespoon water

Instructions

Grease a large baking sheet and sprinkle with cornmeal. Set aside.

Combine 2 cups flour, yeast, and salt in the bowl of a stand mixer. Stir in 2 cups warm water; beat with the dough hook attachment until blended. Continue adding remaining flour, a little at a time, until incorporated.

Knead dough on a lightly floured surface until smooth and elastic, 8 to 10 minutes. Shape into a ball, place in a greased bowl, and turn once. Cover and let rise in a warm place until doubled in size, about 1 hour.

Punch dough down and divide in half. Turn out onto a lightly floured surface. Cover and let rest for 10 minutes.

Roll each half into a large rectangle. Roll up, starting from a long side. Moisten edge with water and seal. Taper ends.

Place loaves, seam-side down, on the prepared baking sheet. Lightly beat egg white with 1 tablespoon water and brush over loaves.

Cover with a damp cloth and let rise until nearly doubled, 35 to 40 minutes.

Preheat the oven to 375°F/190°C.

Use a sharp knife to make three or four diagonal cuts, about ¼-inch deep, across the top of each loaf. Bake in the preheated oven for 20 minutes. Brush loaves with egg white mixture. Continue baking until an instant-read thermometer inserted into the center reads 190°F/88°C or loaves sound hollow when tapped, 15 to 20 minutes more. If necessary, cover loosely with foil to prevent over-browning.

Remove loaves from the baking sheet and cool on a wire rack.

GREASE

Timothy gave him the information for James's match. Reassured him that it wasn't a big deal. Even rode the bus over with him after school, but Hollis still felt out of place.

He wasn't someone who went to the gym. Much less a sport-specific gym like this, where it was an open-plan space and people noticed when strangers walked inside.

Walt, on the other hand, smelled the sweat and metal and men and said, *I'd rather jump ship than spend the rest of my time with you hanging around in a place like this.*

James was talking to his coach. He glanced over at Hollis and Tim, and nodded.

Walt watched the fight keenly, tracked James's strengths and weaknesses. Spoke to Timothy for them when the situation required it. Waved off the membership discount James's coach offered them, as well as the sad look in James's eyes, inevitable and kind.

This really isn't your thing, huh?

Y'don't have to like everything you're good at. I don't like to hurt people if I can manage it.

James and Timothy didn't let him leave afterward. They took him to a nearby bar and crowded him into a booth like this was something they did every day.

It felt strange, but they weren't letting it get awkward, they filled the silence easily, like they'd talked about doing this and were determined to make sure it went well no matter what Hollis did.

James ordered them three nonalcoholic lagers and shook his head when Hollis took out his wallet.

"Why are you guys being so nice to me?"

James shrugged one shoulder. "You came all the way out here 'cause I wanted you to. Least I can do is buy you a drink."

"He wants to know why you're turning all this down," Timothy said, straight to the point, the way Hollis liked it.

Hollis shrugged. "Don't like hurting people."

"What are you going to do after we graduate?" James asked. "I keep thinking about that time . . . at the beginning of the year. You've gotta have some hard opinions about that if you said what you said and you did what you did. That's why I thought maybe this whole thing would help."

Hollis could feel Walt's curiosity.

Tell you later.

"I mean, yeah. I was . . . projecting. But I'm fine now, I'll just do what everyone else does. I'm sure my pa's work has some openings, we can head up to the city together. It's common enough; I'm not better than anyone else here; I'm not too good for factory work."

Timothy's face twisted. "No one is saying that. But you should at least try. I applied to a bunch of schools and got in, but my scholarships weren't enough to make up the difference, so I'm headed to the city like you."

Hollis was horrified, he assumed Timothy would have been all right. He was a star athlete, popular, James's best friend . . .

"I can talk to Yulia if you want," he said urgently. "See if maybe we can figure out something that works for you?"

Timothy shook his head. "No, man, it's not even that. I don't even want . . . People don't leave here because they really want to go to school most of the time, they leave because there's nothing here anymore. People want to stay with their families. You *know* this shit. If I had a job I could work around here that paid enough, I'd take it in a heartbeat. When Yulia's family came to work nearby, we all thought things might change and we could rebuild, but nothing happened."

"That's not her fault," James replied, rolling his eyes. "You should take him up on his offer. Yulia's nice enough. Her dad probably is too. Paid for new supplies for all our school's teams the year they moved here and no one's seen him at a single game."

Hollis smirked. "Mr. Egunyemi doesn't like sports. He's more of a musical theater guy."

James laughed, bright and free, and took a long drink. "Good guy. Nice enough."

Walt took over without warning. "Would you really stay here and work here if there was somewhere for you to do it?" he asked.

Jeez, calm down.

Timothy shrugged. "I'm sure if you asked around, most of us would. My dad takes a bus three hours both ways, man. But like I said, nothing has changed."

Walt tapped his fingers against the side of their bottle.

"I'll ask Yulia about your situation, Timothy; we'll see what we can do. I'm sure if you talked to Mr. Egunyemi about your situation, we can figure something out. It's not an easy fix for everyone, but—"

James cleared his throat. He glanced at Timothy.

Timothy tapped the side of his bottle against Hollis's and took a swig.

"Musical theater, huh." Tim grinned. "Well, I'll be."

GROAN

Hollis's trial loaves of French bread were a little hard, but his second batch came out light and fluffy. He made six, froze three, and saved one for the house. Sliced them and put them in ziplock bags for the next night.

What was that bread you made when you first came here?

I like that, "first came here," Walt said, soft. I don't know, it was some Depression-era bread. I hadn't made bread in forty years; I was just trying my best.

Hollis hmmed. He turned on the bathroom light and started the tub.

Walt leaned them against the sink so he could inspect Hollis's pores.

I love your eyes.

Yeah? What color were yours?

Green.

Walt paused, then continued squeezing the sides of Hollis's nose.

Surprised no one's noticed yet.

I'm not. No one looks at me close enough.

Walt swiped a towel and threw it at the bottom of the door, pushing through the crevices until it was close to airtight. Then he opened the window and turned off the light.

The moon was full and bright out, but still Walt didn't look at him.

Hollis lay there in his skin and boiled with want.

He flicked on Jorge's lighter for Walt but let him take care of the rest, leaning their head back on the lip of the tub.

Tell me about someone else you rode in. How far did you go with them and their wives?

Walt crossed their ankles.

You're not slick, Walt said, and blew smoke toward the window. **It's not the same as what you're asking from me.**

Is it because it's not acting? You said this is like being on a stage for you. Pretending to be someone else, to like someone in another person's life for their sake. Is it scarier to . . . to like me for your own sake. Or is it like . . .

What?

Is it because I'm just a house? For you?

"No," Walt said into the smoke and the gloom of the bathroom. "You're not just a house to me."

Hollis wished he could press his forehead against Walt's collarbone, drag his nose up his neck, taste the skin behind his ear.

Why d'you even . . . Hollis, what is wrong with you?

Hollis had thought about it. Quiet one night, when Walt was asleep and he'd stopped trying to reach his phone.

I like your face. I don't move mine the way you do, the way you make our eyes crinkle when you feel like smiling but don't want to go all the way. Your expressions are pretty. You have a . . . The way you stand, it's . . . strong. I could imagine it before you even told me what you looked like. I like your voice, and I want to hear it all the time; it drives me crazy. Even on the first day.

I don't need to touch you to know that I want to.

It was easy to be honest when he didn't have to speak out loud. When these felt more like wishes than admissions.

"Christ."

You say the Lord's name in vain a lot for someone religious.

Your bad behavior is inspirational.

Mm. More than that, Hollis continued. *I just like you. You're funny, you're kind. When you bitch about things you do it in a way that makes me want to laugh. When you're scared or sad, you make me feel glad that you're here in me and not in anyone else. You make me want to take care of you. I want to take care of you.*

Walt didn't say anything to that, but he was thinking. Hollis could feel it.

He brought his hand to the curve of Walt's neck, grazed the edge of his finger against their skin. Walt flinched and hissed. Hollis did it again, and the water slopped out of the tub onto the floor.

I'm not a coward, Walt.

You make me feel weak.

Is that so. Do I still make you feel sad?

Hollis scraped a line up his neck, and Walt slammed their head back against the tile. Teeth clenched tight.

Shit. Walt hissed.

That's better. Be quiet for me for a bit.

Hollis clamped his hand around the back of his own neck, cupped it like Yulia did when she thought he needed grounding. Not rough and mean.

Sweet.

Walt slipped them beneath the water to scream.

KISS

How come it didn't feel that way the first night, when I bruised us?

We are sharing, always. But I took it in, so you wouldn't have to feel it. I pretended, for your sake, that it didn't hurt to hold all of it.

Don't hide it from me like that ever again.

Why?

How can I take care of you if you don't let me know when you're hurting?

It wasn't fair. I couldn't take away your chance to be angry. You deserved to be angry.

I can be angry, and worried. I can be angry and care about you too.

Walt made a wounded sound, deep in Hollis's throat, and buried their face in the sheets.

I didn't know you were going to be like this. I didn't know this would happen. I wouldn't have . . . I wish I could . . .

Quieter, like it wasn't intended for Hollis to hear, he said, **Forgive me, God, come to my assistance; Lord, make haste to help me.**

Hollis laughed.

I'm wicked enough for prayer? What's the rest?

Don't mock me Hollis. Not now, when I feel so small.

Let them be confounded and ashamed that seek my soul. Let them be turned backward and blush for shame, that desire evils to me. Let them be presently turned away,

blushing for shame, that desire evils to me. Let all that seek thee rejoice and be glad in thee. And let such as love thy salvation say always:

The Lord be magnified.

But I am needy and poor: Help me.

Hollis put a hand to their face through the sheets, brushed a thumb over their cheekbone, tender and cruel.

Thou art my helper and my deliverer: Lord, make no delay.

Glory be to the Father, and to the Son, and to the Holy Ghost.

As it was in the beginning, is now, and ever shall be, world without end.

STARING DOWN THE SUN

Hollis knew then that he couldn't give this up. He needed this in a real way and he wasn't ashamed of it, it wasn't in his nature to feel ashamed. Like being born to drink gasoline on a planet of people who needed water.

He wondered if Walt had felt that way too. Living rough in the final years of that brittle last millennium, did Walt lie in bed in his tenement and stare at his ceiling in the middle of the night and just feel thirsty? Off-balance without Hollis crowded in beneath his skin.

It was greedy. But Hollis had been greedy before.

FLOAT

Friday went better than they thought.

There were two weeks before winter break started, and they had papers and projects due.

Walt was always amused at Hollis's homework. He was better at history for predictable reasons, but math and science worked well for him too. English was his only sore point, but that was Hollis's best subject, so it evened out.

They had to swing home and pick up the French bread and Hollis's clothes and toothbrush before heading to Yulia's. Technically, the slumber party didn't start until 8:00 p.m., so they had time for dinner too, but Hollis liked food at Yulia's house better than anything they ate at his.

Usually Yulia's parents were home when they came over for dinner, but Yulia knew how to make stew and fufu and pounded yam and dodo herself. Nigerian food had a decent amount of ingredients that Yulia's family had to get in the mail.

Early the year before, Hollis had managed to grow them some yams, but a decent amount of them had gotten too green in the Michigan spring sun. They only got them a single pound of flour.

The ordeal made him one of Yulia's pa's favorite people though, so Hollis still tried planting both yams and Scotch bonnet peppers for him every so often.

INDIGO

Hollis cocked his hip and leaned against Yulia's stairwell. She kicked open the door and turned back inside.

"Get the stew off the fire," she shouted. "Annie's here early, we're almost done with dinner. Come fry plantain." She took Hollis's bag off his shoulder and dropped it in the living room by the couch.

Annie was poking at the stew with a fork and looking dubious. She wasn't a good cook. Her parents handled most of that at her house.

"Scrape the bottom, but be careful if it's nonstick," Walt told her. Hollis grabbed the bag of fufu and started handling that, making sure to whip it hard, the way Mr. Egunyemi showed him.

Yulia slid in next to him and dunked a chicken in a boiled pot of water, then rapidly began plucking the feathers off.

It's been a while since I've seen something like that.

We don't usually have chicken and fish in the same dish.

"Need any help?" Hollis wondered.

Yulia shrugged one shoulder. "It doesn't have to be perfect. This isn't for tonight's dinner."

Please marry her, Hollis.

Literally everyone in town can do that. It's not special.

Hollis scowled. *And for the last time, Yulia doesn't like guys.*

Whatever. Where is Yulia's cooking oil?

Hollis opened the cabinet above the stove and took out the canola.

"This the pan we using?" Walt asked, and Yulia nodded.

I've never had Nigerian food, is it spicy?

It can be, Yulia's is all right though.

Hollis realized how quiet it was in the kitchen.

"So, James invited me to see him do MMA. He's really focused on trying to get me involved in something positive."

"I think it's wild that you're hanging out with him at all," Annie said.

Hollis shrugged. "It's not really hanging out. Tim sits next to me in history and he's kind of being a go-between. It's not like we talk a bunch or anything. It's just weird to me that they seem to care so much. They wouldn't let me turn the invitation down."

Yulia hazarded a glance away from the chicken to check on the plantain.

"You're better at this than usual, Hollis. You practicing at home?"

Hollis shrugged. "When you leave, who else is gonna make this for me?"

Yulia laughed and picked up the chicken to take it somewhere deep into the house. "If you visit, I will. But I'll figure out how to write all this down in a recipe. Measurements will vary."

"Why does James care?" Annie brought them back to the topic when the table was set and Walt was staring dubiously at the red stew sauce.

"He . . . thinks I bait people into beating me up as a form of self-harm and is really freaked out by it. I got lucky with Jorge, but he actually thinks I'm a good fighter and just letting people lay me out."

Yulia glanced at Annie. "He's not wrong though, if we're being honest. Not the fighting part obviously . . . but . . ."

Hollis put down his fork.

237

"It's not. It's more like the price of getting to say what I want has been people reacting however they see fit. I'm not cashing checks my ass can't pay for if my ass knows the bill is coming."

Annie snorted.

Yulia sucked her teeth. "Still fucked, babes."

"Well, we're not doing that anymore, so it shouldn't be an issue," Walt said. He speared a piece of plantain and ate it.

Annie made a face but stopped bothering them about it.

NIGERIAN FISH STEW

Ingredients

1 kilogram (roughly 2 pounds) fish steaks (I am using red headless, but you can use hake, mackerel, or croaker fish)

1 cup vegetable oil, or palm oil, or groundnut oil

1 ¾ medium onions, chopped, reserve ¼ of 1 onion for later

2 large red bell peppers

1 can chopped tomatoes or 6 medium Roma tomatoes

1 Scotch bonnet chili pepper

Salt to taste

1½ tablespoons chicken bouillon powder, or any stock cube of choice

1 lemon

Fresh basil or scent leaves

Fish Marinade

1 teaspoon garlic granules

1 teaspoon ginger powder

1 teaspoon dried parsley

1 teaspoon onion powder

1 teaspoon of bouillon powder

Instructions

Prep the fish: Descale fish and cut into steaks, add to a bowl, and rinse with water and lemon juice. Then transfer the fish to a colander to drain excess moisture.

Marinate the fish: Add garlic granules, ginger powder, parsley, onion powder, and 1 teaspoon of bouillon powder to the fish and mix to combine. Cover it with Saran Wrap and marinate for at least 30 minutes. After 30 minutes, grill or fry the fish for a total of 20 minutes, 10 minutes on each side.

While waiting for the fish to finish grilling or frying, blend the peppers and bring to boil on medium heat for about 10 minutes.

Cook the stew: Place a pan on medium heat, add oil, and heat until hot. Add chopped onions and stir-fry until translucent. Then carefully add the Scotch bonnet chili pepper, tomatoes, and large red bell peppers to the oil and bring to boil for about 10 minutes.

Season the stew with salt and bouillon powder to taste, stir to combine, and continue to cook for another 10 minutes, or until you can see the oil floating on top of the stew.

Add the grilled fish to the stew and carefully mix to combine. Shred fresh basil or scent leaves to the stew and cover the pan with its lid. Continue to cook on low heat for another 5 minutes. Take it off the heat and serve immediately.

STRAIN

After dinner Yulia wanted to show him something she and Annie had been working on in art, the one class they had together. They made Hollis wait upstairs while they set up in the basement.

I like Yulia's house. She definitely has money.

They're from the city. Her pa's a civil engineer, and they're working on building a development near Rose Town, but not, like, on the haunted soil. It's just taking a while. They've been here for a little over three years.

Walt went so quiet that it felt like he was screaming.

What?

How do you mean, "haunted"?

What? We've talked about this. I told you about Jorge—

No. The night we met, you said, "Jorge was cut up by ghosts or whatever" and you said it very sarcastically. I assumed another kid did it and you said that because you didn't care who.

Hollis rolled his eyes.

No. Rose Town is definitely haunted; no one has been able to build there for years. Like almost a hundred years. There's all these accidents and stuff. A bunch of people have died.

But you said you went there to get fruit sometimes, that first night. That's what you told me the night we met.

Yeah . . . during the daytime. And it's reckless to even be doing that. Why does this matter so much to you? Stop freaking out, I can literally feel our blood pressure going up.

Hollis, we need to talk when we get home. I don't want to ruin this slumber party, but I have some things to tell you.

Or you could just tell me now.

I can't—

"We're ready!"

Fuck. Hollis—

Just calm down before you give my body a heart attack. We can do this later.

PULP

There was a glow coming up the stairs.

"I know it's cringe, but don't laugh at it or anything," Annie said. "Close your eyes."

"I can either walk down the stairs or close my eyes, you gotta choose."

There was some whispering, then Annie darted up the stairs, red-faced and grinning. She clasped his arm.

Hollis closed their eyes.

He was led to the middle of the room, and Annie guided him to sit down. It was bright and warm.

"Can I open my eyes now?"

"Not yet."

Annie scrambled across from him.

It smelled like burning herbs.

"Okay . . . now."

Hollis opened his eyes.

There were candles everywhere, on every surface.

Yulia and Annie were sitting in front of him. Yulia had a hollowed calabash and the chicken from earlier for whatever reason, and Annie had a necklace wrapped around her arm. Yulia had painted her face in white chalk stripes, which was as disorienting to see as it was beautiful.

Wow.

"This is cool, but I think it's going to be a fire hazard," Hollis said.

Yulia didn't respond. Instead, she threw the contents of the calabash over him, then chanted, "Ku ro nbe ye!"

"What the fuck—" It was burning their eyes. "Is there some kind of oil in this?"

"GET OUT OF HIM!" Annie shrieked.

Shit!

Hollis started to stand, but their knees were so weak suddenly. Walt was drowning them in terror so deep Hollis could hardly breathe.

Hollis, what's happening?

He didn't know.

Everything hurt, the room tilted, and then their forehead was pressed to the floor. The sound of Annie's and Yulia's yelling was drowned out by Hollis's own scream. It felt like his spine was being torn out.

Annie pressed her hand to his forehead, and something hard dug into his skin. But that didn't matter; the crucifix didn't do anything; it was the *touch*. They made contact, and Hollis felt Walt leave.

Roughly, Walt was torn from him.

Hollis's skull pounded, excruciating, and he collapsed to the floor from the weight of holding his own body alone again, and he hated it.

He *hated* it.

"Walt!"

"Annie?! Annie!" Yulia was shrieking.

Hollis opened his eyes, and through the haze of tears, he could see Annie curled over herself, arms wrapped around her stomach.

"Come back." Hollis reached out for Walt, but he was too far.

Annie vomited. First orange and full of fish stew, then foamy and yellow. Her face was white, eyes rolling.

Hollis dragged his body across the ground. Each heave of his legs felt like dragging bricks. He was so heavy; how could he have forgotten? Everything hurt, but the silence of his head was worse, the rattling emptiness of it; his heart was breaking.

Yulia was picking up Annie, moving her, moving Walt away from him.

Hollis stretched out his hand and hooked the corner of Annie's sneaker and pulled as hard as he could.

"Get away from her!" Yulia screamed.

Hollis didn't care.

With one last effort, he grabbed Annie's ankle.

"We had—

a deal!

Walt slammed back into him so hard, Hollis sat up and skidded a foot backward. Annie immediately returned back to normal and took a deep breath. She pushed herself out of Yulia's lap and coughed the vomit out of her mouth.

Hollis was shaking. He wanted to run but didn't think he could take the stairs. Walt was sobbing inside him. Hollis hadn't had control of his entire body like this in too long, and it felt wrong. It felt unnatural.

Yulia was rubbing Annie's back and gaping at Hollis in terror.

"I'm sorry," Hollis said. "I'm . . . I'll be back."

He stumbled a few times but managed to make it across the room into the downstairs bathroom, then he locked the door.

ROCK

It was pink and terrible in there, shag rug and mildew, but Hollis clung to the privacy like a lifeline.

Walt was crying too hard to talk, and Hollis melted, curling his legs up to his chest. He laid his cheek on his knee and put a hand into his hair, petting it the way Walt had that the first night.

"Shh, shhh, I've got you. I've got you," he crooned. "You're safe, I've got you."

He could feel Walt flashing in and out of him. His face, his fingers, his legs, his elbows, his palms. Rattled and running through his body like a cat.

Hollis sat still, and let him. Scraping a hand over his scalp, very careful not to invoke that shivery feeling Walt was still learning to like.

"Sweetheart," he said, the way Walt did when he was crying.

Are you all right? he asked. *Are you going to be all right?*

Walt wept desperately still, so Hollis let him cry. Let him cover their face in tears and sob loud enough that Annie and Yulia could probably hear them.

But he didn't stay his hand until Walt finished.

TREMBLE

I didn't mean for that to happen to Annie. I'm so sorry.

It's okay.

You've gotta understand, she got sick because we didn't have a deal the way you and I do. It was only for a second, but I didn't want it to happen at all. She doesn't feel like you, I can't . . . she wasn't.

I'm sorry that happened to us, Hollis said gently. *It won't happen again.*

Hollis, this is my fault. All of it is my fault, you don't understand.

I don't care. You're back with me and I—

Hollis was too thankful that Walt was back inside him to be angry, too desperate. He wanted to tear Walt out of him so he could eat him back up like a beast. He wanted and wanted until it made him feel grotesque.

Hollis had their arms and their mouth, so he kissed their wrist so Walt could feel the heat of it. His own skin. Licked it, lush and greedy until the slime of it choked and doubled them over and Walt's breath came fast in his head.

I didn't know you could . . . How does it feel like that? You touching you. How is that worse than when we're touching each other?

Hollis ignored Walt, raked his teeth across their palm, then sucked hard enough to bruise.

We're going to the hollow when this is done. And then you're going to tell me your story and face the music.

Oh God, oh God.

When you're done, we'll make a new deal, and we'll figure out how this works best for us.

Hollis rubbed his mouth against his purpling wrist until the shocks of it made Walt twitch.

Hollis!

Fine.

He stopped and breathed until their heart slowed. Waited until they were presentable.

Then he wiped their tears with Yulia's scented toilet paper and stood up and faced the mirror.

Walt gazed back at him with brown, bloodshot eyes.

BREAK

Hollis pulled the towel from the rung and unlocked the door. He opened it slowly, and as he expected, Yulia and Annie were waiting for him.

Annie was crouched low, Bible in one hand, crucifix in the other. Yulia threw the remaining herb water at him, and he skidded back, caught drops of it in the towel.

"STOP!" he shouted, before she could begin chanting. "This isn't working the way you think!"

"How does it work, then, demon?" Yulia said, her eyes flat and cold.

"Just give me a minute to explain."

"Fuck you, Hollis!" Annie shouted.

In his panic, he'd missed the steak knife in Yulia's other hand, but he was definitely noticing it now.

"Just put the knife down and give me five seconds," he begged.

Yulia twisted her wrist, fluorescent light flashing off the blade. "No."

Things were rapidly getting out of control again. Hollis could feel the sweat sliding between their shoulder blades. Walt was, mercifully, silent.

"I know this is fucked up. I know and I'm sorry, I just didn't know what to do. You don't understand—"

"Then explain it, for fuck's sake, what the hell happened to me?" Annie sobbed.

"I'm trying!" Hollis cried. "I don't know what you want me to say. Oh, I got possessed, but we figured things out. How would you even have reacted to that? Realistically, what would have happened?"

"You could have told us!"

"No, I couldn't! By the time that was even an option, I . . . we . . . Annie, it's so much more complicated than that." Hollis shook his head.

"How do we even know who we're talking to?" Annie was starting to hyperventilate. "Does your mom know? Does anyone know? What the fuck, Hollis! What's wrong with you?!"

"HEY," Yulia barked over Annie's hysterics. "You keep saying we won't understand, but you haven't even tried. Try."

Hollis took a breath.

"First, how did you figure it out?" he asked. "It's been happening for so long. . . . On the first day I hoped you would somehow know it wasn't me. That you'd . . . save me or something, I don't know. What happened that made you—"

"The day we took you to get drug tested, your eyes were a different color. I told Yulia and she . . . she wanted to try this to be sure," Annie said.

"At dinner." Yulia stabbed the point of the knife into the ground. "It said we."

"What?"

"It said, *We're not doing that anymore.*" Yulia stared at him, unblinking. "How long has it been, Hollis?"

Hollis closed his eyes for a moment, opened them to study the floor.

"That day I went into the woods and didn't come out until late, when I stopped answering your calls. That was the night we met. He was . . . shivering and cold. He was scared. And he was desperate.

He was dying, and I was kind and thoughtless."

Walt was quiet, listening. Hollis put a hand on his knee and squeezed.

"It's been a little over three months. For the first month it was all him. He walked me around and used my voice. Asking questions in my head to make sure he got things right. He was . . . kind and thoughtless too. Every day, he tried hard to make sure he didn't scare anyone. He was patient at school, sweet to my ma, helped out around the house. Followed any strong rules I gave him, he's . . . It's not what you think at all, and I understand why you feel the way you do, but I've had time to—"

Annie's face was twisting in concern, and Yulia's eyes got even harder. So Hollis paused and tried again.

"Never mind. Eventually, we just worked things out, figured out a way for both of us to . . . be me, I guess. We're sharing, for now, and I'm fine the way things are. If I wasn't, I would have asked. By the time I could physically ask you to help, I already *knew* him, Yulia."

"How come you aren't like Annie was?" Yulia asked, unmoved. "You're not sick."

"You have to make a deal with him. Like a crossroads demon, but I think getting sick is our fault. I think maybe there's a certain suspension of belief that our minds and bodies can't handle and when there's discord with that, we get sick." Hollis shook his head, exhausted.

"When I made my deal with him, my first thought was *What have I done?* I knew that in some small way, it was my fault, and there was a moment when I surrendered to it. But Annie was doing something else, she wasn't ready when she took him from me."

"I didn't take him from you; he jumped into me."

Hollis met her gaze.

"No, you *took* him from me. Yulia somehow severed whatever part of this that makes the transfer voluntary and made it involuntary. Whoever touched me would have taken him. It could have been anyone, he could have been lost, it could have—"

Annie pointed, scared.

Hollis looked down to see his left hand over his heart.

"That was me, not him. You can talk to him if you want, but he's really upset, and to be honest, I . . . I don't want you to."

"Annie could have been hurt, you mean," Yulia said slowly. "Annie could have *died*. If he's a ghost, he's already dead, Annie was the one at risk. Why don't you like her anymore?"

"I don't dislike Annie . . . *he* doesn't like her actually. He likes you though. He . . . he actually thinks you're really hot. It's fucking . . . embarrassing." Hollis didn't know what else to say about that.

Yulia looked pensive, but that confession seemed to break the tension enough for her to put the knife down.

"There was a day. You were acting . . . I mean, we flirt, but you seemed serious," she said, uncomfortable. "I didn't know what to think."

"He *was* being serious. I was screaming at him to stop. I think that was in the first week or something. God, you have no idea how bad it was in the beginning, I don't even know how to articulate it. But if I could have talked to you and asked you for help, I would have. You've got to believe me."

"Why doesn't he like me?" Annie asked, soft and sad.

Hollis sighed and leaned back against the bathroom door. "You look like someone he knew."

Tell her I'll talk to her about it later.

"He says he'll explain it later. Maybe tomorrow or something, I'm sorry."

Yulia settled down and held the knife in her lap. She looked around the room at the candles still burning bright, at the chicken who died to make this exorcism possible. At the rosary that hadn't worked at all.

Hollis followed her gaze to Annie's wrist. "I don't know. Maybe the crucifix and candles didn't work and your stuff did because he's not a demon . . . and he's Catholic."

Yulia's frown got deeper.

"Was Catholic?" Hollis tried.

"Give me a second to think," Yulia finished resolutely.

"Is he telling you that we can't be friends anymore?" Annie pressed.

Hollis shook his head. "No, it's not that, it just . . . He feels sad and anxious whenever we look at you. It wore on me, I guess. I'm sorry, Annie. . . . I should have been a better friend. To both of you."

Yulia got up and started blowing out the candles.

"I think it would be good if you left for now, Hollis. Annie and I need some time to talk and think. You should come back tomorrow."

SPACE

Yulia said two things as she closed the door behind them.

"We still love you" and "You can't stay like this forever."

Hollis didn't expect the anger he felt at that, but he kept his mouth shut.

They went down Yulia's stairs and stood in the dark on the sidewalk. The light from her windows was dim with the shadows of his friends watching him walk away.

And you, he whispered into the dark where Walt lived.

Hollis.

Yulia's house was far from the hollow, and the buses had stopped running, so Hollis took them on foot. Walt stayed quiet, curled in his chest, or warm in his stomach, as they traveled. Didn't even have the decency to carry Hollis this distance, but Hollis already knew Walt was a coward.

He knew that.

They passed through the living houses filled with people to the abandoned dead ones. Walked down the street they met and down the street where Walt had taken him. Where the dust of Sam's body was still frozen in between pieces of pavement.

Went from buildings to gravel to trees dark and tall. And Hollis wasn't afraid in this forest any more than Walt was. When it got too dark to see, Walt took their legs and guided them to where the ground was warm and soft and wanting.

CAUGHT

Hollis dragged their fingertips around the side of the hill until they dipped into the hollow, then Walt crawled inside.

The trees stopped at the edge, clearing space for the wild Michigan sky. The moon was too new for light, there was nothing but stars.

Hollis put their arms into their coat so he could tuck one hand around his side and rest the other heavy over their throat.

Tell me.

I don't want to.

Tell me, Walt, stop hiding from me. I can't hide from you; it isn't fair.

You're going to be angry with me.

Probably.

He could feel Walt's anxiety like a stomach full of snakes, and there was probably a good reason for it.

What do you think is going to happen? Yeah, I'll be angry at you, but what then? Will we yell at each other a bit? Maybe I'll give you the silent treatment? I'm struggling to imagine what is so much more horrible than what's already happened. I think even if you told me you killed people, I'm already kind of prepared for that, seeing as though you jumped out of a dead guy and then made me hide the evidence. You don't leave much to the imagination.

That situation was different.

Not for me it wasn't. I had nightmares about it, I'm still sort of worried about it.

I don't want you to hate me. I'm afraid that you're going to hate me, and I don't think I can handle that. Not now.

Hollis sighed and looked up at the trees.

You're scared of me getting so angry I turn into another Sam, he said simply.

Walt didn't answer.

I won't, Walt. I promise.

THIS IS HOME

Walt was right, he was fucking furious.

> **I came here to die,** Walt started. Like saying that to Hollis meant nothing.

This was his last stop. Sam was supposed to get him all the way to the end, but Sam started breaking down before Walt could do what needed to be done.

When Walt met Hollis, he thought he'd won something.

He had one last chance to do what he loved: To make someone's life better in the place he was born and the place he would die. To shepherd someone so much like him to a future better than he deserved, then settle into the soil of Rose Town like a bad dream and fade.

> **In 1931, I was a mess. I . . . stole something I shouldn't have, and a lot of people died.**

> **Everyone worked at the factory in Rose Town. You had to if you weren't a grocer or a tailor or whatever else people needed. No one ever had enough money; we didn't own the land, so we weren't allowed to farm it. We didn't have houses the way you do; we had these terrible buildings like apartments, with three to four families on each floor. Children in drawers, packed like sardines. Everyone was always sick, always hungry, whatever. The fruit trees helped, but there were just too many people.**

> **We had two crime families: the Rossis and the Callaghans. They got along better than most; they didn't**

feud over territory, and smuggled in low-cost beef and booze. The Callaghans had the police, and the Rossis owned the factory. Of course, they both got a little competitive with entertainment and nightlife. A cat and mouse sort of situation that benefited mostly them and sometimes us.

If you were young and tough, you found other kinds of work. Some people did hard things. Stole, sold parts of themselves, hair, teeth. Me and Toji fought.

You fought?

Yeah. They had betting rings. I was good, but Toji was better. He's the one who looks like Annie. Maybe a great-great-uncle or great-great-grandpa of hers or something, but they have the same face. Earnest, kind, selfish, and careful. Toji's ears stuck out just a bit too much, just like Annie's.

Anyway, we needed cash so we fought. Me more than him.

So, what, you fought and threw a fight? Bet against yourself or something?

No. Who has time to throw fights? If you got too thrown around, you couldn't get up for work in the morning. Fighting's technically illegal, so you might even earn a night in jail on top of it. No, Hollis, I didn't throw a fight, I robbed the Rossi family.

Walt rubbed his palms into their eyes.

Only Toji knew I was going to do it, and he begged me not to. He was scared, but I was determined. I'd been to their main offices; I knew where they kept winnings. I knew the man who handled security would work a double shift and be too tired to be good at his job for one night a month, every month.

I needed cash because I wanted to leave town. No one ever left. You couldn't because we were paid too little to be able to start over anywhere else. You have no idea how depressing it is to know that hasn't changed.

Hollis sighed and put a hand over their heart.

I wanted to leave because I wanted to find a new place for my family to live. My pa was getting too old to support us, and they paid women practically nothing back then. If we could move to the city, maybe things would be better and I wouldn't have to watch them waste away before my eyes.

So. I did it. I got away with it for a while. There was no such thing as security cameras, and detectives were half the men they are today. I got away with two thousand dollars, close to forty grand today, and booked it to Chicago.

I spent a week eating good food and sleeping in nice hotels, lying low, then I called my ma. She begged me to come back and said they were looking for the thief and not being too kind about it. Both families, for whatever reason.

And I was . . . I just.

You were a coward.

I couldn't go back. They *killed* men for this, Hollis. They didn't just throw them in prison and fine them, you *died*. I cut off all contact after that call. I left my ma half, took

259

what was left and split that in half and handed it to a banker for Toji, asked them to call him to pick it up after a year. Then I changed my name. Got a regular job at a meatpacking factory and held my breath.

But thing is, Chicago is a town of connections, and somehow they found me out. Rose Town reached its hand across so many borders and gripped the back of my collar.

I woke up one night with a barrel in my face and a serious man at the end of my bed.

Walt swallowed hard.

They drove me back to town through the night and walked me up the street. They weren't Rossi or Callaghan, but that didn't matter, Hollis. I was a country boy, and I didn't understand favors and connections between crime families.

They put me back in that town, handed me right to my maker. Then I was dragged down into hell, to a room where Toji was waiting.

His face was black and blue; he was barely breathing. The way I heard it, he hadn't said a word. People just knew we stuck together, so he was paying for my crimes.

They took a moment to give me the same treatment. Boxed my ears so hard they took to ringing and I could barely hear their questions. They wanted the money of course, but I had less than a quarter left, and there are things worse than death. I knew I was as good as gone, but I couldn't let them get Toji's cut, his family needed it as much as mine.

They broke my ribs and fingers and jaw, cut beneath

my nails and burned me something fierce.

But, Hollis, I couldn't die. I was so angry at being poor and hungry, at fighting for nothing but greed. At seeing Toji's little sister's hair getting thin and my own blood, my family get so weak from not having enough meat.

Walt looked up at the sky. The moonlight threaded through the trees, and the hollow filled with light.

When you die, there's a moment everything goes still in the room.

There's a door that you didn't see before and you know that it's where you gotta go. There's no singing angels, no bright light. Just the door and the feeling that you've got an appointment, and the knowledge that if you keep standing there you'll be late.

But I stood next to my body and ignored that door. I stared at the man holding the pistol that killed me and I *hated*. I hated harder than I ever had in my entire life.

Then I walked right into him.

We didn't shake hands, didn't make no kind of a deal, I just took him like he was mine. Like I took that money.

I took his hand and I bent it toward his own face and I shot him.

Then I walked into the man who was guarding the door. Bent his screaming body to untie Toji.

And Toji looked into my eyes and saw *me*.

He wasn't afraid. Somehow, he just knew.

The body I was in was dying again, quick just like Annie, so I opened the door and found myself another. I wanted to tell Toji that I left him some money. I wanted to tell him sorry, but the bodies kept vomiting and dying too fast.

I slid into your body like putting on an old jacket, Hollis, but I've had practice. I've had time to learn how to do it right.

Back then, I tore them apart and didn't even know I was doing it.

I knew this would end real bad, so I left Toji behind. I jumped into enough people to get to a guard and then threatened my way into my first deal. He lasted long enough for me to write out a confession implicating me and the two men they'd kept in the room with Toji. This body was even polite enough not to expire for the length of a car ride back to Chicago.

The early days were such a blur that I don't count them in my tally of bodies. I can't.

I was living like a beast.

After a year though, things settled and Toji got his call. I'd figured it out by then, managed to settle in a street cleaner and hung around the bank to see if Toji would come pick his money up.

When Toji walked up the street, I could tell he was different. He was dressed finer, stood taller, looked prouder. He was older, and I knew then that I *wasn't*. I knew, looking at him and seeing time on his face, that I was stuck.

Toji went inside and got his money and walked out. Stopped on the curb to smoke. I didn't even have to call him for Toji to know I was there. He just turned to me and said, "How are you holding up?"

The way he used to after work, when we finished our shifts, still covered in steel dust and aching.

"Fine," I said. "Just fine." But I was lying, and he knew it.

He shook his head like he was disappointed in me. Then he told me the Callaghans killed them. Killed them all.

Who?

Everyone. My ma, my pa, my sisters, my grandfather who had been living with us. They wiped them from the face of the earth and there was a new family already living in our house.

Walt was crying. Hollis pushed down his anger and rocked him.

I was an orphan in an old man's body, in the center of a city I didn't love. I had no one and I am no one and I should be dead and I'm too much a coward to even do that right.

All this has just been wasting time.

I just . . . I figured if I came back to Rose Town, I could go to that room and find that door, and if I was lucky enough it would be there waiting for me.

But now, you tell me—you *told* me—that there are spirits not at rest in this place that I left. Ghosts that are angry and confused and destroying anything that tries to take root there, and it's my fault. Everything is always my fault.

PYROMANIA

They didn't speak for a half hour. Hollis just stared at the ground.

He wiped their nose with the sleeve of their coat and leaned back into the hollow.

I don't know what to say, Walt.

Hollis.

Everything bad that's ever happened to everyone I know . . .

I know.

I can't even be like "Oh, how come you didn't tell me?" because I know why you didn't say anything. I get it.

Walt didn't respond, but Hollis could hear him thinking, hear him worry.

You understand now why I . . . can't. Why I don't deserve you.

Yeah, I get why you feel that way too.

Hollis wiped their face again.

Stop fucking making us cry, I'm not going to turn into Sam, but I don't feel like crying for you right now.

I'm sorry.

What happened with Toji. Did you ever see him again?

Walt shook their head.

I looked him up once, just to see how he was doing, back in the 1960s, but he'd already passed. Y'know he didn't even live in Rose Town anymore when he came to pick up his cash? He'd moved to Chicago. We just never managed to run into each other again.

Hollis sighed, rubbed their temples.

He hugged me though, right there in the middle of the street. In the body of that street sweeper. Let me cry and apologize and say goodbye even though I was getting his suit all dirty and people were looking hard.

He knew I was weak; he got it. He's better than me, always will be.

I get why looking at Annie fucks you up now, I guess.

I didn't expect his family to still be here. That hurt me worse than his eyes in her head. Toji might have gotten out, but he either moved back for some reason, or he was the only one who ever got to leave.

Ninety-two years, huh?

Hollis dug in their pocket and pulled out the pack of cigarettes. There were only four left.

I understand this now too. Fucking need one after that fucking shit.

Walt took their arms and face.

I can do it myself.

It means something when you do it for me. I don't want this to ruin that.

Hollis huffed.

And this situation is what it takes for you to admit that? You're a fucking asshole.

Walt smoked in silence, wiping his own nose and face when he needed it. The night sky was turning purple. Not dawn, but close to it. The stars were harder to see.

Why are we still out here, Hollis?

I had things I wanted to do to you that would make you too loud to keep in my house. But now I'm too angry for that.

Walt tapped ash and shook his head, dragged a hand through Hollis's hair.

What now, Walt? What do you want to do now?

Walt shrugged.

If you don't mind me working rough, I can pick someone up at the bus stop. Someone not from here and ride them to Rose Town. You can be yourself by the time the sun's high in the sky. Swing by Yulia's, green-eyed and pretty.

That was it.

Hollis stood. He took a few steps from the hollow and then turned his head up to the sky, furious.

Is that what you want? To leave me? That's what you want, more than anything?

It's what I came here to do. Not leave you, Hollis, but to eventually go back to Rose Town. I've overstayed my welcome long enough. I have to pay my debts.

You're such a coward, Walt. This is so fucking convenient.

What?

Hollis closed their eyes and crouched in the grass.

You did something selfless, got scared and ran. Did something selfless again for Toji, then got scared and ran. Spent ninety-two years doing something selfless, then ran home to Rose Town. Then you met me. And you think you're changing, turning over a new leaf to go find your eternity door or whatever the fuck, but you're just running again.

You came to this town and you found out that it's the same as when you left it. All of us are still poor and struggling and eating fruit from hundred-year-old trees. You stood in my pantry

and tried not to weep at the sight of it. You spent a month fixing
a home fifty years younger than you are, and I know what that
means now, I do.

But you came home to Rose Town, and you found **me.** *And*
I'm a part of this place, and we fit. And I scare you.

You scare me because you keep doing things I don't—

"Don't say it, Walt, don't say it if you don't mean it. Because you
and I both know you like it. We like it," Hollis snapped out loud.

I scare you because for the first time in ninety-two years,
this isn't about anyone else, it's about you. You're not on a stage,
you're not in a house, you're with me, and I can see you and I'm
not screaming.

You don't know what to do with that, so you want to run,
and I'm not pissed off that you're scared. It's okay to be scared.
But running from that to go die isn't any different from what
you've been doing for the past hundred years.

You have no idea what I— You don't know what it felt like!
You don't know how bad it was, how could you say that to
me?!

Walt pushed them to the ground. Their anger doubled in the
way Walt warned him it would and it made them feel reckless.
Walt flipped them flat on their back, pinned their wrists to the
ground. Hollis pushed against it, struggling. Hollis was so fucking furious, he could barely see. Everything was black, and Walt
was winning.

FUCK YOU, WALT. YOU'RE A GODDAMN COWARD. You
didn't learn anything!

Stop saying that! Stop it!

FUCK YOU, FUCK YOU, FUCK YOU.

Shut up, stop saying that!

Hollis couldn't handle this sanctimonious fucking martyr bullshit. So fucking lost in his own head he couldn't fucking figure out how to handle what was in front of him. Drowning Hollis's body with his yearning and his sorrow and his shyness and all of these things, like Hollis wouldn't fucking feel it every day and didn't know him. How could he act like Hollis didn't know him? How could he—

"Why can't you just fucking want me back? Is this really that bad?" Hollis screamed into the woods. "Am I worse than death? I fucking need you! Is staying with me worse to you than death?"

Walt immediately stopped fighting and let go of their wrists, horrified.

No, Hollis, no no no. I'm sorry, I didn't mean that.

How could you think I would be okay hearing you act like you don't mean anything to anyone. How many times do I have to choose you, over and over again, before you understand? I thought we were on the same page with this shit, I thought—

Hollis, I understand, but you need to understand me too. You need to listen. I don't think you understand how much all of this scares me. I'm scared because you make me feel small. I'm scared because your friends don't recognize you anymore. I'm scared because it isn't a good life, the kind you'd live with me. You deserve more than this, you deserve more than *me*, and I don't deserve anything at all. You're not worse than death, Hollis.

Don't you ever think that again. I don't feel that way about you, but I'm *scared*.

They curled on their knees, forehead to the frozen ground,

hands clasped tight beneath them. Hollis breathed steam out into the cold air. Listened, really listened and thought.

Okay, I'm sorry. You're right, it's not about me. We . . . we just met. This has been something important for you for a long time, and it's not fair for me to just . . . act like everything is going to change just because I showed up one day.

Walt filled Hollis's eyes with his own tears, and Hollis let them wet the ground.

But is it so bad that I wish I could? I know it doesn't work this way, but I wish I could love you big enough to make you happy in a way that sticks. I'm not an idiot, I know these things don't work like that.

Walt sobbed.

I can't have more bad things happen because of me, Hollis. I can't take it anymore, I just want it to be over.

Hollis curled an arm around them.

It's okay to want that. It's okay to feel that way. Yulia likes to say, "You don't want to die, you're just very sad right now," and she's mad as fuck at us, but she's right. Yeah, you can't take it anymore, you want it to be over, you're scared because you think you're hurting me and ruining me, but I'm not the one who's crying.

You have a lot of problems, and I can't claim to know every last one of them. But if we went down the line and solved them one by one, would you still want to die?

What?

They were getting too cold. Hollis sat them back up. He walked them to the hollow and nestled in before he continued.

If you knew you weren't hurting me. If my friends got used to us.

If we figured out how to fix Rose Town and completed the terms of our original contract. If you got the chance to redeem yourself and give back to the community afterward. Hell, if you got a chance to learn more about Toji from Annie and figure out if he had as good of a life as you intended him to, would you still want to die?

I . . . I don't know. I'm not sure, maybe not. But I don't know, I've never thought about it like that.

Hollis pressed their hands against the walls of the hollow, trying to get some warmth back into their cramping fingers.

We can also go on meds if that helps. Antidepressants. Who's to say they'll work on my brain, but we can always give it a try. I don't mind figuring that out, if it's for you.

Walt was quiet, Hollis could hear him thinking, feel him turning this over in the back of their head.

You don't have to tell me an answer today or anything. I just want you to know that I'm willing to work with you on this. You're not alone anymore; we're together in this. We'll figure it out.

I promise.

MOON

Mr. and Mrs. Brown were asleep when they came in.

They didn't have to explain themselves to anyone. They didn't turn on any lights.

They slithered upstairs, took off their clothes, turned on the bath, and settled into the gloom.

Soaked the cold from their bones.

Anointed, rose petal and freesia like frankincense and myrrh.

Washed off ice and salt and grass and herbs, diluted purification.

Slipped beneath the tincture to come out new.

Then, in the murky space before sleep, when Hollis was limp in Walt's grasp and warmer than the hollow on a summer day, Walt pulled him back to the surface. He kissed the curve of their palm, and then licked it just once.

You make me shiver.

SILT

Yulia opened her door and stared at them. They stared back.

"I'm sorry," Hollis said. "I shouldn't have kept this from you. I should have trusted you."

"Stay here," she said, and opened the door wider.

There was a tape square drawn out on the living room floor and several bundles of herbs and sticks laid carefully on the border. Annie was seated in the middle of it. Yulia backed away, slow and without blinking until she too was inside the square.

"Close the door. Go sit on the couch."

Hollis followed her instructions, taking off his shoes by the door politely, then settled in front of them. Annie still looked like she'd been crying.

"We can't tell who we are talking to, so we have a few tests. It's obvious that you guys can talk to each other, and I assume you've been doing so for the past few months. I wouldn't be surprised if you know enough about each other to answer anything basic and even some unique things without us being able to tell. However, what's most important to us—more than anything—is that Hollis is even in there at all. Do you understand?"

Hollis nodded.

"Okay," Yulia said. "Finish this poem."

To his surprise, it was Annie who started reciting. "'I met the most beautiful turtle today. Her head was hidden in her shell. Those lovely eyes were peeking at me. She was scared I could tell.'"

Hollis immediately covered his face with his hands.

"'I . . . I'm . . . a dime-a-dozen toad. Nothing . . . super special about me. I seem the same as everyone here, in the toad community?'"

I haven't heard this since I was nine. Our teacher would sing it when kids fought each other, until everyone sang together and didn't want to fight anymore. Even Yulia wouldn't know this song.

They waited for him, Yulia angry and Annie afraid.

"'Will you be my friend . . . ,'" Hollis whispered. "'Oh, toad, nobody talks to me here, and I beg you it's been a long time. I have been waiting on the sidelines wishing for someone so kind.'"

Annie reached a hand past the circle, so brave it made Hollis want to cry. He wanted to take her hand, but Yulia tugged Annie back.

"We're not finished," she snapped. "You're in Hollis's body. Even if Hollis is in there, we don't know if he can control it. Last year when our other PE teacher broke his leg skiing, we had a sub who forced us all to learn how to square-dance for a semester. I want you to do the square dance."

Hollis was horrified. "Like . . . from memory? Without music?"

Yulia held her phone up. "You'd better."

"Yulia, I'm not good at dancing, and I barely remember it."

"Try." She pushed play.

Hollis stood up by the door.

If you laugh at me I'll kill you.

He bumbled through a few steps until he could manage some of the routine. Yulia's face slowly shifted from anger to amusement.

273

"Can I stop now?"

"No. Finish it," she said, holding up her phone higher.

"Are you recording me?"

Annie was watching the video from over Yulia's shoulder. "That's fucking terrifying."

"I'm not that bad!" Hollis yelled. "You're lucky I remember any of it at all!"

"No, your eyes kind of reflect like a cat's sometimes now."

Hollis scowled. He quickly finished the dance and crossed his arms.

Yulia glanced back at Annie for reassurance.

"Okay. We need some safeguards. When you're talking, hold up one finger and when it's talking it has to hold up two."

That's reasonable.

"He says he doesn't mind that. Also please stop calling him an it; he's a person," Hollis said.

"I'm not doing it any favors," Yulia said dryly.

"He didn't ask for that, *I* did." Hollis sat down on the couch. "He's a person, and I care about him, and it feels like you're calling me 'it' when you do that, so *stop*."

Yulia scrunched her nose in distaste.

"You care about him?"

"He's with me all the time. We wake up together and go to sleep together; he's with me when I eat breakfast, lunch, and dinner; when I'm sad and when I'm happy. In just hours spent together alone. I know him well enough to . . . to choose that."

Yulia looked a bit sour, but she didn't complain.

"Given the circumstances . . . and the whole . . . yesterday . . . ," Annie started. "Has it occurred to you that maybe you could have

274

dissociative identity disorder? It's like when your brain decides to have multiple personalities and—"

"No." Walt cut her off, raising his fingers like Yulia asked him to. "That's a fine guess, but I would appreciate it if you didn't spend much time pursuing it. I've spent a few years in a hospital because of that mistake, and I've no interest in going back."

"Do you have any interest in getting out of our friend?" Yulia asked immediately.

Walt shook his head. "I made him that offer last night. Didn't seem too keen on it, Hollis. Personal reasons."

"We didn't test him," Annie said urgently. "We should test *him*."

Walt stood up. "I can do a fair amount of things Hollis can't. His dancing is abysmal. If doing a few steps will save me from a fortnight in your version of Bellevue, I'm willing to shuffle."

He didn't even need music.

Walt danced so much better than Hollis that it was as humiliating to him as it was vaguely arousing.

"It's better with a partner," Walt said, breathless. "But I'm not raring to touch either of you until I know that potion is done working. Not to offend, but your body doesn't feel like home, Ann. I'm not looking to come back."

"But Hollis's does?" Yulia spat.

Walt shrugged and settled back down onto the couch.

"He's taller than I am, but I like the room," he said, merciless, then turned to Annie. "Who is Toji to you?"

"What?"

"Toji Watanabe, the guy you look like. I don't know if he died before you could meet him or see pictures." Walt sounded casual but Hollis could feel his heart racing.

Annie looked surprised, then concerned, then offended. "Why?"

"We were close. Need to know if I'm talking to a great-granddaughter, or great-grandniece."

"To what end?" Yulia snapped, but Annie answered anyway.

"Toji was my great-grandma's brother. . . . You knew him?"

Walt frowned. "Oh . . . you're Fumiko's . . ."

Annie curled up tight, arms folded around her knees. "How old are you? Why do you know us?"

"I grew up with Toji and Fumi," Walt said. "You look like him a lot. More than you do Fumiko. I doubt he ever mentioned me, but if he did, did he say anything about a Walt Eidelman?"

Annie shook her head, and Hollis reeled at the wave of Walt's disappointment.

"How old are you?" Yulia echoed, impatient.

Hollis interrupted and held up his finger. "That's not important. I have to tell you about him and Rose Town, and I want it to come from me."

BRUISE

Yulia got up and left the room when Hollis finished explaining, and he wasn't surprised. He was kind of shocked that she stayed through the whole thing. But Annie didn't leave, she just sat there processing it and looking curious.

"Are you all right?" Walt asked.

She tilted her head to one side, then the other.

"These past few months haven't been great for me. I thought you were mad at me because of what we talked about at the pond. After that, I thought you were doing something dangerous and secret. Then for the past few weeks I just thought you were sick," Annie said hesitantly. "This isn't the best thing I've ever learned, but . . . at least for *me*, this is better. You don't seem like anything is wrong with you physically, so I'm relieved about that. But now that I know why you were avoiding looking at me, I don't feel as bad. I might get angry about it later though."

"That's okay. I'm sorry. I really didn't mean it," Hollis said.

Annie stuck her legs over the edge of the protective circle, smudging it on purpose, and then lay back and closed her eyes.

"I spent all of last night thinking about what I would do if this were happening to me. I think I wouldn't know how to approach it either. I know you wouldn't believe me, and Yulia would have freaked out so bad. Worse than this," she whispered. "I don't think I'm a person who could have figured out a way to live the way you guys are. I know I should probably be more upset, but I'm just really glad you're okay, Hollis. I'm really glad you're doing okay."

Hollis was ashamed.

"I'm sorry, Annie. I haven't been a good friend," he admitted.

Annie shrugged.

"Who's to say this isn't the best kind of friend someone going through this can be?" she said. "Come lie down, Holly."

Hollis waited a moment, to see if she would change her mind, but Annie didn't say anything. He lowered himself to the hardwood floor and crossed the broken circle line. Lay on his side, head by her shoulder, curled up like a crescent roll.

"Can I talk to Walt?"

"You can talk to Walt," Hollis said. "He's listening."

"Hey." Annie turned her head, and Hollis could feel her breath rustling his hair. "Great-Uncle Toji wouldn't be mad at you still. You should stop feeling so bad. It was a long time ago, and you were just a kid."

"I can't, and I wasn't a kid," Walt said. "You weren't there."

Annie sighed.

"It's self-centered to think everything that happened is because of you. Yeah, you were a major catalyst, but they didn't have to kill your family. They didn't have to do any of it. They could have just hauled you back to town and handled it on an individual basis. You're not responsible for the actions of others, you're just responsible for you.

"I'm sure you have other things you probably need to apologize for, and I definitely don't want to know about them. But, this? It's whatever. Great-Uncle Toji was fine, he died old and made a bunch of my aunts and uncles. I never met him, but I'm sure he probably forgave you ages ago."

Walt was quiet.

278

Hollis reached up and brushed his hand through their hair. He could feel the weight of Annie's gaze, so he looked up at her.

"He's sad. I . . . This helps."

Annie reached over, and Walt froze.

"I'll give him back if. If . . . ?" Annie let her fingertips graze Hollis's forehead.

Nothing happened.

Walt relaxed, and Annie traveled the path Hollis took. Her fingers following the furrows and waves.

"I missed you, Annie," Hollis confessed.

"I missed you too."

NEED

Do your friends know what you're like?

What?

Do your friends know what you're really like? With me? In the hollow, in the bath, in our bed.

Do they know what I'm—?

Have they seen your face, lit by moonlight, terrible and grinning? Seen you laugh to harmonize with screams? Felt what it is to be small and in your hands?

That's not very romantic. You say that like I'm the one haunting you.

Walt projected the deepest frown he could manage, and Hollis grinned, under the soft weight of Annie's fingers.

Annie is so kind.

Told you so.

JAVELIN

Yulia needed more time than Annie. She kicked him out again, and Hollis couldn't hide how much that hurt him.

This time Annie left with him, even though she didn't have to. Looked up at the two of them as they walked home together. Studied them, and they let her; it was the least they could do.

"When you guys eat, do you both taste the food?"

"Yeah."

"Do you use each other to cheat on tests?"

"Not really, but we do have different subjects we're better at."

"Is one of you stronger than the other? I imagine the Jorge fight was you, Walt?"

"No, we're the same. It's not magic. Hollis's body is Hollis's body, I'm not doing anything to enhance it. But, yeah, I did fight Jorge."

Annie rolled her eyes. "How can you say it's not magic when it's literally magic? Textbook supernatural. This is fantasy."

"I like to think of it as science fiction," Hollis interjected. "It doesn't seem to be common, but there aren't a lot of other fantasy creatures around or anything. We just don't have a way to explain it yet."

Annie bit her lip.

"You also must be the reason for the smoking . . . What else can you do that Hollis can't do?"

Walt smirked. "Dance, of course. Knit, I'm a good fisherman. A bonny fighter. I know a lot of games. Passable at chess, ace at baseball. I'm fair at building things out of wood, but it's been about fifty years since I've had to. I play the violin, some Spanish guitar, but not enough to brag about it—"

"You play the violin?" Annie gasped. "Whoa, can you come over? My dad has one. It will be freaky to watch Hollis do that."

Walt laughed. "Sure. If Hollis gives me permission."

Permission? Do what you want. We were supposed to be at Yulia's all weekend. We don't have anywhere else to be.

"He's fine with it, kind of."

FLY

Annie dragged them into her house. Rushed them through the living room and up to her bedroom. Mr. Watanabe was eating lunch in the front room.

Good God.

Does he look like Toji too?

What do you think?

Walt stared warily at Annie's pink-and-green bedroom. Her walls were covered in film posters and photographs she'd taken. There was a mountain of fabric scraps next to her sewing machine and clothes all over the floor. It was a mess, but a good-smelling mess.

Hollis pushed some of the debris off her bed and sat down.

Annie was struggling with her pa's violin case.

"Here, let me—" Walt grabbed it from her delicately. "You sure your old man's not bothered we're touchin' this?"

"He hasn't touched it himself in, like, ten years," Annie said.

Hollis watched as Walt took the violin out and brushed the dust off it with one of Annie's loose bundled-up socks. He tuned it, checked the bow for damage, and then scrubbed at the strings with some small block.

"No promises if it squeaks. Y'all took awful care of this."

Walt settled their face in the chin rest and put the bow to the strings.

Hollis didn't expect the vibration and how it buzzed through their jaw. Didn't expect his arm to ache deep in the bicep from the awkward angle. Didn't expect the homesickness that welled up in their chest until their throat got tight and their stomach felt like it was full of bees.

Annie was sitting cross-legged on the bed, eyes lingering on Hollis's flying fingers. She looked a bit disturbed.

What song is this?

"Road to Lisdoonvarna." I used to play it after dinner oftentimes. Not a perfect rendition.

How could your family afford a violin, aren't they like a bajillion dollars?

My grandfather made them. The strings and some parts of the bow we had to order in. But wood and metal were plenty.

"I can see you talking," Annie murmured. "Now that I know what to look for. Your eyes kind of . . . dim. It's more obvious when you're caught off guard though."

Walt gritted their teeth and finished the piece. He didn't like feeling like a specimen.

"I think I get what you meant when you said 'he's a person,' Hollis." Annie leaned back and put her hands behind her head. "It's weird but you're definitely two different guys in one guy. So, what are you going to do?"

"I . . . I don't know. Go home or something? I'm not due back until later so—"

"You can stay for dinner, sleep over, it's whatever. But I mean, what are you going to do about Rose Town?"

Walt put the violin back in its case.

"We haven't decided."

THE STARS

Mr. Watanabe said they could take the violin home. It wasn't an expensive one, and he was pleased someone was taking interest. He'd hoped Annie would pick it up, but she never did.

Annie's father would never pressure her into doing anything she didn't want to do. And Hollis was as close to a son as he was going to get.

Mrs. Watanabe made cast-iron pizza for dinner, excited to have Hollis over. They didn't spend much time at Annie's because Yulia's house was so nice, while Hollis's house was shabbier and easier to relax in.

When her parents went up to bed, Annie pulled some blankets out of the hall closet and made a camp for them on the living room floor in front of the TV.

Walt watched warily as Annie flopped down next to them and turned on *The Matrix*.

She's so comfortable. I don't understand.

She's not comfortable; she's adaptable. Annie was my best friend for nine years before you got here. This isn't her worst nightmare. Me leaving or hating her probably was.

And now everything is okay because she knows me? And you're doing okay with it?

Yeah. Yulia was always going to be the hard sell. She hates stuff like this. She's never stepped a foot into Rose Town, and she was better prepared than Annie ever was to handle you.

"Do it out loud," Annie demanded, annoyed.

"We're talking about Yulia," Hollis said immediately. "Walt is confused about why you're here. But she's still mad at us, so I'm telling him."

Annie gazed up at them from her spot on the floor. Then she bit her lip, hesitant.

"You know. There were a lot of small changes to you at first, not ones to really worry about. But the first made me happy."

"What was it?" Walt asked.

"You stopped going to see the train," Annie said, plain.

Hollis froze. He had just . . . forgotten. Hadn't needed to. Hadn't had that buzz at the back of his brain, the craving.

What does she mean, Hollis?

"Your clothes stopped reeking of oil and steel and you came out in the morning smelling like laundry detergent and flowery shampoo every day," Annie said, drumming her fingers against her knee. "And I just thought. Well. Something is different, but at least it's a good different. At least he's happy now."

"I . . . I didn't . . . notice," Hollis said.

Tell me, *now*.

"I never. Walt doesn't know about that, give us a second," Hollis whispered, and turned away from Annie.

In the mornings, I would go to the train tracks and watch a train go by and then walk to school with Annie. She doesn't like it.

As a hobby? What did she mean by you're "happy now"?

Hollis shrugged.

You were planning on train hopping before I arrived? That's not safe. I knew three men who died doing that.

I know. I know it's not safe. That was the point. To stand there

286

and know I could do it and not do it. It made me feel . . . calm.

How could something like that make you feel calm?

Walt was upset, their chest hurt enough to make their eyes prickle.

I can't explain it in detail, I just know it worked. You can't judge me for this after everything we've done.

I'm not. I'm not judging you. Christ, Hollis. Ain't I allowed to be worried?

It's not even happening anymore.

BUT IT WAS! It *was* and you were doing it, like it was nothing. Like you were nothing and I—

Hollis got up.

"We're fine, but we're gonna do this in the bathroom."

Annie nodded. She didn't pause the movie.

He closed the door behind them and sank down to sit on Annie's mom's pristine cream-colored bath mat.

Why does this bother you?

You're not supposed to want to die. You have everything. *Everything*, Hollis. I'm the worst thing that's ever happened to you.

You're not, Walt. Not even close.

What if I came two months too late, would you still be out there? You can't make me the only reason why you don't . . . why you can't.

How come you're allowed to want to die and I'm not? How come I'm supposed to sit there and listen to you talk about coming here to figure out how to disappear permanently, and you can't handle the idea of me going to the train when I don't even do that anymore.

Hollis, please. Please, it's different for me. I'm not, it's not the same.

Walt was so distressed, their heart was beating rabbit fast.

Walt, please calm down. I feel like I'm about to have a stroke. I won't go there again. We won't go there.

Walt's hand shot out and grabbed Hollis's hand, held it close to their chest, desperately. He was shaking, he wouldn't let go, and it hurt.

Oh, sweetheart.

Hollis curled his knees up close and sighed.

DREAM

The movie was half done when they came out. Annie had gotten some Twizzlers while they were gone. She offered him one, eyes still glued to the screen.

"He yell at you about it?"

"Something like that."

Annie snorted.

"You gonna listen to him as well as you listened to me?"

"I have to. We always compromise."

"At least he's teaching you something," Annie muttered.

When the screen faded to black and the credits scrolled by in green, Annie tossed her side of the blanket over his shoulder and pulled him close.

"Come here, Hollis."

They curled close and didn't think about how they still hadn't brushed their teeth and were wearing jeans.

Annie's strawberry Twizzler breath skated over their eyelids and her soft small hands wound themselves over his shoulder.

"Go to sleep," Annie whispered. "I love you still."

RIB

In the morning, when the sun was half up and everything was purple and pink, Hollis got out of the pile of blankets.

He covered Annie with his side of the quilt and kissed her on the forehead. Left a note. Turned off the TV. Grabbed Mr. Watanabe's violin and went next door.

They took a quick shower and got dressed.

You should take me.

To the train?

I want to understand you. The way you were before I arrived.

You sure?

Yes.

Hollis put his fingertips to their mouth. Kissed them quick and sweet.

Anything you want.

RIOT

Yulia wasn't waiting for either of them when they got to school. Annie scowled.

"What a bitch."

"She's not a bitch, she's being normal. You're the one being weirdly okay about this. As thankful as I am that you are," Hollis said.

"What do you think, Walt? Is Yulia being a bitch?" Annie tugged the tassels on either side of her hat angrily.

Walt rubbed the top of their nose.

"She's got spark. You get yourself a girl with spark, you can't go around bein' shocked by fire."

"Do I have spark?"

"You're a cream puff through and through," Walt said, grinning. "Even angry I think."

Annie stuck her tongue out at him, until he laughed raw and sweet.

Timothy flicked his eyes over to Hollis as soon as they sat down in English.

"Jorge is back," he said.

"Wasn't he supposed to be back last week?" Walt asked.

Timothy shrugged. "Don't know. I don't really talk to him much now. He's beefing with James, and to be honest, we're both kind of done with him. I'm telling you—"

"Timothy, please stop talking." Their English teacher put a finger to her lips.

Timothy narrowed his eyes at her, before turning back to Hollis.

"I'm telling you 'cause if he acts up again, we don't got nothing to do with it. We've tried to help, you're always supposed to try to help. But now he's on his own until he gets his shit together." Timothy jerked his chin at Mrs. Feldman. "I'm done. Sorry about that."

Walt and Hollis mulled about it for the rest of the day, but they didn't see Jorge at all. Not in the hallways, not outside, not even in PE—the one class they had together.

Ten minutes before the bell rang for lunch, he was called to Mr. Feehan's office.

GRIEVE

The principal looked exasperated, and again, Hollis was surprised by who else was there.

He should have guessed that this was where Jorge had been this whole time. He was sitting there in his gray sweatshirt and sweatpants, arms folded, chin tilted away from the door so he didn't have to watch Hollis walk in. Skin still pink and scarred.

Who he didn't expect to see was Clementine.

"Hollis," Mr. Feehan said. "I'm sure you know what we're all here for."

Walt sat down next to Clementine.

"I don't."

Mr. Feehan sighed.

"Normally, things that occur off school grounds are none of my business, but you seem to be on a roll when it comes to creating new and exciting exceptions, Hollis Brown. Clementine Robertson has brought to my attention some kind of video of a fight that's been circulating?"

"Oh," Walt said. "Okay."

God I hate her.

"In this fight, it brings to question a decent amount of the statements you made in this room about the history of bullying you've received. Namely, the frequency and your ability to . . . handle such things?"

"Isn't it *your* job to handle stuff like this? I've gotten my ass kicked six ways from Sunday for four solid years, and the first time

I've made it into this office for retribution it's for a single punch for a fight that I didn't start or even want to be in?" Hollis said, before Walt could stop him.

Mr. Feehan stared at him in silence until Hollis felt foolish.

"See, Hollis, I'm not exactly sure what to think. Because from where I'm sitting it looks like only two options are available to you. In the first, it's a straightforward story about jealousy and luck in which you and your friends coordinated together to victimize Jorge for the purpose of humiliation because of his . . . unfortunate treatment of your friend Annie. Which I don't condone, by the way.

"The second option, and much more concerning, is that you have, for some reason, been allowing many members of the student body to enact violence upon your person without getting the authorities—myself or any other teachers—involved, while being entirely capable of defending yourself. And this—"

Mr. Feehan held up Clementine's phone.

"—is the only proof that you could, all along. Now you understand why this would be more concerning. 'Mandated appointment with a social worker' concerning, right, Hollis?"

Hollis glanced over at Jorge. He was still refusing to look at him.

"Why is *he* here?" Hollis asked instead of answering the principal's question.

"Hollis."

Walt gritted their teeth.

"I don't want to talk about this with *him* here," Walt said.

Mr. Feehan sighed. "Well, it's a good thing you're not in charge and I am. Answer the question, Hollis."

Hollis glanced over at Clementine. She sneered at him.

Great.

"Fine. Yeah, I let people beat me up for fun or whatever. You happy? Does it make you feel better to know that no one, not even a single teacher cared because I could have knocked everyone out myself? I'm not the kind of person who asks for help, and I'm not the kind of person who doesn't pay my debts.

"I like to say what I want. I'm doing better these days, but I can be a bastard and I know that. A part of that is understanding that people can react whatever way they see fit. This shouldn't even be a problem anymore. I'm being nice; the fights stopped. Whether they stopped because I'm genuinely trying, or they stopped because no one liked watching that video and imagining themselves on the ground, the end goal is the same," Hollis said, frustrated.

"I could say sorry to Jorge, but what does that even matter? None of this has ever been my fault when it comes to him, and I don't get why he's so focused on me anyway. I don't like him or dislike him, he's just always there making things slightly worse for no reason.

"We can do the whole social worker/shrink meetings thing, but we've got like five months of school left before graduation, and the problem has already stopped. How much more of this am I supposed to have to take? Who else that's kicked my ass do you want me to talk about being self-destructive in front of? Why do I have to keep doing this in front of people that hate me?"

"No one here hates you—" Mr. Feehan started, but Hollis cut him off.

"*Surely* you do. Why else would you force me to talk about feeling a way about myself that . . . that got me here in the first place?"

Oh, Hollis.

Hollis, I'm *sorry*.

Mr. Feehan opened his mouth, then closed it. He looked down at Clementine's phone, then got up and handed it to her.

"You can go."

"But!" Clementine looked horrified.

"Clementine Robertson," Mr. Feehan said quietly. "You have the rest of your life to learn to think of someone other than yourself. Hopefully this . . . helped. Now go."

Clementine rushed from the room, pink-faced, and closed the door hard.

Mr. Feehan rubbed his eyes.

"Hollis, you're not going to like this, but it's the best I can offer. Since this is a piece of media and I'm certain someone higher than me is going to see it, we can't just do nothing and act like this isn't repeated behavior. On paper it doesn't look good. The district leadership isn't from this town, they don't know our struggles, and unless you're prepared to give that speech to some city folk, you're going to have to swallow this:

"We're doing three weeks out-of-school suspension. Just enough to keep the district satisfied and eyes off the situation. We'll also have to get your mother to sign off on this one, Jorge. Hollis, yours already knows. I wish she was more concerned, but she knows. As you both are aware, winter break starts this Wednesday. I'm going to arrange the suspension to take place largely over the break. It will start this afternoon, you've got the rest of this week, then the two weeks of break where everyone is off with two days left of it when we start back in January."

"Oh."

"When you get back we'll have a meeting with the social worker, and she'll assess whether the situation has resolved so we can send a formal statement to the district about the incident—but we both know it will be, correct?"

"Yeah."

"Yes," Jorge said, to their surprise.

Mr. Feehan nodded. He grabbed a tissue from his desk and patted his sweaty forehead.

"This stops now. I want you both to have a good vacation, and when the new year starts, I want a brand-new Jorge and Hollis. We're not doing this again; they don't pay me enough."

"Is this going to go on my record or be purged like that other thing?" Hollis asked, just to be sure.

Mr. Feehan shook his head. "This one will stick, kid. But if you spend the next five months on the straight and narrow, I'll write you a letter of recommendation that will make your head spin. Might even leave you better off."

STEP

When they left, Jorge was following too close behind him. Hollis whirled around.

"What?!"

Jorge shrugged. "I don't know. I wanted to say something."

Hollis rubbed his hands over his face.

"Why are you doing this to me, man? I have literally never done anything to you; I don't even know you."

"I didn't do this; Clementine did. They brought me in as a witness or whatever." Jorge frowned. "Did you mean what you said in there, or were you just trying to get out of shit?"

Hollis turned around and started walking away.

"Hey, wait," Jorge said. "Wait, it was Annie—"

"I *know* this was about Annie," Hollis called over his shoulder. "Just leave me alone."

"I—I didn't understand why she was so happy with you and not with me," Jorge yelled after him. Bold in the empty hallway.

Hollis stopped.

"Well, you could have started by not being mean to her," he said.

"It's more than that, man." Jorge caught up with him. "She seems . . . With you she's just way more happy. I just. What have you got that I don't got, you know? You always seemed so . . . I didn't know why she liked you. Why she canceled on me to see you all the time. When you showed up with her at Rose Town, I just couldn't take it."

"I'm not dating Annie, I already told you that. We're just friends."

"But you liked her. I'm not stupid, Hollis. You're so fucking frustrating sometimes. I don't understand you."

"I used to, yeah, but she isn't interested in me, dumbass. How do you even know it was me she's trying to see all the time? It could just as easily have been Yulia. We go everywhere together."

Jorge's face went slack so quickly it would have been funny if Hollis hadn't also been experiencing a similar revelation.

"Oh," Jorge said.

Oh my God. The pond. That's what she was trying to say at the pond.

What? What pond? How are you surprised? You were the one who said that. Plus the way they're all over each other is very obvious.

What do you mean why am I surprised?! I would bet every single cent in my bank account that Annie herself might be surprised that anyone noticed.

Are you about to tell her?

No! I have enough journeys of comphet to handle dealing with you.

Excuse me? What's that supposed to mean?

Just let me handle this so we can leave.

"Look, Jorge," Hollis said, impatient. "Whatever's going on with Annie, I really can't help you there, but I can tell you two things: one, I've known Annie since we were nine and if there had been an opportunity there for me to succeed where you failed, we wouldn't be having this conversation, because you never would have had the opportunity to date her at all.

"And two: girls don't like feeling like they're in a cage. The more you push them and give them orders and try to trap them, the more they'll focus on getting away from you. You can't force anyone to like you, they have to be begging for it."

Jorge's face soured. "Gross."

"Whatever. Just don't talk to me again."

RAKE

Hollis texted the group chat about the situation. Annie got back to him quickly with a bunch of frowny faces, but Yulia didn't respond.

It was still so early in the day. Lunch was already over, but school wouldn't be out for a full three hours.

Hollis started walking home.

Take us to the train tracks.

Now?

You said you would.

Hollis shook their head and changed direction. The woods around their town was different depending on what side you went to. The trees were big and close together by the abandoned houses. They formed a canopy above your head that got so dark it almost looked like nighttime during the day. The forest by the train tracks was the exact opposite. The trees were thinner, lighter, the sun filtered through the leaves, bathing the wood in a calm green light. People hiked around here. No one hiked at the other side of town.

How long did you do this before we met?

Five years. I'm not the only one in my family who did. My mom's brother did it too.

Did he teach you or something? I should kick his ass.

Hollis laughed.

No, no. My ma just told us about it. He's dead now, so I guess you'll get your chance at that sometime. She told us about it, and then when I had a hard day, I got desperate enough to want to figure out if it would help.

301

You must have been twelve, maybe thirteen. You were just a little kid. . . .

Hollis shrugged one shoulder. Walt had their other arm, and he was using it to trail their fingers across the plants and pull leaves off every so often.

They sat down on the embankment by the tracks; Walt tucked Hollis's shoulder bag beneath them so they wouldn't get wet.

There should be a fence here. People shouldn't be allowed to get this close.

There should be a lot of things that we don't have in this town.

RADIANT

It took an hour, but it came. On time, as expected.

Walt let Hollis pull them up from the ground, knees creaking from the cold. Let him walk them down to the embankment, where the dead leaves had gathered in damp fragrant piles next to the steel and the mud squelched beneath their boots.

He pulled himself deep inside to give Hollis control of their arms, their legs, their back, the nervousness in their gut, because Hollis knew this trick. Hollis knew how to react.

He'd keep them safe.

Walt startled at the sound of the whistle.

Hollis brushed two fingers against their palm.

Shh.

Time is relative. It slows and speeds when it wants to. It took a week of waiting as the ground shook and the sweat took a year to drip down the back of their neck.

Come on.

Their bones rattled. Bones Walt loved so dearly, and their teeth hurt more than when they'd been torn apart.

It's called the Venturi effect. As the air velocity goes up, the static pressure goes down, it pushes things in its vicinity toward the reduced pressure. If you don't stand far enough away, it will pull you in. That's why people keep dying.

Hollis spread his legs, kicked one back for stability, and closed their eyes.

The train screamed like a thousand horses and snatched the

breath from their lungs. The gaps between cars flashed sunlight like strobe on the backs of their eyelids as they stood.

Walt cried out in terror.

Hollis laughed at the joy of it.

Winning against terrible pressure and the hand of fate. Laughed that he was loved so sweetly by a God that chose him to live, again and again. That the muscles in his legs were strong and his balance was true, and that for once he was being witnessed at the very pinnacle of himself:

A boy versus the relentless march of gravity.

Grand and terrible.

Like Holst's Jupiter.

ETERNITY

They fell back into the dust. Hollis pulled himself in so that Walt could have their arms and legs, and they immediately started shaking from adrenaline.

Hollis hadn't shook after doing this in years.

Hollis! *Hollis!*

Mmm. What did you think?

We are never fucking doing that again, but Hollis, fuck. I understand.

Hollis turned their face so the warmth of their hair protected them from the ground, and panted the way Walt wanted them to.

It felt like us! Walt cried, hysterical.

It really felt like us!

Walt didn't wait to resolve Hollis's confusion about what that meant. He snatched off Hollis's mitten and shoved his hand up their coat, skin to skin, spreading his fingers wide across their chest. Tore himself from that place so Hollis had no choice but to flood into it.

Hollis arched off the ground and moaned, greedy and unashamed.

It was similar. The way their souls jangled together, like hot steel touching cold steel, steam trapped in a bottle. There wasn't enough room under his skin. They ricocheted off the walls of that space between his spirit and flesh. Too close, scraping the way humans were never supposed to touch as long as their feet were still standing on God's green earth. And by God, did he love the sweetness of it.

Jeez, Walt. Hollis laughed.

No, stop laughing. Don't laugh at me.

Hollis pulled off his other mitten and pushed his hand into their mouth. Sucked hard and ignored Walt's racket. Kissed him the way he knew how. The button on the bottom of their coat surrendered, pinging off the train track. Walt scrabbled to open the rest.

You're sewing that back on.

Shut up, shut up, shut up!

Walt forced Hollis out, made them switch sides, gave him the hand that was making them shake and took over sloppily kissing him back.

And still, he was modest. Untrained—even in this—and Hollis's heart *ached*.

Hollis curled his fingers and raked them down the center of their chest. Walt snatched their hand out of their mouth so he didn't bite down, didn't ruin this, and yelled so loud the birds left the trees.

Noisy.

Walt burst into tears. Sobbed into the darkness inside them.

"I was looking for you this whole time, I think," Hollis whispered, out loud so the words were real.

So they floated in steam above them in the cold.

"I'm sorry it took so long. I'm sorry you were waiting a few years for me."

Hollis!

I would have come faster, if I could. If I knew. Taken you right out of whoever you were riding in, put you back where you belong.

Walt curled them up and huffed into the dirt. Rolled their eyes into the back of their head, as Hollis slid his hand up their neck. Closed his fingers around his throat like he had months ago. Wrapped them up, temple to the ground, knees bent in supplication.

This is a good thing. We're a good thing.

Please don't leave, please please.

What did you say, back then? When you were praying me away? When you were being a coward, running from me, and even still you couldn't stop yourself from saying it. Begging for it.

What?

Tell me, Walt. I know you remember, because I can't forget.

Walt shuddered, opened their eyes, glassy and wild.

As it was in the beginning—

Is now, and ever shall be . . .

Hollis shoved his hand into their jeans.

A world without end.

YGGDRASIL

"We're the same age, you know," Hollis said, staring up at the blue sky.

I know.

Do you? Have you thought about it?

What do you mean?

Hollis closed their eyes and took a deep breath, smelled the salt and sweat on their skin, the sweet brown leaves and metallic winter, and tried to make Walt understand.

If you stay, we could grow up together, he said.

> *You can have your years slowly like everyone else. We can turn eighteen in a few weeks and learn what that's like, turn nineteen the next year. We can move into our own house, be at work, come home, cook dinner, do the dishes, till the soil, and sleep in our own bed until we grow old. We can get married if you want, have children if you want. You can be a father; you can kiss our wife and know we earned her by ourselves and she loves you for you and me for me.*

> *Or you can just have me. We'll never be alone. We can be in our house and be strange and be loud and lasso a hurricane whenever we feel like.*

> *We can lie in the hollow all weekend, and go to Rose Town without being scared. Swim in the pond. Eat from the trees. Find your door so we can admire it and know that we can open it whenever we want to.*

Hollis—

We can leave if you want. Walk straight out of here and never come back. We can go to the city and learn a new trade, figure out how to be a man and be reliable. Be quiet in an apartment—I won't let you make a sound. Muffle your wailing so the neighbors won't hear. And we'll get older, and time will pass, and I'll never have the wrinkles I would have had on my own.

You'll make your stupid expressions for decades, and they'll dig into my face until it's our face. Really ours.

And no one will know.

No one will know that I ever had green eyes when I was a stupid kid back in our stupid hometown, before we ever met.

Walt moaned, dug their fingers into the ground.

Walt, we can live, really live.

We'll be a monster, Walt whispered, scared again.

Hollis was calm, waited for their heart to slow, waited for Walt's anxiety to crest.

We'll just be something new.

I'm not afraid of being new. You were something new once, and you can do it again, if you're brave enough.

It was terrible, I can't—

I know, but you're not by yourself, we're together.

If you just stop running, you can walk with me.

Hollis pulled their fingers, smarting and half-frozen, out of the ground and blew on them. Took care of them.

I'm scared.

It's okay to be scared. Do you want this?

I can't.

*I didn't ask if you could, I asked if you **did**.*

Hollis, I—

Do you want to wake up with me on Saturdays? Have our own pantry? Maybe have chickens so we can have fresh eggs?

We can eat what we like every day, go where we want.

It's too selfish.

It's not. Not to me. And even so, I'm being selfish too.
Be selfish with me.

Be selfish?

Let's be together and be selfish and loud. I'm asking you out, Walt. I want to make us honest.

Walt curled up tight, hiding his face again, too weak for ecstasy as he always was.

And you'll tell me if you're not happy? God, please tell me, if years down the line you decide you don't want me.

I'll tell you. I'll tell you, and if you want, I'll even take you back home. I'll walk you all the way there, from the hollow to Rose Town and I'll walk you to your door and I'll kiss you the way we kiss before you go. Even if we hate each other by then, I'll still do it.

I can't be happy if we leave that place the way it is right now, Hollis. I can't be that selfish, if it was my fault.

Then we'll find a way to fix it. Tomorrow, we'll talk to Annie and Yulia and we'll make a plan and we'll figure it out. I'm not in the habit of breaking promises.

All right . . . all right.

Together?

Yes.

Come on, let's go home.

HOLY

The sun was still high in the sky when they crossed back into town.

One sleeve of their coat was empty, arm wrapped around their middle.

SWALLOW

Yulia was sitting on Hollis's front stairs, bundled up warm.

She met their gaze as they opened the gate.

"Hollis," she said, frosty.

"Yulia . . . are you all right?"

She was having difficulty looking at him now, staring beyond him to the sun lighting up the grass.

Walt held up two fingers.

"Thanks for coming. Hollis missed you. He's worried."

Yulia bit her lip.

"I don't trust you," she said.

That, they understood.

"I'm sorry—" Hollis started.

"But you didn't trust me first," Yulia interrupted. "And that's the main problem. I've just been thinking all this time about the opportunities you've had to try to figure this out with us. Walt's a stranger, he doesn't know us, but *you* do. When you got close enough to get some control, you should have called me or called Annie and talked to us. We could have figured this out together. Found a way to . . . help him move on to someone else."

Hollis closed the gate behind them, crossing his arms.

"Yulia, I don't want him to move on to anyone else," Hollis said. "I want him here. That's harder to explain than what you're describing."

He leaned against the fence, a fence he had put up himself a few years ago. Stamped each post in hard, covered in sweat while Annie

312

and Yulia watched and mixed up Kool-Aid on the porch.

"How would you have handled that, Yulia? By the time I was able to decide to call you about it, I knew him. One couldn't exist without the other: knowing him is getting the freedom to leave, but to know him is to . . . not want what you're wanting for me."

Yulia made a face. She walked down Hollis's steps, closer and closer until they were sharing air. Then she leaned up and clasped his cheeks between her two hands. She turned his head this way and that, looking at him closely.

"It's not that I didn't trust you," Hollis said. "I'll always trust you. I'm trusting you now. We trust you."

Yulia bit her lip.

"I don't like demons, Hollis. I don't like this and it's not from a lack of familiarity."

He didn't correct her.

"I know. I'm sorry."

Yulia pressed their foreheads together, up on her tiptoes to close the few inches that separated their height.

"Why do you *like* him, Holly?"

"We're . . . so similar. He . . ."

Forgive me.

"It's like . . . having someone inside you seeing everything that you are. All of it. The good parts, the bad parts, the disgusting parts, your weaknesses. All the things you're afraid of, all the things that turn you on. Everything you're ashamed of, everything that you wish for, every part.

"And they hold these pieces up to the sun, in the light. And it's so bright that no part of it goes unexplored. Nothing can hide. And you're there. You. Not the you that you are at school or the you that you are for your parents, or the multitude of other yous that exist for everyone that knows you. There's just you. As you are.

"And they tally everything up, and they just kind of . . . accept it. Walt looked at what I was and said, *'It's fine. This is okay.'*

"You don't know how much that meant. And yeah, it's selfish and weird and fucked-up and definitely supernatural, I guess. But I feel . . . lucky. I don't feel cursed, and I don't feel possessed, I feel lucky," he finished.

He held her back. Tucked his arms around her fluffy puffer coat, and Yulia let him.

"He has nowhere else to go," Hollis said against her cheek. Like he rarely did, like she rarely let him. "I wouldn't want him to if he did."

And Walt stood back, silent.

"I don't want you to get hurt," she said.

Hollis swallowed hard.

"You're my best friend, Yulia. The only thing that hurts has been the past forty-eight hours without getting to see you. I'm sorry I kept this a secret. You deserve better than that and I won't do it again. How can I fix this?"

Yulia pulled back and looked at him hard. Took in the dirt scrubbed across his face and Walt's brown eyes.

"Christmas cookies," she said, very serious. "I want six different kinds; I want them tonight, and I don't want you to skimp on toppings. I want you to come with me to the winter fair this weekend and carry all my bags. I want you to—"

Hollis scooped her up and swung her around, let her heels dangle and ignored the ache in his arms and back. Held her close because she was precious.

"Anything, Yulia. Anything you want."

FLANNEL

Yulia went to Annie's so that Hollis could shower before baking began.

Apparently he smelled "disgusting" and would have to text when he'd fixed it so that they could come over.

Hollis slung his bag into their bedroom and headed for the bathroom.

"Can Yulia and Annie stay over?" he yelled.

"You cooking?" his ma yelled back through her bedroom door.

"Yeah, I'll handle it."

Walt reflexively turned off the light to start getting undressed.

We can probably stop doing that at this point.

Walt shrugged and threw their shirt on the ground.

You want it to stop, you turn it back on.

Hollis hummed and left the light. The day had been enough.

She really just forgives stuff when you feed her?

Hollis shook their head.

No, Yulia is from the richest family in the whole town. When she asks for bread it's because she knows that's what I can give. She doesn't ask for anything I can't give her if I work hard enough. It's not the food, it's the labor. She wants to know that I was thinking about her when I made her something. That I tried my best to make it good. That I remember her favorite flavors and thought about what she likes.

The Christmas cookies aren't just . . . it's not about the cookies. It's about being with me as we make them. Watching me do something she's seen me do before while she feels insecure about who we are. The winter fair is because she knows I would never say no to her. I'd carry her bags from here to Chicago if she needed me to. It's reassurance that I'm the same person, that me being "we" hasn't changed the things that matter.

Walt was quiet as he scrubbed a loofah over their shoulder.

You give a lot of speeches.

I don't like being misunderstood.

SPECIAL

Annie bounced into his house, Yulia right behind her. Settled down for a dinner of fish and root vegetables with Hollis and Mrs. Brown.

Yulia sat across from them. Her eyes weren't cold as flint anymore. She separated out all the pieces of chopped beets to the corner of her plate, then reached over the table and dumped them onto Hollis's. Mrs. Brown didn't even flinch at it.

Okay.

Hollis smirked and began eating.

Bad table manners or more incomprehensible subtext?

Subtext. She wouldn't have done that if she was still pissed.

Mrs. Brown left them and went up to her room. Annie washed dishes, while Hollis and Yulia cleaned the table and set out ingredients.

"We're doing chocolate chip, iced sugar cookies, peppermint chocolate cookies, thumbprint jam cookies, oatmeal spice cookies, and gingerbread brownies," Walt announced.

"Hollis is doing the first five, and I'm handling the last. We're starting with sugar, so you gals can ice 'em if you want while you wait."

"What are gingerbread brownies?" Annie asked.

"S'thing I learned from a kid in the eighties. They're like gingerbread with the same texture as brownies. They've got spiced icing on the top, hard like sugar cookies do," Walt explained, while Hollis washed their hands. "I'm not a whiz in the kitchen like your boy, but I do know a few things."

Yulia pursed her lips together dubiously but didn't say a word.

In the end, it took about four hours to finish them. Even with a baking sheet on all three levels of the oven.

Hollis put the last batch in and settled down at the dining table to help decorate.

"Walt, you have an accent," Annie announced. "You didn't have it when you were pretending to be Hollis, but you have it now. Is that what he sounds like inside, Hollis?"

"Yup. Drove me crazy trying to figure out where he was from. Time period and location. In the end he just told me."

"Have . . ." Yulia seemed reluctant, but she powered through. "Have you traveled anywhere outside of the United States?"

Walt welled up with joy at being addressed directly, and Hollis suppressed a grin.

"Not on purpose. Got drafted once, and ended up in Indonesia before I was able to strike another deal and get back. I like the US. I'm not fond of the unfamiliar."

Bolder, Yulia asked. "What does it feel like, being a ghost?"

You don't have to answer that.

"It's . . ." Walt put down the wax paper they were piping with and put his chin in their hands. "There's a lot about it I don't really care to dwell on. It's frightening at times, lonesome. I get home-sick from time to time. But every day I get a new sunrise. Things keep growing and changing, and it's good seeing people doing better than we ever were. When things are going well and I get to talk to someone who likes me, that's nice."

"Oh," Yulia said, frowning.

"What was the Great Depression like?" Annie asked, unaware of the shift in mood.

Walt laughed, dry as sand. "A lot like this, actually," he said, gesturing to Hollis's entire house. "And I don't mean to offend."

He picked the wax paper back up. "I was already dead when it happened. Didn't even have ten years in. Everything was like this, but more manual, and shit didn't work half the time. Desperation exists in isolation. If near everyone is desperate, you don't call it that anymore. You don't call it anything. During the worst of it, I had to eat grass. You've got to boil it first though. Learned that the hard way."

Yulia tilted her head to the side.

"What do you look like? Are there pictures?"

Walt shrugged. "Might be. We didn't have many, photography was expensive. But my ma got one taken of me when I started my first job. If what I did made the papers and it was a slow day, it might still be around."

Yulia took out her phone. "When did it happen?"

Walt set his cookie on the rack to dry. "December of '31. I doubt there would be any of those still kickin' unless someone local is a pack rat. You don't even have museums round here."

Yulia shook her head. "Not a museum. The libraries keep old papers and file them. If they're really old, you have to visit in person to see them though. You might not have done something big enough to make local papers, but your family's murders absolutely would have made a splash. If you were at the core of it, we might just get lucky."

You're nervous. Why are you nervous?

It never occurred to me that you'd get to see my face. What if you don't like it?

Walt, I would never—

319

"Do it out loud," Annie said, scowling.

"What?" Yulia looked up from her phone.

She pointed at Hollis. "They're talking to each other. It's rude to do it in front of us, just do it out loud."

Hollis drummed his fingers on the table and bit his lip.

"Walt's . . . hmm. Walt's nervous about me seeing what he looks like."

"Why does that matter?" Yulia went back to researching.

"He thinks I won't like it. Or won't like *him* anymore when I see him specifically. He's already described it though, and unless he was lying, I don't see what the problem is. And even if he was lying, we look like me now, anyway."

Hollis didn't care, but Walt was making their face burn pink and hot.

"It's creepy to put it that way." Annie grimaced. "Why is he so embarrassed?"

"It's been a hundred years," Walt said, defensive. "I didn't expect to be doing any of this. Much less looking at a picture of me all dressed up for work—"

"*Well*," Yulia interrupted loudly. "We can solve this once and for all. There's a library about fifty miles from here with an archive as far back as 1910. Later this week, we're all off school for break. My daddy's using my car for work so we'll have to take the bus, but we can definitely just go there."

Walt frowned.

"Do we have to?"

Yulia turned off her phone and put it on the table. "If I'm going to help you do what needs to be done, I want to see your face. Hollis and I have mended fences, but you and me? We're strangers."

GINGERBREAD BROWNIES

Ingredients

1½ cups all-purpose flour

1 cup sugar

1 teaspoon ground ginger

1 teaspoon ground cinnamon

½ teaspoon baking soda

½ teaspoon ground cloves

¼ cup butter, melted

⅓ cup molasses

2 eggs

Powdered sugar

Instructions

Preheat oven to 350°F/180°C. In a large mixing bowl combine flour, sugar, ginger, cinnamon, baking soda, and cloves.

Combine melted butter, molasses, and eggs in a separate bowl. Add to flour mixture, stirring until thoroughly combined. Do not beat (the batter will be thick).

Spread batter in a greased 13 x 9 x 2–inch baking pan. Bake for 20 minutes or until center is softly firm. Do not overbake.

Cool on wire rack.

Dust with powdered sugar.

Cut into squares. Makes 24 brownies.

CORNUCOPIA

They slept under Hollis's roof, curled up on the floor in the living room. Even though Yulia and Annie could have easily gone next door and shared Annie's giant soft bed.

For all that Yulia was still not exactly satisfied, she still fell asleep quickly. Hollis was glad she was comfortable enough to let them watch over her.

Annie lay between them, bundled up in the blanket from Hollis's bed. It was too quiet for her to be asleep. Hollis knew her snores too well.

"Hollis," she whispered, turning over.

"Hmm?"

"Can I ask you something?"

Hollis scooted closer so Annie could talk even quieter. Shimmying down until his forehead was near Annie's shoulder and their breath was blocked out by the folds of their covers.

"Do you still like-like me?"

There was a thrum of terror in Hollis's chest, but it didn't belong to him. Walt was quiet and heavy, watching. Insecure.

"Is it important to you that I do?" Hollis asked, instead of answering. "Does it mean something if I don't? It doesn't mean I don't love you anymore."

Annie's brown eyes were black in the dark.

"What did it feel like?"

"Liking you? Frustrating," Hollis said immediately.

"No, I mean what did it *feel* like?" Annie insisted.

Oh.

"To like-like anyone?" Hollis whispered. "God, Annie, what a question. Um. It's like . . . Everything feels high stakes. When you see them, if they're going to text you back, what you're wearing around them, how you act. It's exciting but scary at the same time, and whatever they do can shift your mood really fast. Some people feel it more in their stomach, the nervousness. Some people feel it in their chest. But when they're nice to you, or smile, it's like . . . ten birthdays all at once."

"I made you feel like that?" Annie said, quiet and mournful.

Hollis shrugged. "Yeah."

Annie sniffled, and Hollis pressed their head against her shoulder.

"It's fine to not know. It . . . definitely puts some things you've done into perspective. But you didn't hurt my feelings or anything, I could have said something about it at any time. I just liked being your friend, most of all."

"Is Walt listening?" she said, so small Hollis almost didn't hear.

"He's always listening, did you want to talk to him or—?"

"No. It's . . . you used to make this face at me. Your eyes would get kind of . . . soft, and you looked like you weren't sure whether to smile or frown."

"Wistful?"

"Something like that. You used to do it all the time, you did it for years, and then you did it less and less and then, eventually, you stopped."

"I'm sorry," Hollis said.

"No, it's not that, it just . . ." Annie burrowed even closer, spoke even quieter. "You started doing it again, but not at me. You do it when you think you're alone, and I wasn't sure what to make of it. What should I make of it, Hollis?"

Hollis stared into the darkness between them.

"Don't tell Yulia."

Annie closed her eyes.

"I won't," she said. "The whole time I've known you, you've liked dangerous things."

Walt flinched, and Hollis didn't like that.

He rolled over onto his back, curled his arms behind his head, and decided to be kind instead of nice for the first time in ages.

"I won't tell her either."

"What?"

"Yulia. I won't tell her about the way you feel. But *you* should, Annie. We have five months left until graduation. You're brave enough. Make them matter."

PARKING LOT

They got on the bus early, groggy and full of Christmas cookies.

Yulia really liked Walt's gingerbread brownies, to her chagrin and Walt's delight. She brought a hefty chunk of them with her to snack on.

Hollis had been to a large city before. His pa brought him up to Chicago for a birthday a few years back. He would never get used to how tall the buildings were or the press of so many people close by.

Annie and Yulia seemed much more in their element. Annie kept making them stop to look into store windows as they walked from the bus stop.

The library was huge, with a giant domed ceiling and multiple floors. Hollis felt small and out of place. Yulia asked the librarian about records and archives. Then led them up to a quieter space where they were located.

Walt's anxiety had been slowly growing throughout the day, but now that they were there, he was making Hollis want to pace.

Calm down, it's fine.

I haven't seen myself in ages. I don't remember—well, I remember my own face, but not the details of it.

Walt, I wouldn't care if you looked completely different than you described. As long as you didn't lie about your age we'll be okay.

"Ah, I think I went a bit too far. They're talking about the mill closure though, so I think they definitely wrote an article about it," Yulia said.

Walt swung them around so they were facing the wall instead of the giant clunky "microfilm viewer machine," as Yulia described it.

We rode a bus for three hours in traffic, we can't just turn around and avoid this.

We can do whatever we want. *You're* **the one who said that.**

Hollis rolled their eyes.

Good grief.

Annie was holding the film to the light and squinting at it, an objectively worse way to look than Yulia.

"Here's a few maybes," she said.

Hollis could hear her handing her pieces to Yulia.

They were quiet for a while. A sweat broke out on their neck.

"Did you find it?" Hollis called over their shoulder, a prisoner to Walt's insistence at facing the wall.

"Yeah," Yulia said, flabbergasted. "Yeah, we did."

LOVE

It was three pages long. In the paper dated for the day after, there were four more pages about Walt's family and the criminal charges involved with their murders, and two pages about Toji's, which Annie ran to go print.

Yulia got up from the worn-down library chair so Hollis could sit.

So he could stare at Walt's face without crumpling to the floor.

Hollis touched the screen even though he knew they weren't allowed to, and Yulia didn't say a single word about it.

She was watching him. He could feel her eyes burning into the side of his head, but it was hard to focus on that when everything was roaring, static, blackening at the edges.

Walt was making an expression Hollis had only ever seen him make with their face.

Eyebrow raised as if to say *Get a load of this shit*, with a twist to his mouth that betrayed how nervous he was to start work. His hair was greased down, and it was curly, just as he promised.

His jaw was a bit stronger than Hollis anticipated, his ears stuck out a little more. It made Hollis want to weep.

Walt looked terribly young and incomprehensibly old. The soft collar of his work uniform was a bit scrunched and messy.

We couldn't afford starch.

Shh.

More than anything, Hollis focused on Walt's eyes. Eyes he'd been staring at for months. His own eyes, now.

The only picture of Walt his mother had: A "missing" photo on yellowing paper, from a moment when he'd been happy. And he had dimples, just like he'd said.

Yulia put a hand on their shoulder. Walt jerked, startled, and looked up at her.

She was smiling.

"Nice to finally meet you, Walter Eidelman. I'm Yulia."

FOUND

Annie sat between them on the ride back to town. She couldn't handle buses, always fell asleep in them even back when they were kids on field trips. She was currently drooling on their shoulder.

Yulia had relaxed considerably and was reading through more material that they'd printed.

Walt was thinking hard and Hollis didn't want to interrupt him. There was a conversation brewing that should wait until they got home, and he didn't want to start it here, in public.

Walt surprised Hollis by turning to Yulia.

"Was there anything in there about what happened to my family that I should look at?"

Yulia grimaced at him.

"Takin' that as a no." Walt leaned back against the seat and closed his eyes.

"It's detailed and bad," Yulia said, turning a page. "I'm upset just knowing about it."

"Hollis and I . . . Well, we don't know much about what you did in your basement. But I think you're our best bet when it comes to figuring out how I can make amends. I need to go back home and face the music."

"You guys haven't gone to Rose Town since you've been together?"

Walt glanced at Yulia without turning their head.

"If this situation is my doing, I should be there to figure it out," Walt said instead of answering. "Now, I'm no expert on this, but I can guess that we probably need a circle of protection like the one you did for you and Ann. One that I can stay inside but that other things can't cross. We need something that can bind or banish spirits, maybe a cleansing incantation or— I don't know. But if your magic works on me it might work on that, and I owe it to a lot of people to try."

Yulia closed the files and laid them out flat on her lap. She gazed out the front window at the trees going by in the setting sun.

"I'm not a witch or anything. I just got scared enough to ask my daddy about Isese. He'd left that life behind in Nigeria, and he was really mad and asking a lot of questions, but I can't fumble around with this. It's serious. I don't know how any of this works, I was just hoping for a solution."

Walt laughed, soft, quiet so he wouldn't wake Annie up.

"That's all right, sweetheart. Your best is good enough for me. Trying is better than nothing."

"I can't promise things won't go wrong," Yulia explained. "I don't know if whatever I make will banish you and the spirits at Rose Town together, or just piss them off. So, you and Hollis should talk about that. It's one thing to go in knowing that anything can happen and another thing to be surprised by it."

Walt nodded.

"What do you think will happen when Rose Town is free of all this? You think people will move back?"

Yulia snorted. "Absolutely not. It will take at least fifty years for its reputation to change in any real way. Maybe someone will try to build there again and nothing will go wrong, but people will probably still be freaked out until all the old people who remember it are dead, at least."

Interesting.

What?

"Do you know how much that land is worth?" Walt asked.

"No, but I could probably look it up."

Walt closed their eyes again.

"If it's not too much, and things work themselves out, your family should buy it. Turn it into something new. It's got good soil from the fruit trees dropping produce for decades. The mill itself can be sold for parts.

"There's room for a dairy, you could keep chickens and rabbits. Some of the mill is set underground, so there's potential for that too. It's a gold mine with no guards, Yulia. Your old man might be hard to convince, but the potential is there. With good farmland like that, no one nearby would ever go hungry again," he said.

"I mean, the land is cheap at this point, and my dad is the only adult on earth who would believe us about the haunting," Yulia said with a scrunch of her nose. "Probably uninsurable though. Anyway, but what about people to work there? Who is going to want to run the dairy or any of that stuff?"

"Lotta kids round here gonna be looking for work when school's out," Walt said with a yawn. "If they're brave enough to joke around while the spirits are angry, they'll be brave enough for this."

SMOKE

When the bus dropped them off, Walt got a hug from Yulia, the very first one just for him. They walked back to Hollis's so Yulia could take all the cookies she wanted back home with her, then promised to meet up Saturday morning for the winter fair.

Hollis's ma had made grilled cheese and roasted tomato soup for dinner, and they ate it with her homemade country rolls.

"Do you want to make any cookies to sell at the winter fair?" Mrs. Brown asked. "I had some of those brownies, and they were fantastic."

Hollis shook his head. "I want to go with Annie and Yulia this year, not sit at a booth. It's the last year we'll be able to just hang out there unless they come home from college in time enough for it."

Mrs. Brown collected their plates and dropped a kiss on his crown as she headed to the sink.

"You make another few batches and me and your dad can hawk them for you," she said. "I want you to have a bit more cash in your pocket this time of year."

Is that all right?

Fine.

"Okay, I'll have them done by Friday."

"Do some with nuts." Mrs. Brown squeezed his shoulder, then went into the living room to watch TV.

Hollis washed the dishes, even though he knew they could wait, then they went upstairs to talk.

PYGMALION AND GALATEA

Walt slid down Hollis's bedroom door to sit on the ground. They pulled out the picture of Walt's face that Yulia had printed and cut out for them in the library.

What are you thinking about?

You. You were very brave today.

That's all you've got to say about it? Second-worst day of my life.

Hollis smirked.

You don't mean that. Besides, there's still time left.

He traced the edges of the photograph, then folded it up and put it in their wallet.

Walt was still nervous, Hollis could feel it rolling around in their chest.

Calm down, it's fine.

I can't. Sorry. I'm trying.

Hollis sighed. He stood up and turned on the lamp by his bed. He closed the shades, ran a finger down them so there were no more gaps. Then he locked their bedroom door.

What are you doing?

Hollis sat on the edge of their bed and took off his socks. Took off his watch and belt, put their phone on the nightstand. Then he went to stand in front of their full-length mirror.

Hollis had never liked what he looked like.

He tried not to think about it most days. Even after Walt blew in and made a bunch of nonconsensual changes, Hollis still felt apathetic about the whole thing. But this was different, it wasn't about him.

He peeled off his sweater and stood there in his T-shirt and jeans.

Hollis, you don't have to—

It's time, I think.

Hollis tugged his shirt over his head, unbuttoned his jeans and the rest, and threw it in a pile by the bed. The way he knew Walt hated, did it that way just to make Walt angrier than he was scared.

Hollis pushed all the opinions he'd gathered about himself away until their head was silent. Then he tucked himself in deep inside, pulled himself back to the place he'd been trapped in on the first night they met. Sitting in a prison in his face, a witness. Shrank even smaller when Walt tried to tug him out.

Go on. Do it.

Walt used Hollis's face to grimace, but eventually looked down.

Oh.

Walt darted closer to the mirror, the way Hollis had when he noticed Walt's eyes. Touched the surface, smearing it, careless.

You have freckles! They're everywhere . . .

They're on my face too, I don't know why that's what you're surprised about.

Hollis leaned back into the darkness and felt Walt's joy. His curiosity and the rightness of his satisfaction. Walt turned Hollis's arms so he could study the fronts and backs, gave them goose bumps accidentally when he skimmed the hair on their bicep while checking a scar.

Broke my arm while falling out of a tree. They had to put in a rod.

Jesus.

Walt twisted to look at Hollis's back, the long curve of his thigh and the rough patch of skin at the back of their ankles.

You've already seen that.

It's different with context.

Walt tilted their head from side to side, angled their shoulders, checked under their arms, touched all their crevices, respectful and exploratory. The museum of him.

Do you like it?

Of course, I like it—

*Do you like our **house**?* Hollis clarified.

Hollis reached out and took himself back in all the ways that mattered, settled down on the hardwood floor. Crossed his legs and leaned back on his palms to look Walt in the eye. Immodest and indolent.

Do you like our house? Is there a garden for your roses? Do you want to paint my fences white?

Walt wrinkled their nose.

You talk like no one else I've ever met. How did you get like this, Hollis Brown?

Hollis tilted their head to one side and then the other. Licked at their eyeteeth the way Walt had once, when he was in Sam. Careless. The way a human never thinks to.

Walt made a small wistful sound, then palmed the side of their face. Hollis pressed into it with a sigh.

ANISE

The weekend before Christmas, everyone always gathered in the neighborhood of abandoned houses at twilight.

It was good to have a place to be noisy and bright until late and know that no one was being disturbed. This year they were lucky and there was no snow. Last year Hollis had almost gotten frostbite from his wet boots. But it was too cold for that, and he was thankful.

They couldn't afford those heat lamps Hollis had seen in the city. But there were trash can fires with clean slow-burning wood every half block or so, with a responsible person to keep watch over each and free marshmallows for those who wanted to roast them.

It was a good way for people to make some money before the holidays and get in some last-minute Christmas shopping. People sold things they knit or carved. There was a toy maker, a soap maker, a man who somehow managed to keep bees and had honey and wax. Some locals had garage sales and offered barters instead of money.

There was a family who came up from several towns over to sell tallow and lanolin, sheep cheese and jerky. An apple farm that brought juice, cider, butters, and apple pie doughnuts that sold so quick you had to come early just to get one.

The school had games, and some of the teachers did contests, trivia, cornhole, mock gambling. The band usually played a live song or two before the kids scampered off to have fun with the rest of the town. If the old people stepped in, there would be string music and dancing.

It was good. Worth waiting for. There was nothing there that anyone couldn't afford.

VELVET

Walt managed to bake enough gingerbread brownies to keep Mr. and Mrs. Brown occupied for at least one full day. Hollis's parents headed out to set up shop a couple of hours before Hollis and Walt were supposed to arrive with Annie and Yulia.

Annie came over early, tapping her acrylics against his screen door until he rolled out of bed to let her in.

She was already bundled up warmly, dressed for endurance not fashion, in thick sweatpants and multiple sweaters with earmuffs under her hat.

Annie peeled off all her layers and stood in the foyer, huffing and sweaty.

"We have about a half hour before we go; you're going to have to put all that back on," Walt said.

"Don't tell me what to do." Annie scowled.

She followed them upstairs into Hollis's room and sprawled out on his bed like she owned it. Socked feet dangling off the edge, arms spread out wide.

Hollis searched his room for cash. He had about $30, but that wasn't enough for all the gifts he was planning to buy.

"Can I ask you a question, Walt?"

"Shoot."

"Do you think you'll stay here with Hollis after graduation? Or are you guys going to try to move away?"

Walt stopped rummaging through the pant pockets from their pile of dirty laundry.

"To be truthful, I'm not sure. You askin' 'cause you wanna keep track of me?"

"No, she wants to know if we're going to disappear and she's never going to see us again," Hollis clarified. He glanced over his shoulder at her. "We haven't talked about it. But I'm not going to just not visit you when school's out."

Annie sighed. "Yulia is almost done with that stuff you asked for. You guys should probably sort out a bunch of things before you head over to Rose Town. She told me what you said about what you guys want to do with the land, and it just doesn't sound realistic to me."

Hollis pulled a few more singles out of a pair of unwashed jeans and tucked them into his wallet.

"It will be hard to pull off, sure. But we have the raw materials. It's one thing to try and use that land to make money exporting goods to people not from here. It's another to use it to subsidize what people here need.

"We only have about ten thousand people who live in this town. Half of them have their own places where they grow and preserve things; the other half have important skills. The rest of them work construction and wish they could work closer to home. Subsistence isn't glamorous, but it's an old way to live, and it *works*.

"We already know how to share, and we're already working hard. This'll just—I don't know. But it would be so much better if Rose Town could *help* us instead of *haunting* us all the time."

Annie sat up and folded her hands in her lap.

"And if Walt isn't there to help you?" she said bluntly. "What if you do this exorcism or whatever and he dies for real. What then?"

Even the thought. Just the *thought*, made them curl close, hand against their chest like they were trying to hold themselves in. Annie didn't comment on it, terribly kind.

"I . . . ," Hollis started. "I would leave, make some money and then come back and try on my own. Someone has to. We would be the only ones who knew things were safe, that the haunting is over. Me and you and Yulia."

Hollis stood and tugged an extra sweater over their head. Started getting ready to leave.

"It will be fine," Hollis said, to both of them. To himself. "Even if it takes a few years, I think it will be all right. It's the right thing to do. I . . . I'll be all right."

I love you.

Tell me again later when I can do something about it.

Annie watched him dress for long minutes.

"You're really brave, Hollis," she said. "I don't think I've said that yet."

He shoved his feet into thick winter socks.

"I wish I was as brave as you."

DOORKNOB

Yulia didn't bring up what they spoke about on the bus. She just slid down her front stairs in Cole Haan and fox fur, and handed them both wicker baskets.

"We can get things for each other tomorrow if we go by ourselves," she said. "That way we don't have to guard any secrets. Remember, Hollis: you're on holding duty when my basket gets too heavy."

There were more people on the first day anyway, and way more this year than the past year, because it wasn't as wet.

As always, they stopped and got candied nuts at the entrance. Hollis could see his ma and pa's booth farther down, and they had a very long line.

Don't get a big head about that. I'm still better at cooking than you.

Didn't say a thing.

But Hollis could feel how proud he was anyway.

Annie wanted to focus on getting food first, so they cut across from the crafts and headed to get those German sausages she liked that Yulia thought were too salty. Pino's had come out and had fair food too, and Annie mocked him for choosing to get mozzarella sticks again instead of something more festive.

Yulia managed to snag more of Walt's gingerbread.

"You will make this every year and mail me some if I can't come home from college," she announced.

"That's fine. Happy to." Walt used Hollis's face to blush like he always did, and Hollis was just glad he no longer had to explain why.

They got a cow-bone hair stick for Mrs. Brown, 'cause her hair ties were all over the house, and some menthol tallow cream for Mr. Brown's bad back. Hollis got a set of pencils for Timothy, who always asked him for one, and hand chalk for James, because he'd always be in need of more.

Hollis thought for a fleeting second about getting something for Jorge but decided against it because that meant they'd have to talk to him again at some point.

He got Yulia's pa a "just add water" bread-making kit, and Yulia's ma some honey soap and hand cream. Annie's ma a book of poetry the school library was going to throw out and Annie's pa some jars of pickled radishes and hot peppers.

Yulia's basket was twice as heavy as theirs because she kept buying things in glass containers. But Hollis and Walt gritted their teeth and hefted it on their shoulder so that it wouldn't cut into their hands.

"You should get something for the principal," Annie said. "Or would that look like bribery?"

"It would probably look like bribery," Walt replied, but Hollis threw a small bottle of cherry moonshine in his basket and thanked God no one ever cared to card around here.

LAVENDER

They dropped their baskets off at Hollis's parents' stand when they got too heavy and went to go watch the band play.

Annie should have been up there with the rest of the drummers, and she knew it. Their band teacher took a moment to scowl at her over his shoulder when they settled in to stand at the front. They were playing a quick big band song, and most of the townspeople were dancing.

Yulia nodded out to the crowd, but Hollis folded his arms.

"I've already done enough swing dancing."

"I want to dance with Walt, not *you*. You're going to step all over my shoes," Yulia said in a huff.

Hollis rolled his eyes.

"Whatever."

He let Yulia pull them over to an empty space and then curled up tight inside so he didn't have to participate. Walt took Yulia's request with a surge of joy that made Hollis roll his eyes even harder.

What happened to "I love you I love you."

Walt spun Yulia around.

> **As much as I would like to show you a good time, we quite literally can't dance together. We can do other things, but this one is impossible, I think.**

Hollis leaned back into the darkness and watched Yulia shriek with laughter. Watched the crowd blur behind her as Walt did something completely out of Hollis's character in front of the whole town. Too happy to care. Too free.

We'll see, he answered, aching. *I think we'll figure it out.*

When the song ended, the band switched to something slow. Walt wiggled his eyebrows at her, but Yulia wanted to go back to Annie.

She know how to dance?

She's not too bad. Band kids got to miss PE sometimes, so she's not as good as Yulia, but I don't think that's the point of this.

Hollis stepped them back into the crowd and watched as Yulia tried to get Annie on rhythm. It took a bit longer than he'd thought, but they figured it out and started to sway.

Can we go somewhere after this? I want to talk.

Where do you want to go?

RIDE

"Come by mine tomorrow, I have what you need," she said, hot into the shell of their ear.

Hollis's heart sped up, and Walt shivered.

Yulia and Annie scampered away, and Hollis watched them go, feeling warmer than he had in months. They turned to grab one more thing from Hollis's parents' stall.

"Hey!"

Timothy jogged over, James not far behind him. "Hollis, man, what's up! You heading to Clementine's after this? They're doing some kind of Christmas rager."

Hollis shook his head. He didn't even know that was happening.

"Absolutely not. Clementine hates me, and she definitely didn't invite me." He grimaced. "But since you're here I might as well give you your gifts. I don't know if I'll see you again before break."

"Gifts?" Timothy looked startled.

"Don't get your jock in a twist, it's nothing big," Hollis said. He rummaged in the baskets behind his parents' stall and pulled out the pencils and chalk. "I'm not wrapping them either so—"

Timothy held the pencils in both hands for a moment, then looked over his shoulder at James.

"Hey, man, you gotta—now is a better time than any."

James flushed and cleared his throat.

"I've been thinking . . . ," he started. "I was gonna leave my car here when I went to school and I was going to just give it to Tim, but we talked about it and decided it might be nice if you wanted to share it and carpool together. Just so you have some more job options in case you don't wind up working where your old man works. You guys don't have to get along or anything, but no one in this town is a stranger to sharing."

Wow.

Hollis shook his head. "That's too much, James."

James shrugged and looked a little awkward. "No, it's not. It's just an old shitty car, and I'm not using it anyway. Can't even sell it, it's worth so little. I know we're not friends or anything and you're not really a part of what happened with me, Tim, and Jorge, but it did have an impact. No one ever thanked you for helping Jorge when he was in bad shape. When everyone else was too chicken-shit to think of anyone but themselves. I doubt his parents are good enough to admit they were wrong, so I bet they didn't apologize either."

Hollis still felt uncomfortable.

You don't have to use it, just let it go. They're trying to make it up to you, you deserve that.

Not this much.

"It's probably too soon to tell," Timothy continued with a grin. "But I think Jorge calmed down on using gear after you knocked him flat too. He's still an asshole, but he's not flying off the handle all the time like a maniac. Embarrassed the shit out of him. You just about saved that boy's life twice and saved me the stress of worrying. Sharing a few rides until we can both buy better than James's old Toyota isn't that big of a deal."

"Okay, okay, fine," Hollis said, embarrassed. "I didn't do any of that on purpose; I wasn't even thinking about him."

James shrugged. "Who cares. The means justifies the end. I'm sure Jorge will be thankful too in a few years."

He slapped Hollis on the shoulder. "Thanks for the chalk. Merry Christmas."

Tim grinned and gave Hollis a one-armed hug. "See you round."

Yulia and Annie held hands for the rest of the winter fair. Hollis and Walt politely pretended not to notice.

They went back to Mr. and Mrs. Brown's booth and negotiated where their baskets would be dropped off. Hollis felt the side of his coat to make sure his ma's hair stick and his pa's cream hadn't fallen out during the dance.

"Annie and I want to go back to mine. Do you want to come?" Yulia asked. She was flush and beaming. He could tell she wanted them to say no so badly.

"It's all right," Walt said, pulling Annie in for a quick hug. "We have our own plans."

Yulia kissed him on the cheek.

FIDDLER'S GREEN

Any other night it would have been too cold to go on a long walk. But they didn't wear twice as much clothing every night.

Hollis and Walt took a ride back home from the abandoned houses with Hollis's parents, so it cut the time in half, but it was still a bit of a hike.

He wished he'd thought to ask Yulia if her pa was finished with her car.

I thought you'd be more nervous.

Walt shrugged their shoulders.

I did too. It doesn't seem as scary now that I'm not alone.

It was a bright night, not a cloud in the sky. The moon wasn't full, but without buildings or dense foliage, there was nothing to block the light.

What kind of buildings were here?

I'm not sure. I don't know where the demo started. But at the edge of town, there should be a grocery store. Maybe a church.

Hollis had never seen a church in Rose Town.

When the buildings pierced the horizon, Hollis crossed the road and trudged through the field. They were near the gravel lot, where everyone had parked their cars so many months ago.

They walked as close as they could manage before Walt's hands started shaking.

Hollis sat them down on the cold ground.

Is it as bad as you thought?

It's too dark; I've never seen it with the lights put out. No candles in the windows, no streetlamps, no fires. It's a grave.

Walt rubbed their mittened hands together; heated the wool with their breath.

People were always in the streets, day and night. It was loud all the time. The sidewalks were loud, the bars were loud, the clanging and forge at the factory were loud. People were always yelling and crying and laughing. Trying to sell stuff in the street, having a good time with their friends. It was loud even when we tried to sleep.

My pa used to snore like a bear. Kept the whole house up for years until we started shoving sponge in our ears.

What were they like?

Walt brought their knees up high so he could rest their head on them.

My ma was big. We barely had enough to eat, but she was big and stout. She worked as a seamstress, and she was very quiet. Very kind. My pa should have been a violin maker like his pa. But that paid less than factory work, so he ruined his hands so we could keep the lights on.

One of my sisters was nine when we left, the other was nineteen. Unmarried, so she stayed with us. They were both mean the way Yulia's mean. Viper-tongued and sweet, despite it.

We lived in that house there.

Walt pointed down the main street at a place five houses down from where Jorge had nearly died.

It looks like the edge of town now, but it wasn't. It was near the middle. If I told you how much of this place was carved

away. If you could have shown me on a map where the line was. Where they cut this town to quarantine what was safe from what wasn't, Hollis, I would have already known this was on me.

Walt pointed farther down the street.

You go a ways that way, you'll hit the place I used to fight. It was a dance hall on the first floor and matches were in the basement. Way down nearer to the factory is where the Callaghans liked to gather. But the Rossis' territory is field and farmland now.

Wonder if they relocated, or sold . . .

Anyhow, some guys, low-down guys who worked the line with me during the day were all right. They weren't all bad, not the Rossis or the Callaghans on the bottom level. They were just hungry, like me. From families just a bit worse off.

I don't know, Hollis. I wanted a minute to just take it in before we came here to do what needs to be done. I didn't want my first shot back in town to be my last.

I get that.

Hmm. Lie down with me.

Walt let him carry them down, arm behind their head to cushion them from the frozen grass. They looked up at the sky.

I'm glad you came here. I'm glad we ran into each other that night. I'm glad I stopped and gave you my coat.

Walt laughed soft and private into the night.

Best, worst decision you ever made. If anything happens, I'll miss you. I miss you right now.

Hollis slid off their mitten and kissed their fingertips.

350

You know, I think even if this place wasn't full of ghosts things would be the same.

What's that?

There are so many places like this out there, towns like ours. We're not special. Just because Rose Town is full of angry spirits doesn't make this more or less of a haunting than any other town with an empty shut-down factory and a bunch of poor people.

There's land all over the place that's so ruined no one can step foot on it. Signs around it talking about toxic poison and danger, parents worried their kids will sneak over to have fun and get hurt.

It's not the same.

*It **is** the same thing, Walt. It's the **same**. We just have the luxury of calling it a haunting. We're lucky enough to have nothing but ghosts in our way, not like . . . the brute force of environmental exploitation. But materially speaking, it's the same. The American nightmare or whatever.*

Big words.

Hollis grinned.

Shut up. I'm being serious. We all kind of know it too. That's why no one really complains about it. Having ghosts is not so different from having nothing at all.

But, what if—

Yeah, Walt. What if. I'm sure there's half a million people around this country with the same question. At least we might have a way out. At least you came back to help.

I didn't come back to help, I came back to die.

Hollis closed their eyes.

You can't make me hate you for that. Stop trying.

DIADEM

They got home late to an empty house. Mr. and Mrs. Brown must have gone back out to enjoy the festival with their friends now that selling was finished.

What time does that thing end?

Maybe 2 or 3 a.m.? Most of the food stands close and the sellers shut up shop, but the bar and band stay open and the old people keep playing until everyone feels like going home. We should have a lot of time. Those guys are my parents' high school friends after all.

Like that cop?

Hollis chuckled. *Yup. No one ever leaves. I'm surprised you remember that.*

They peeled off all their layers and tossed their dusty clothes directly into the washing machine, and went upstairs.

Hollis grabbed the last of Jorge's cigarettes and lit one as they waited for the tub to fill. Held it between their teeth as they got undressed.

I'm still not used to this.

You have time. Hollis winked at Walt in the mirror, but Walt didn't take the bait.

I might not, sweetheart.

Hollis didn't take that bait either.

Let's say you do. I have a question. Did your mom ever pick up the money you left her? The half of it that you put in an account in Chicago?

Nope. And it won't still be there neither. Great Depression ate that up quick. The banks were just doing whatever. We gonna buy this town, we gotta do it through hard work. No free lunches. You still wanna do that, by the way? I thought maybe you were just . . .

Hollis shrugged, took a quick drag, and folded their arms, leaned back to watch Walt in the mirror.

I keep my promises. Food, shelter, and all that.

Walt sucked his teeth, their teeth.

Turn off the light, Hollis Brown, I can see you better in the dark.

They sank into the water, one knee bent, one ankle hanging off the edge, and Walt promised them he'd get them a bigger tub in their own house.

Tell me it again.

Tell you what?

Tell me about how you love me.

Walt took their face, let Hollis brush a thumb against their mouth for the shock of it. Blew smoke out into the dark and closed their eyes against the ash.

In the pantry, old things are in your pa's handwriting, some in your ma's. Most of it is in yours now. If anything happened, your family could survive for months on jars of your cursive.

Your . . . room is filled with hand-knit things: sweaters, mittens, scarves, socks. The ones with holes are misshapen, just real bad beginner's stuff. But you wore them out. You kept them, and I know your lazy ass never learned to knit.

Under your bed, you've got books. Not the kind you'd put on display to show off. *Little Women, The Water Babies*, at least four from the Little House series, some absolutely shocking romance rags. All from before the 1980s, yellow and smelling like vanilla. I knew your ma's name before that cop said it. She wrote it in the back.

Last week you restocked the shampoo and conditioner. Not the cheap shit from before I arrived. The good stuff, even though it costs more, and I didn't have to ask.

You just bought a guy who broke your nose a jar of pencils, for no reason other than that you thought he needed them.

It's enough. You've always been enough, even before I got here.

Hollis leaned their head back and swallowed hard. Blinked fast.

Okay. I'll try not to forget that.

But you are still an asshole, Walt said, taking another drag.

Be boring if you were any less.

Yeah, yeah. Okay. You know what it was for me?

I'm afraid to ask.

It was too early to know you yet, but that first night, when I woke up scared and you put me back to bed.

That was so long ago, Hollis.

Hollis laughed, wet.

Yeah. We weren't there yet, and I was still angry. But I knew and it was the only thing that let me sleep.

I knew you were once scared of this too, and then I couldn't be afraid of you.

SHIMMER

Yulia looked at him hard, hands framing his face.

"I don't want to forget what your eyes looked like, when you were like this. If anything happens."

"You could take a picture." Walt grinned.

"It's not the same."

They took her binder of instructions and bag of ingredients.

"Thank you for this, Yulia. You're a real pal."

Hollis kissed her on the cheek. "Thanks, Yulia," he echoed.

Yulia opened her front door for them.

"My dad helped out a little. He wasn't exactly . . . happy, but he loves you, Hollis. He did say something about how you shouldn't be in the room when it happens, for safety or something," she said. "Not that we know enough about this to be giving out advice. . . . My dad's smart, but we're all just making conjectures.

"Anyway, I hope you don't immediately get sucked into hell, Walt. You're a really good dancer."

Walt threw their head back and laughed, full and throaty.

"I'll try my best, ma'am."

Yulia scrunched her nose.

"If everything goes all right, you should come to Annie's after. We might be asleep, but you're welcome to pile in. Tomorrow morning, my dad wants to talk to you; he's taking us to brunch in the city."

"We in trouble?" Hollis asked, leaning against the doorframe.

"Depends on your definition of it." Yulia smiled, fond. "Get off my porch, Hollis Brown. And good luck."

ROSE TOWN

Hollis tried to force himself not to imagine Walt living in this house, but he was failing.

The last owners hadn't fled without warning. They'd gently packed everything they could afford to move with and left. Everything inside was untouched.

There was still furniture: a couch and chairs, a dining room table, stove and icebox. The bedrooms with doors open still had beds and dressers. All the surfaces scrubbed clean before they left, the layer of dust on everything was smooth like a blanket of snow.

Hollis hadn't spent much time thinking about what tenements looked like when he was learning about them in school. He knew it wasn't his turn to be upset, but he was anyway.

It's okay. Most people lived two families to one house. Toji said the people we lived with, the Robinsons, moved out shortly after my family died. None of this stuff is theirs, all of it belongs to strangers.

Hollis could see particles floating in the air. It probably wasn't safe to be breathing all this in.

Check the bag. Yulia's smart enough to think of this.

And he was right. Hollis put on the mask, goggles, and gloves Yulia no doubt pestered out of her father and read the handwritten instructions she'd taped to them so he'd put them on right.

How do you feel?

Like standing on a table with two broken legs. Unsteady.

That was better than before.

Where do you think we should do this?

The basement. It's always the basement. Heart of the house.

Walt took their legs and walked them to a door in the hallway that Hollis had just assumed was a closet, and it opened to a set of stairs. He turned on Yulia's flashlight.

"Okay . . . okay. Fuck. Okay," Hollis muttered.

The air was very dry, the stairs might not be safe. They sat down on the first step and eased their way down slow. They clung to the metal railing and skipped stairs that seemed a bit brittle.

Their foot finally touched the ground, and they scampered off the stairs to stand in the center of the room.

"Okay." Hollis gasped again, out loud.

Candles first.

The flashlight was bright enough to get a sense of the size of the space. It was more like a storage room than a traditional basement: a combination of Hollis's house's root cellar and pantry. There were jars still filled with food lined up against the walls, shining in the light. Every inch of it was covered in cobwebs, but it had been long enough that even those had begun to rot and fall to the floor.

Hollis had expected mice since there was so much food, but it was so still. So quiet.

Nothing lived in here.

Are cobwebs flammable?

Stop paying attention to that and be careful. I don't want anything to happen to you.

Us, Hollis corrected.

He kicked a clean space big enough for them to work safely.

They weren't going to use nearly as many candles as Yulia and Annie had. That had been overkill, a bit dramatic and definitely Annie's idea.

You know, I didn't think I'd get this far, to be honest. I half expected to be "Jorged" on the stairs before we even got started.

They've done that to anyone who came down those stairs. We're fine 'cause I'm here. It's watchin' me.

Us, Hollis corrected again, irritated.

He spread the herbs Yulia packed in a circle and walked inside without hesitation because he trusted her. Sat down and opened the gallon of spiced water. Soaked the large paintbrush Yulia had packed and painted a large rectangle on the wall in front of the circle. Then he dipped his hands in the white chalk Yulia had painted herself with and tried his level best not to fuck that up.

"Okay," Hollis said again. "Okay, I think I have to let you to handle the rest in a sec."

Savior of all men, you that have all virtue and power, Father of our Lord and Savior Jesus Christ—

Are you fucking kidding me?

No, shut up.

Hollis rolled their eyes but let Walt continue the sacrament. He didn't tease him. Not when he could feel the echoes of Walt's fear.

He opened the audio file Yulia had sent him with, and her voice filled the room, soft and sure.

"Ilẹ̀ mo pe o! Dá mi l'óhún!"

Walt moved restlessly from their stomach to their chest, down their hands and up to their face.

Settle down.

Hollis, I'm scared.

Don't think about it. Focus.

Yulia's voice stopped, and to their surprise, her father cut in and finished the rest of the incantation. His voice was strong and for the first time Hollis could tell that he was very upset. He wondered what it cost Yulia to ask him for this. To open that door from a past he'd closed so firmly.

Hollis started to say something else to calm Walt down, but he couldn't.

He finally was able to understand what Walt meant, why he was scared. Hollis felt heavy now, unsteady. Like he was at a great height or beneath a very large tree.

Redwood leviathan, old as fern.

There was no breath on the back of their neck, but it felt like someone was standing behind them. First at a distance and then— with a crack—so close that Hollis wanted to flinch forward away from it.

But he couldn't move.

He couldn't do anything. Couldn't shift Walt to the surface, couldn't scream, couldn't sweat. And the worst part of it all was how familiar this felt.

It was like there was a miasma over Rose Town. He breathed it in while he picked fruit, thin enough to walk through, diluted. Strange enough to raise Annie's hackles in the car, but light enough that everyone could play games in it, light fires in it.

But in the basement in Walt's house, it had concentrated to this one spot. Like a man-shaped black star, and Hollis knew that outside this place, Rose Town was safer than it had been in a hundred years.

Hollis couldn't move his eyes, but he could see a shadow of it, blurring and moving at the bottom of the wall. Like it was struggling to hold shape.

Walt came to the surface slow. Wrapped his arms around Hollis and buried him inside. Deep enough that he didn't have to see, that he could barely hear, where it was warm and safe beneath his own heart, and Hollis looked up at the candlelight like looking at the sun underwater.

The instant Walt hit the surface of Hollis's skin, the room imploded. Shards of wood and rock, sharp and heavy, jutted in toward the middle of the room. Horizontal the way they never should be, like a great lamprey's mouth, all the way up to the edge of the circle and around the rectangle on the wall.

The noise was indescribable. A roar organic and mechanical, musical and discordant, the press of a thousand voices, a howl like the wind during a house fire.

Hollis knew Walt was screaming only because their throat hurt so bad and their lungs cramped with the pressure.

Then it touched them.

Walked over Yulia's protective charms and spun them around, and Hollis knew it wasn't because she failed them.

Look away.

Hollis wasn't a coward. He stared harder. Looked at this thing that was pulling in the candlelight. So heavy it belonged in space, not the basement of a house.

It didn't have a face, but it left the impression of one. The way Hollis knew where things were when he was going downstairs in the pitch blackness to get a cup of water.

Walt was talking now. Apologizing, trying to explain. Tears

and sweat stained their clothes as they shook. But the thing wasn't paying attention to Walt. Somehow Hollis could tell that it was looking at him instead. Head tilted to the side.

Walt changed tactics. He covered their chest where Hollis was hidden and began begging. He scooted back to the edge of the circle to try to escape it, but it moved toward them, relentless as orbit, reaching forward.

Hollis screamed alongside him when it connected with their chest. When it reached inside, parting veins and tendon and muscle to close its fingers around the back of Hollis's spine and begin to tug.

It placed a hand on their shoulder, gentle, and leaned forward close enough to kiss, then tore Walt out of Hollis's body like a poison.

Walt clung to him, to his legs, and Hollis scrabbled to hold him in.

"Please!" Hollis shrieked.

It stared at him, burning his skin radiation hot. It didn't respond to Hollis's request. It paused and then kept pulling harder.

Hollis had never been strong.

But he was ready.

When the weakness of losing Walt came as he knew it would, he caught himself on one knee and hurtled his arm like a comet toward the tincture. Grabbed the handle and threw the entire thing.

The liquid flew in an arc, wetting the entire room. Then, with a noise like tearing the sky apart, the creature split into pieces. Into *people*.

Hollis could see the shape of them all in suspended droplets, shimmering in midair, and for the first time in a thousand years, it was silent.

Hollis knew which one was Walt, knew the shape of him. Knew those shoulders and that stance and the feeling of him curled up as he was now.

He could tell Walt was crying, but Hollis couldn't hear it. He couldn't hear anything at all.

The largest shade dipped down, reached with an invisible hand to touch Hollis.

"Please," Hollis asked again.

The smallest turned to the rectangle on the wall, the only space of untouched brick, and vanished. The next began to fade as well.

Hollis lunged forward, connecting with Walt again at last, but he couldn't hold him inside. They faded in and out of each other like a hologram—nothing at all the way Yulia's tincture had worked the first time—and Hollis's heart raced with terror.

Walt's parents were left, and they were watching them. Tall and thin, short and stout, just like Walt described.

They want me to go. Walt's voice hit him with great and terrible relief now that they were touching. But it still sounded so far away.

"Is this your door?"

What? No, Hollis, mine is—

"This isn't your door," Hollis interrupted him. "I don't think they know or care whether you leave the right way. I don't know if there is anything left of them that can remember."

But they're my ma and pa! Walt cried.

Hollis looked at the tincture suspended and leaned down to fit it, put his arms where Walt's arms were, legs bent beneath them, leaned his face where Walt's face was, merged them manually.

Looked up at Walt's parents with Walt's eyes.

"He apologized. This wasn't his fault, he was just a kid. If you still remembered how to love him, you would already know that. Go home. You don't belong here."

The taller shape hesitated, then phased through the wall, leaving Walt's ma.

I'm sorry, I'm sorry. Walt sobbed. **I didn't know. I never should have done it, and I never should have left. I'm sorry.**

Hollis held his breath, but she didn't disappear.

Instead of following the rest of the family through the door, she turned and started gliding up the stairs.

What—

Hollis grabbed his phone and stood up. "Come on. You have to move with me."

They followed her up the stairs and through the living room, jogging as she got closer to the exit. It was so hard to see her in the brightness of the daytime. The tincture was drying and Hollis had to slow and squint. Then, just like Hollis thought they would, the foundations of the house began to shake.

"Shit. Shit!" Hollis took off in a sprint.

Wait!

Walt's mom reached the threshold of the house, and the door burst wide open.

Immediately, the floor behind them tilted with a sickening whine, and Hollis slipped, sliding backward. Walt caught up with him, and they scrabbled up the flexing floorboards. Walt scraped their fingers against the doorstop, took every ounce of strength he had left and threw them outside just as the house began to crumble.

Hollis landed on his shoulder and bounced down the stairs violently, arms wrapped around his head, grit stinging his eyes.

He managed to look up in time to watch the rest of the building slide into the basement. All three floors of it, flimsy without the load-bearing supports that had been obliterated completely.

It made a sound that set his ears to ringing, loud enough to be heard over the city line, loud enough to be heard back home.

It was a long moment before he noticed the shade of Walt's mom still next to him. Five feet tall and sweet and wide, looking down at him.

"Thanks for that," Hollis said.

She didn't answer. She turned and went back to the rubble. Sinking into the basement to answer the call of her door.

FAIR

Hollis lay out flat. Everything hurt.

He'd lost all of Yulia's stuff under the house, barely managed to get his phone and wallet. His shoulder was bruised enough that he thought it might be bleeding, his lungs burned from all of Walt's shouting. Throat still ached from whatever that spirit did, his skull pounded with what was sure to be a terrible migraine, and his ears were still ringing.

It took far too long for him to notice that he was alone.

Walt.

Hollis looked at the collapsed building.

"Walt," he said, out loud this time.

He forced himself to sit up.

He couldn't even scream because he'd done enough of that already. It was too dusty to pick out water droplets in the bright midday sun. He didn't know what to do. He tried not to think about how Yulia's solution had worked. How if he'd gone to Yulia and her pa to begin with, he and Walt could have been separated months ago. He could have placed Walt in this house with the rest of the ghosts and gone home like nothing happened.

Hollis didn't think about that. He couldn't.

Rose Town was finally quiet, and it was cold.

Hollis covered his face with his hands.

BLUE

It was night by the time Hollis made it back home. His fingers and face were smarting with cold and red enough to warrant a trip somewhere medical. He went around the back and opened the gate, trudged through the garden.

He didn't want to startle his ma, and he didn't have enough energy to answer any questions.

He didn't think anyone heard the building collapse now that he was here. It wasn't exactly a skyscraper, and it was far away. The police should have at least come to the city limits to check something like that out, but no one showed up. Even after he sat there for an hour.

Waiting.

FOOD AND SHELTER

Hollis managed to make it up the stairs and into the bathroom.

Closed the door and locked it.

Stared at himself.

Hollis took off his coat and let it fall to the floor. Peeled all the rest of it off until he was naked, dusty, and shaking with exhaustion. He washed his face, wiped it clean with his ma's decorative hand towels until he could see himself as he was again.

Hollis sniffed and dashed his palms across his eyes.

Thought about gouging them out, but he stopped.

Turned around quick.

It was so hard to see dust suspended in the air. The tincture was almost too dry to track, but he knew.

Heart racing, he walked backward into place until they fit.

"Walt," Hollis breathed, and it choked him sweet. "Fuck, I just—"

Wait a second. Let me look.

"At what?"

Your eyes. I want to remember them.

Hollis stood there unbound until he shivered with need. Stared at himself in the mirror for Walt, green-eyed and filthy.

All right, I'm ready.

Hollis turned on the shower and turned off the lights. Drew the shower curtain back like a veil and carried them over the threshold.

Waited until Yulia's good work ran down the drain and Walt settled into him again.

Together together together, like a promise.

Walt's wrists, Hollis's hands, their neck, their feet. They twisted together beneath their skin like a pit of snakes, delirious. They pressed their forehead against the tile and breathed hard so they could focus on the feel of it.

The rightness of what they should be. Full to bursting and complete. Greedy.

Then Hollis Brown washed them clean.

AVE MARIA

Hollis turned the shower off and let the tub fill. Now that everything was over, his entire body ached from all the running, from carrying every last one of his old bones all on his own. Walt was so amused at that, thought it was so fucking funny that they were too lazy now to work a body on their own.

Anyway, my old man was pissed, Walt said as they settled into the gloom. **Claimed he raised me better and didn't like the look of you. Seemed more important to him that I know that more than anything else.**

I don't care, Hollis said firmly. *I would never have asked for his blessing anyway.*

You'd have taken me shamefully? No dowry or nothing?

Hollis stopped and turned off the faucet.

I want to be clear with you, Walt Eidelman: If I was a boy back in your time, I would have crawled in your window in the dead of night and made you loud enough to cause a scandal.

Walt laughed loud and free while Hollis shivered and gripped the edge of the sink.

I would have dragged you outside and driven you to a town where no one knew us. Gotten us paperwork with new first names and the same last name. I would have hauled cargo until we could buy a bit of land, built you a house out in the fields, and made you loud all over again, Walt. Do not test me. I am not a coward.

Walt's joy battered at his edges, delirious, reckless, shot through with tenderness, rich enough to lick from a spoon.

Jesus, Hollis, you'd have gotten us hanged. . . . My sister would have visited us though, in that brand-new house you'd build me. What would it look like?

I'd make it however you like. You've gotta know that. White shutters? Wraparound porch? All it is, is work. I'm not afraid of work.

She laughed at us, right before everyone passed on. I wish you could have seen her. Walt sounded so wistful.

I will, Hollis promised. *Someday.*

Walt settled them down into the water and draped their leg over the side.

Give my right arm for a cigarette.

Hollis snorted and rolled their eyes.

We can do a year of that and then we're quitting. Yulia won't stand for it, and we'll be seeing a lot of her soon, I expect. Birthday's in a week or so though. We'll buy them honest and legal.

Walt hummed. He placed a hand in the center of their chest and closed their eyes.

Hollis felt it in his bones, Walt's love. That soft whisper behind his ribs, the ache, the fondness, where it belonged.

When I was down there, I saw my door.

What?

On the other side of the wall, next to the other one. Looked at it hard before I turned to follow you.

Jesus, Walt. What was that like?

Are you sure you want to know? You'll have your own someday.

Hollis snorted. Typical.

370

Be kinder to your last ride, give me some hints.

Walt huffed and shifted, stretching their legs out. Twitched their top finger like he already had the cigarette he desperately wanted, and tried:

> **You ever get in from a long night out and stand in your doorway with the lights off? It's dark, but it smells like home, it feels warm even if it's cold as a winter with no firewood. You know that everyone you love is in there fast asleep and you don't want to wake them too early. Doesn't matter if it's a mansion or a hovel, it's where you live and you're glad to be back.**
>
> **There's no one tryna rush you, or people behind pushing, but it would never occur to you not to put your foot over the threshold and stumble inside. Your heart wants to kick off its shoes and fold up under the quilts.**
>
> **You don't even think about it, you just go.**
>
> **That's it. No more, no less.**

Hollis breathed in the thick stale air and let it go in a whoosh.

Oh. Wow.

> **Yeah.**

Hollis swallowed.

If . . . if you really wanted to, you should. Me needing you isn't as important—

> **You promised me years. That creepy wrinkle thing you said, way back when. I want that. You fixin' to break that promise?**

No! I just meant—

> **I know what you meant.**

Hollis heard Walt start to grin, felt it in his voice.

Don't get cold feet on this. Let me linger on the porch and look back at you, waitin'. Let me close the screen quiet enough that my ma won't hear, before I follow you back to your place for a nightcap.

I'll just be a little late. The old man'll understand.

NEW

They hopped Annie's fence and pried her window open. Shed their shoes and outside layers and traveled miles across the room to the harbor of Annie Watanabe's bed. Yulia turned over to gaze at them in the moonlight.

They pulled off their sweater, unbuttoned their jeans, and tossed them in with Annie's dirty clothes. Yulia scooted over as they crawled across her tangled pile of sheets and comforters, making room between her and Annie for them to fit.

Annie snored softly as Hollis bent their long arms and legs, shifting until they were under the covers. Then Yulia wrapped an arm around their waist and hooked her chin over their shoulder.

"Are you all right?" she whispered.

"Yeah. It's over, one haunt-free town for yours truly. Bottom-barrel-priced."

Yulia grinned against their neck.

"Are you in pieces?"

"Just the one."

"Mmm. My dad's not happy. You should have heard him yelling, he almost drove all the way up to Rose Town to do the exorcism for you. You're supposed to do it with elders, not alone—"

"It was too dangerous," Hollis interrupted. "I wouldn't have wanted him there. I couldn't handle it if anything happened to him."

Yulia snorted. "I know. That's what I told him. That won't get you out of the doghouse though, and he does think you're an abomination now. He said, ""kò sí ìpàdé láàrín òkú àti aláàyè."" *There is/should be no meeting/meeting place for/of the dead and the living.* So he and Walt are going to have to have an argument at some point."

Walt grinned. Yulia tightened her arms around them.

"Five bucks says I'll win."

"You might, who knows, but don't underestimate him. He does think our plans have legs though. He agreed to let me use what was set aside for this year's tuition for down payment on the land if you managed to pull this off. Made me promise to graduate in three years instead of four. He's gambling on us."

"Shrewd businessman." Walt huffed. "I'll have to thank him in person."

Yulia yawned, she was fading fast.

"What will you build, Wallis Brown, to make my efforts worth it? What will we make of that wreckage with my money . . . ?"

They shivered. Wallis. Wallis wallis wallis.

Threaded their fingers through Yulia's and closed their eyes.

"Everything for you, sweetheart. We'll build it all."

WALLIS BROWN

Mr. Egunyemi wasn't happy, but Walt grew on him. He watched them with deep eyes, suspicious and terrible until Walt figured out Hollis's Scotch bonnet problem: indoors instead of outdoors, right before the last frost, in front of a window with the heat jacked up all the way to 85 degrees.

Now he kept bothering them about going to college instead of helping with the build. "Give Walt's problem-solving brain the workout it deserves," he said.

But Walt and Hollis wanted to look over blueprints, talk to contractors, test soil, and choose brick. They wanted to feel the sweat slide between their shoulders during a hard day's labor, wanted to wet the ground with the want of something better. Something new. That made Mr. Egunyemi like them better too.

It took a year for Mrs. Brown to notice their eyes. When they had enough money for her to rest a bit and slow down. They'd come home to drop off some building permits quick before heading off to meet Yulia in the city, when Hollis's mother caught them by the arm and hauled them close.

"Oh," she said, leaning in to look. "That's so strange, Holly. I've never seen anything like that before. We should get you checked out, take you to an optometrist or something."

They looked down at her and shrugged. "I've already seen someone about it; it's not a problem. Doesn't hurt."

"Still." She frowned.

Their ma tilted her head to one side, then the other, looking at them. Then she ruffled their hair and kissed them, whole.

RECIPE RESOURCES

Sweet Potato Bread

www.littlesunnykitchen.com/sweet-potato-bread/

Mozzarella

www.thekitchn.com/how-to-make-homemade-mozzarella-cooking
-lessons-from-the-kitchn-174355

Walt's Bread

www.busymomrecipes.com/snacks/simple-homemade-bread-great
-depression-era/

French Bread

www.allrecipes.com/recipe/6882/french-bread/

Nigerian Fish Stew

www.myactivekitchen.com/nigerian-fish-stew-recipe/

Gingerbread Brownies

www.bhg.com/recipe/cookies/gingerbread-brownies/

AUTHOR'S NOTE

When I was a little girl, my mother read me a book called *Stone Soup*. It was a story about a starving community; each family only had some small bit of dross—old, wilted carrots; flowering broccoli; potatoes about to turn. But together, with a bit of salt, an old stone, and desperation, they pooled their resources and were able to eat.

Understanding the metaphor about community unity was easy, but I cared more about the stone part. I went to find a pebble, carefully washed it, dried it in the sun, then placed it on my tongue. Held it in my mouth until my mom saw the bulge and forced me to spit it out.

"It's not about the rock!" she cried. "It didn't even add anything to the soup. Don't eat things that aren't food!"

There is nothing on earth that tastes the way a rock tastes, except for a rock. You know what a rock tastes like. I know you do.

It tastes like grit.

The people of that town who ate stone soup were willing to swallow the taste of grit with their food because they made it, because they needed it, because they were starving, and I promise it made a difference. It is difficult to describe what having nothing is like to someone who has never experienced it. The way it sharpens your teeth.

Hollis Brown is a story about American resilience.

It's a tall tale, a parable.

A ghost story, a mob story, a coming-of-age story, a *love* story—a love story about the love between Hollis and Walt. The love between Hollis's mother and his father, who works terribly hard so far away. Easy love between friends: Annie and Yulia, suspicious and tender. Hard love between enemies: Hollis carrying the loathsome Jorge on his back, James terrified of Hollis's self-destruction. The love of community, brave and steadfast.

The cycle of poverty never-ending, love that keeps people tethered to land.

The love required to wish that things were better and then work to make it so.

The love between me and you.

And hunger.

Please make the recipes provided with the understanding that they are a lifeline and my love language from far away to any child who has very little but needs so much. I am here for you. All of this has always only ever been for you.

Yours,

Kayla Ancrum

ACKNOWLEDGMENTS

With great and terrible love, thank you to my beta readers: Colby Dockery for your steadfast support, Anna Didenkow for your early and necessary analysis, Brendon Zatirka for your academic eye, and Sara St. Taylor for your criticism when I needed it most. With additional riveting commentary by Dorian Webber, Sabina Bailey, Baillie Puckett, Art Rishk, sweet Anna Rodriguez, 2ndthoughtgirl, Megan Bailey, Lorea, the wonderful and dedicated Sofia Espinosa Solar, Artdartcart, Amy "my hometown hero" AyMeeko, Catherine Stewart, Devin, Ginger Tempura, longtime friend Min (and her books), Jess, Paris, Aliyah Symes, Koopins, and last, Natalie S.

To my father, Matthew, Yulia is for you. Thank you for your love, guidance, and strength. Additionally, I would like to thank my three authenticity readers who brought Yulia to life and corrected me where I stumbled. I hope my adjustments did your vision justice.

To Kyle, it was a pleasure to turn your heart from indifference to devotion. Winning your interest is difficult but satisfying every time.

To Eric, Alyson, Karina, and Emilia, thank you for believing in me, and my fervent apologies for the rigidity of my vision. I will always work to make sure it was worth it.